Transcendent

Shevaun DeLucia

Words Written, LLC
Rochester, New York

Karlee -
I so needed you!
tonight. missed you!

XO
[signature]

Words Written, LLC
Rochester, New York
www.shevaundelucia.com

Publisher's Note: This is a work of fiction. Names, characters,
places, and incidents are a product of the author's imagination.
Locales and public names are sometimes used for atmospheric
purposes. Any resemblance to actual people, living or dead, or to
businesses, companies, events, institutions, or locales is completely coincidental.

Book Layout by East Way Photography
www.eastwayphotography.com

Cover Art by George R. Parulski, Jr.
Email: eastwayphoto@aol.com

Transcendent / Shevaun DeLucia
ISBN 978-0-9863951-2-3

Dedication: To my daughter—may you one day find a love like this.

Transcendent
tran·scend·ent
ˌtran(t)ˈsend(ə)nt/
adjective
adjective: **transcendent**

1. beyond or above the range of normal or merely physical human experience.

"the search for a transcendent level of knowledge"

- surpassing the ordinary; exceptional.

Table of Contents

CHAPTER ONE

Jeff

amn! It's almost last call, and I haven't scored a chick to go home with yet. I hate being drunk without a warm body to take home. My thoughts tend to get the best of me in these sorts of hazed, self-loathing moments. The last thing I want to do is be alone, leaving my mind to wander.

I request another shot and a beer. Jenny, the bartender, lays it down in front of me. "Is Kyle here, or do I need to call you a cab?" she asks.

I look around the crowd to see who is left and exhale loudly when all I see is Beth and her friends. Beth used to hook up with Kyle, my best friend. They hung out for a couple of months, and when he made it clear he didn't want anything serious, she went all stalker-mode on him. There is no way I'm going near *that* with a ten-foot pole. You couldn't pay me enough for that, but her friend Carrie? Well, she's another story.

I slam back my shot and take the beer. "Nah, I think I found a ride." I slap my palm down on the bar before I head off into the crowd.

I stroll up behind Carrie like a lion on the prowl. Beth nods her head in my direction to inform her friend that I am approaching. The other girls look me up and down like a piece of juicy meat. I know if Carrie won't leave with me, one of them will. Either way, I score.

I lean against the wall next to Carrie. "Hey beautiful. Can I get you another drink?" I ask her.

She's not as alluring as the other girls, but I don't mind that. It means she's probably had less partners then the rest of them. Usually, I don't go for the blondes with blue eyes. Elise Jewels—the receptionist at Saunders Literary Agency where I work—has been my only exception, but in this case, I'll make another. With these beer goggles on, I will have no problem pretending Carrie is Elise. Sick, I know. But she does have some amazing curves.

She giggles. "No, I'm good, Jeff. I just got this one," Carrie replies, holding up her full, dark pink drink.

"I could use one," Beth chimes in, making sure to puff her chest out so "the girls" are right in my face. It doesn't matter how hard I try not to look, they're just too in-my-face. I break down and take a peek. I'm a man, for Christ's sake! I just can't resist.

Shit! Why did I even come over here? "How about you and your girls go grab a drink from Jenny while I talk to Carrie here," I try to hint.

Beth lifts her right brow at me as she slides her hand across my chest. She leans over so her lips are just inches from my ear. I get goose bumps—and not in a good way. "I'll only leave you two be if you decide to take both of us home tonight," she whispers in a husky tone.

My eyes grow wide with shock. Did she just really offer me a threesome? I look to Carrie quickly and look back to Beth, gulping. Holy shit! I've dreamt of this moment—the thought of two hot babes rubbing and touching me and themselves at the same time is definitely number one on my bucket list. But then reality kicks in. Can I really bring Beth into my bed knowing she's already been with my best friend? Not only that, but she is clearly still strung out on him. What kind of friend would I be if I allowed my "other" head to think for me? I already know the answer: a real shitty one.

I remove her hand from my chest. "I don't think so, Beth."

She sticks her bottom lip out and pouts. "You don't know what you're missing," she says, turning to head for the bar.

I blow out a much-needed breath of air and turn my attention back to Carrie. She watched the whole uncomfortable ordeal unfold, and she holds a grin across her face while shaking her head at me. "Wow! You almost fell for it. But I gotta say, I'm impressed you didn't. Most guys would never deny the chance to sleep with two females in a drunken state," she says.

She is so right, too. "Are you trying to tell me you would have went along with her offer?" I ask with a smirk. What have I done? I should have just accepted.

"Maybe," Carrie replies, clearly getting a kick out of all this back and forth.

I take a swig of my beer. "So, what do you say you and I blow this joint? I can always grab Beth too if you prefer?"

I see her glance over towards the girls at the bar. "How about I take a rain check on that?" she jokes. She looks back at me with a sly grin and asks, "Your place or mine?"

"Yours," I respond. I don't bring girls home. This way, there will be no need for me to think of an excuse to kick her ass out when we're finished. I can get my kicks off and then leave with no hassle. Let's just hope she's not the clingy type. Of course, she is friends with Beth, and crazy bitches seem to stick together.

My thoughts quickly jump to Elise, and for a split second I think maybe I'm making the wrong move by leaving with Carrie. I wish Elise was by my side instead. Elise is unbelievably perfect in every single way, but I would be a complete dick to taint any part of her. That's why I stay away. I shake my head at my ludicrous thoughts and stow them away tightly. Not tonight. I won't go there tonight.

I slam my beer and urge Carrie to drink up. I give her time to say her goodbyes to the other girls, and from a distance, I can still see Beth sulking. How can she claim to be in love with Kyle and still be so willing to sleep with me, his best friend? Isn't it bad enough she has already slept with our other friend, Matt? What the hell happened to make her so fucked up? Most girls don't have dreams of becoming a psychotic skank.

Carrie slides on her purse over her shoulder as she stalks towards me. I wave to the other girls, giving them my sexy grin, and place my hand on the small of her back to walk her out.

I wipe my forehead as the night's heat nestles at my uncovered skin. I walk her to her car first. "I'm going to simply ask you not to fall in love with me after I fuck the shit out of you," I tell her honestly.

Her eyes bulge out and she giggles. At least she has a sense of humor. "I wouldn't dare dream of it, Jeffery."

I cringe at my full name slipping out of her mouth. It reminds me of my mother, and she is the last thing I need on my mind as I head to Carrie's bed for a one-night stand.

"Good. I'll follow you," I slam her car door shut and head to mine. I probably shouldn't be driving, but there's no way I'm getting stuck there.

My eyes snap open, and I look around this dark room, trying to remember where I am. I hear a light moan coming from the female body lying next to me. Suddenly, all flashes of last night come to me. Crap! I can't wake her. I look to her alarm clock and the time shows quarter to four. I have definitely overstayed my welcome. I slowly slip out of Carrie's bed without disturbing her and grab my clothes from the floor. I have to get out of here. I run my hand through my hair and exhale forcefully.

My head is pounding like a wrecking ball against the inside of my head. Why the hell do I drink this much? Oh yes, to sedate my thoughts. Now I remember.

After I quietly get my clothes on, I tiptoe towards her door. The floor creaks. I flinch and stop briefly until I am sure she hasn't woken up. I pull the door open and turn the bottom lock before I pull it closed. *Finally!* Phew! I am free—with no confrontation. Hallelujah!

I jump into my car and crank on the air. My mind drifts back to visions of Carrie. I shiver. It was cold and redundant. Nothing special, just like the rest. It always feels so mechanical. I want so badly to *feel* something—anything—just for one moment. What I'm always left with instead is an unfulfilled void. An emptiness. I want love just like the best of them, but it's inevitable, it's just not in the cards for me. A callous selfishness runs through my blood, and I'm haunted by my parents' past. I am my father's son, after all.

The more I hope that the current hook-up will leave me with some type of unknown emotion, the more I'm let down. I'm always left with just a pointless hook-up. Will this ever change? Will I ever get that twinkle in the eye, that firework spark that I see Kyle get from Max? Yes. I had that with Elise.

I see the way Max and Kyle look at each other when they're in close proximity. It's hypnotizing. And let's not talk about the electricity that charges the room when they're both in it. That's what I want. That's what I crave, but I refuse to let it happen at the expense of someone's innocence.

I am completely ecstatic for my friend. He deserves all kinds of happiness, but the difference between us is that he never wanted it or needed it, and I do. My mother loves to tell me it will come, I am young, and there's much time for all that. She wants me to enjoy my youth and take advantage of it all. Man, I know she's right, but I just know something's missing. Maybe it was my lack of a full-time father growing up that makes me feel incomplete to-day, but I can't help but think over and over that it's something completely different.

I reach my street and turn down my long driveway. This house went on the market the day after my twenty-first birthday, almost like it was meant to be. It's the only contemporary-style house in the area. I bought it on a whim because I could, but mostly because I fell in love with it as a little boy.

I can recall my mother and I driving past this house during the winter season when the leaves were completely fallen from the trees. That was the only time I could steal a peek at the house and the only time most people could tell it even existed. The other months of the year, it was incognito, surrounded and hidden by all its natural surroundings. After my first glimpse, I secretly vowed to myself that one day I would own it, and here I am, pulling up and calling it home. A small proud smile escapes my lips, but it disappears quickly as I enter the large, dark, empty house alone.

I pull up to work the next morning, full of trepidation. My palms get sweaty and my blood pumps furiously through my chest. I can't help it. This happens every time I'm about to be in the same presence as Elise. She's not like the usual girls I have gone for. Elise has a natural beauty that had me hypnotized from the first moment I laid eyes on her. Her blond hair and blue eyes make her look angelic and untouchable—like a beautiful gift from God. She's breathtaking.

I tried so hard to stay away, but her energy is like a magnetic force field drawing me in. Once I got close enough, I was sucked in and it scared the shit out of me. Elise screams innocence and pureness. She is just too perfect to be stained by the hands of someone so unworthy of her, someone like me. She deserves so much more. *I* want to give her so much more, but how do I do that when I can't be positive I won't hurt her?

We hung out a while back with Kyle, Max, and Kinsey. I actually got her to loosen up. She took my breath away. Her laugh was so contagious, so addictive. I was captivated immediately. There was no turning back. The way she looked at me unnerved me but also intoxicated me like a drug as well. I still can't get her out of my head.

After that night, I decided that I would leave her alone. It is what's best for the both of us. It wouldn't take long before I eventually sucked the light from her, and I wouldn't be able to live with myself if I did that. Let's face it: I'm a man-whore. I love the ladies, and my past would come back to haunt us.

I trudge up to the entrance and exhale deeply before entering. Elise looks up at me through her long eyelashes and gives me a faint smile as I walk into the reception area. My dick twitches. I nod my head in her direction—no more small talk or flirty smiles—and swipe myself into work.

Every day that passes becomes that much harder to stay away from her. I've thought about quitting. Lord knows I don't really need the money, and I began working here solely because of her. But I just can't seem to bring myself to do it. I love Kyle's family—the Saunders.

I've known them for years. I work under Maxine now, and they would surely understand if I decided to move on. They would be happy for me. But every time I bring myself to cut the ties, I see Elise and decide the torture is worth it. Even if I'm only able to steal a quick glance of her—it is totally worth it.

I see Kyle packing his stuff up. He just got promoted to literary agent last week and is moving into his new office right around the corner from me. I smack the back of his head.

"What the fuck, bro?" Kyle gripes.

I hang my arms over his cubicle wall. "Stop being a pansy! You need some help?" I ask him.

"Yeah, grab that box," Kyle instructs. "You look like shit. Long night?"

I nod. "You can definitely say that. I'm going on about two hours of sleep."

Kyle shakes his head and laughs. "I'm sure I won't be sleeping either after the baby's born."

We head over to his office, through the cubicle maze, and down the hall. "How's Max feeling this morning?" I ask.

We both nod our heads as we greet our coworkers passing by. "She is miserable today.

She's been cramping, so she's bedbound for a couple of days—doctor's orders. She's not happy about it. I left her with a makeshift office in the bedroom," Kyle says. Maxine became a partner just a couple of months ago after her business merged with Saunders Agency.

I can see the worry prominent on his face. "Man, that's rough. How's the sex going?" I ask as I nudge him with my elbow, trying to lighten the mood.

"Man, listen, it was going great up until this. She's now almost seven months and closing in on her third trimester, and I'm getting cock blocked by my own daughter already," Kyle admits with a smirk.

Deep down, he's got to be going crazy knowing there's nothing he can do to help Max. Since she moved up to Rochester for good, these last couple of months have changed my boy—for the better.

He's a completely new man. But, I'm not going to lie: I miss my wingman by my side. It's been really lonely out in the trenches. What Kyle doesn't know is that I've been hanging out with his brother Junior more, and I've decided he's not so bad after all. Kyle and Junior have a long history of not getting along.

I set the box down on the chair in front of his desk. "Man, that's got to suck. Maybe you need to let some steam off. Come to McGregor's tonight so I can whoop your ass in some pool."

Kyle starts emptying the box onto his desk. "Can't, man. I have to be home to take care of Max. It's bad enough I'm here all day and I can't be there with her. She's only allowed to get up to go to the bathroom. She's probably going crazy right about now," he tells me.

I look to him with pride. It's great to see him so domesticated. "Dude, I still can't believe you're about to be a dad soon. How crazy is that?" I plop my ass down in the other chair.

"Me neither. It only becomes real when I can feel her kicking and moving around in Max's stomach. I've never felt or seen anything like it," Kyle admits.

"That has definitely got to be insane! When's the baby shower?" I ask.

Kyle's face turns intense. "Actually, it's coming up in two weeks. We're making it a co-ed one, which means you will have to endure being in the same room with Elise. You need to play nice," he tells me with an underlying threat.

I put my hands up in defense mode. "Of course I can play nice! Why wouldn't I?" I question, feeling a little hurt.

"Well for starters, she was really feeling you, and you just vanished on her. Tell me again why? I thought you liked her?" Kyle asks, still unpacking.

I rub my right hand over my face. I'm not enjoying where the conversation is headed. "I did. I still do, but you were right. I'm a douche. I eat women up and spit them out. I couldn't live with myself if I did that to her," I answer him honestly.

He stops what he's doing and comes around his desk, leaning against the edge to face me. "Jeff, you *can* be a douche, but that doesn't mean you won't know how to treat a girl right when the special one comes along. Love is about taking a chance. And when she's worth it, you will know, my man. Believe me."

I know Kyle is talking from experience, and I know he's 100 percent right, but it still doesn't make me feel any better. "Yeah, I gotcha. But someone's got to protect Little Red Riding Hood from the Big Bad Wolf. I'm sticking to my guns and staying away. Max doesn't hate me, does she?"

Max, Elise, and Kinsey have gotten real close since Max came back into town. They're almost inseparable. Max doesn't give me any reason to believe she doesn't like me, but a small part of me has some doubts—or maybe it's just guilt.

"Of course she doesn't hate you!" he answers like I have offended him. "You know how girls can be. They get all territorial and protective of the ones they love. Max is actually glad you made the decision to stay away from Elise. Now she doesn't have to kill you if something bad happened," Kyle jokes.

I think about that for a quick moment and shiver. I do not want to piss off Max or Kinsey. They can be pretty scary when they get angry. But I also have to ask myself—what if I'm hurting Elise more by staying away? I shake this thought away. I'm in a lose-lose situation. She probably doesn't even give a damn anyways. She might even be involved with someone else by now. I don't know what I'd do if this were actually true. My blood boils and my heart pumps sporadically just thinking about it.

"Yeah, I'm glad about that one. I don't need the girls after me," I laugh. "How is Elise, anyways?" I try to ask nonchalantly. Kyle knows me better than this.

He stands back up, grinning, and goes back to his boxes to unpack some more. "She's good, but she is just around the corner. You could ask her yourself."

Why does he always do that? He knows where I stand. This is my cue to leave before I just get pissed off. I stand up and stop at the door. "You want to grab some lunch?"

"I can't. I have to run home. Next time," Kyle answers. And there it is. I am officially the outsider.

"Ok, bro. Next time, for sure," I respond and head back towards my desk. I know Junior's a guaranteed shot. He has no life outside of work.

I'll just swing by his office to see if he wants to grab some food with me.

CHAPTER TWO

Seeing Jeff Monday through Friday, two to four times a day hasn't gotten any easier. My breath halts and my heart beats so loud I almost think it's coming out of my ears. I've got it bad, and he barely even notices my existence anymore.

We had a great time that night we all went out and saw the band Crank. Jeff dropped me home, and we sat in his car talking for a while. I didn't want the night to end, and I thought he felt the same, so I went to give him a kiss goodnight. And he froze. Completely seized up. He started his ignition and told me it was a fun night, refusing to look at me. I jumped out of his car before a tear could escape and I could make an ass of myself.

I was humiliated. I've never in my life made the first move. Actually, I've never moved anywhere with anyone. He was going to be my first kiss at twenty-six. I was *so* ready for a first kiss, *finally*. His presence does funny things to me, things I have never felt before. He makes my girlie parts come to life. I never knew that part of my anatomy could ache and literary beg to be touched. This is so foreign to me, but it just feels so right when I'm with him.

He hasn't really talked to me since that night. I get just a quick, uncomfortable smile or maybe a quiet hello. No pointless conversations or fleeting looks any longer. It's almost like it causes him pain to look at me, and for the life of me, I can't figure out why. Was it that bad that I tried to kiss him? Maybe he feels guilty about turning me down or thinks I'm so grotesque that he can't even look at me anymore. He wouldn't be the first person to feel that way. Boys never even gave me a second look growing up.

It's clear I am nowhere near his type. For one split second he had me believing that maybe, just maybe, he saw past my bland complexion and stringy, dull hair. But I should have known. I got my hopes up and knew it was too good to be true. I guess my mother was right for once—men will never stick around too long.

My father walked out on my mother after twenty-two years of marriage when he fell in love with a much younger woman. My mother was devastated. Her whole world turned upside down, and she dragged me down with her. I've been taking care of her ever since. It's been almost eleven years now.

She couldn't bear losing me after my dad walked out on her. Even though it had been years, she begged me to stay. She told me if I left, I would be just like him. What was I supposed to do? Now, all I have for her is resentment and pity. This is my life now. I'm a prisoner of my own guilt.

The reception phone rings. "Good morning, Saunders Literary Agency," I answer.

"Hey, G-friend! Whatcha up too?" Max asks.

An employee walks by, and I buzz him in. "Hey, just working. How are you feeling? Kinsey said you're on bed rest now. What the heck happened, Max? You were fine just the other day."

I hear her sigh. "What happened is Kyle and I were getting it on, and I started cramping. I went to the doctor's yesterday, and she put me on bed rest. That means no physical activities until further notice," she explains.

I can't help but worry and laugh at the same time. "I'm glad you and the baby are OK, but poor Kyle," I say, giggling.

"He's actually been really attentive. It's so cute to observe," she tells me. "We decided to make the baby shower co-ed. I just wanted to give you the heads up—that means Jeff will be there also," Max informs me.

My heart skips a beat with just the mention of his name. "I'll be fine. Don't worry about me. I'm a big girl. I can handle myself," I lie. *Fine* is the very opposite of what I will be, but I can't let Max know this. She has enough stress already, and I won't add to that.

"Good girl. He doesn't deserve a girl like you. Oh! Speaking of—Kroy will be at the shower. I've been dying to introduce the two of you. I think you'll really hit it off," she says.

I groan and slam my head into my palm. "Max—" I whine. "I don't need any pity set-ups."

She laughs. "Elise, this is no pity set-up—*believe* me. Kroy's a good friend of Junior's. They went to high school together, and he is one hot piece of ass. Hopefully, I'm off bed rest before then, because I am totally taking you shopping for one hot, classy dress! In fact, Kinsey and I are setting up a makeover spa day for you. These guys are not gonna know what hit them!"

I have to admit, this sounds like some fun. "Okay, you let me know where and when, and I am there!" I tell her. Mr. Saunders heads up to the front door. "Hey, I gotta go! Boss is here!" I hang up without saying goodbye.

I continue on with my work. "Good morning, Mr. Saunders," I greet him as he passes by my desk.

He gives me a nod. "Good morning, Elise."

I buzz him into the office. Thank God he's not a talker, because quite frankly, he scares me.

The rest of the day goes by without a hitch. I try to time my lunch breaks around Jeff's as much as possible so I can limit the amount of time I cross his path on the daily. Sometimes this works and sometimes it doesn't, but it's better than the alternative. I already feel suffocated when I'm home; the last thing I want is to feel crappy at work.

I stop at the store before heading home to grab some things for dinner. If I don't cook, my mom won't eat. She'd rather drown herself in her sorrows and her bottle of pills. I've tried to get her help, but she refuses to take it. I've even talked her into checking herself into rehab, but she checked herself out with her new druggy boyfriend.

I had to put a lock on my door to keep them from rummaging through my room and pawning my stuff. Of course, this hasn't always stopped them. If they're in desperate need, they'll just kick down the door. I finally stood up to my mom and gave her an ultimatum: either he goes or I do. She chose me—at least I thought she did, until I came home early from work one day and caught him there. I should have known she was lying, since he's clearly the one supplying her habits.

I pull up to the house, grab the grocery bags out of the back, and head inside. As always, the house is stuffy and dark. All the blinds and curtains are drawn closed, and my mom is nowhere to be found. I climb the stairs and walk down the hallway to her room. She's passed out across her bed.

I take a seat next to her. She doesn't even stir. "Mom? You need to get up and eat something," I whisper, shaking her lightly. After a couple of minutes go by, she finally stirs and her eyelids flutter open. "You need to get up, Mom."

She groans. "What time is it?"

I look over to her alarm clock on the nightstand. "It's five o'clock. I'll be downstairs preparing dinner," I tell her and leave the room. No matter how many times I see her like this, it still kills me as much as the first.

I finish putting the groceries away and begin cutting up the vegetables and other ingredients for the chicken soup. It was always one of my favorites growing up. My mother was great in the kitchen. She always had dinner on the table and had the house spotless for my father when he would come home from work.

My father had very particular rules and expected my mother to be compliant and attentive to his every need. He wanted her to dress a certain way, act a certain way, and just exist in a certain way. She forgot how to take care of herself without the approval of my father. She forgot what it was like to live. For so long, everything she did was for him. When he was no longer there, she didn't know how to exist without him.

I never realized this until after everything was said and done and I was grown. I didn't realize how broken my mother already was until I looked back into my past memories and really saw what was going on. He abused her mentally and emotionally and tore her down to nothing, only to rebuild her into what he wanted: a Stepford wife. She no longer has any self-worth, so how was I supposed to break what little she had left by going to college?

The soup has to cook for about an hour, so I do a fast clean-up around the house. I open the blinds and crack the window a bit to let some fresh air in. It's now late July and the weather, like always, is very moody. One day it's eighty degrees outside and the next it's gloomy and chilly—jacket weather. The weather can never seem to make up its mind in Rochester.

I can hear my mother stumbling down the stairs behind me. My whole body tenses up. I never know which side of her I'm going to get. I head towards her to help her to the couch in the living room.

She yanks her arm away from me. "I don't need *your* help!" she snaps.

I can see she is in one of *those* moods. The kind where everything in the world is my fault. I go ahead of her to fix the pillows on the couch and remove the dirty dishes off the coffee table.

She glares at me as she sits. "This house is a mess. Don't you ever clean?"

I don't even bother to look at her, and I take the dishes to the sink. "I work all day. That should be your job since you don't have one," I tell her.

She turns on the TV. "Figures you would say something like that! You're just like your father."

Ouch. That stings. But it's nothing out of the ordinary; she always makes remarks like that to make me feel bad. "Dinner will be ready soon. I'm going to take a shower."

I take off upstairs before she can realize she even affected me. If I show weakness, she'll enjoy it—anything to take the attention off of her. She's cruel and disgustingly mean. I don't know what I did to deserve this, but it's beginning to be too much. People just don't live this way. If I think about my situation any more, I'll crack.

Jeff was like my sanctuary, my getaway. When I was in his presence, even if it was just for a moment, all of this disappeared. I was almost happy. I almost believed life could be normal for me. But like always, my reality came crashing down on me.

I hop out of the shower and hear my mother yelling for me. What the hell could she possibly need now? I dry off fast and throw my T-shirt and sweats on.

"Coming!" I call back to her. I rush downstairs. "What is it, Mom?" I ask, annoyed.

She doesn't even look at me. "I forgot my pills. Be a doll and go get them for me. They're on my bed stand."

Is she serious? This was the emergency? I want to tell her to get them herself, but then I have to endure her mouth even more. It's been a long day, and I'm just ready for it to end. I go upstairs to grab them. Her room smells musty, just like her. I grab the pills from the nightstand, where a letter catches my attention.

It's folded up and tucked halfway underneath a Kleenex box. I pull it out and see my father's handwriting. The envelope underneath it is written out to me. How could she? How could she keep this from me? How many other pieces of mail has she done this with?

I sit down on her bed. I can hear her calling my name in the distance. I open the folded paper. I feel anxious and a little lightheaded as I open it.

My dear Elise,

I know I do not deserve your time, so if you're reading this, thank you. I have made many mistakes in my life, but my biggest one was leaving you. I'm sure you hate me and I don't blame you. You have every right to do so. I was a horrible husband to your mother and left you alone to clean up my mess.

I will be in town next month and I'm hoping you will make the time to see me. I'll be staying at the Crowne Hotel the weekend of the 20th on some business. I will leave Saturday night open for you. I hope to see you.

Love,
Dad

I look at the timestamp on the envelope and see the letter was mailed a week ago. I open her nightstand drawer and rummage through the mess to see if there are any more. The only thing I find is an old newspaper clipping of my father and his new bride. The date is from

2005, a year after he left my mother. He must have married the young bimbo he had an affair with. Great.

I hand my mother the bottle of pills and drop the letter in her lap when I get downstairs. She looks at it and huffs as if it's no big deal.

"Do you care to explain why you didn't give this to me?" I ask. I feel like a mother speaking to her naughty child. My anger spreads through my body like a flame.

She looks up at me with exhaustion in her eyes as though the subject bores her. She is just *so* frustrating! I just want to shake her awake. Shouldn't I be reason enough to live?

"Why would I have given you this? So you can betray me by going to see him?" she spits out.

I can't help but shake my head at her like a disappointed mother. "Mom, he's my father—like it or not. Whether I go to see him or not is none of your business! I'm going to the post office tomorrow to open up my own PO Box. Who knows what else you have kept from me, and I'm honestly sick of it!" I screech.

I rarely have enough courage to stand up to her, but this just has to stop! I stomp over to the kitchen to check on the soup.

"It is my business if you see him! I am your mother, and you would have never been born if it wasn't for me! He wanted me to have an abortion, you know. He didn't want a kid messing up his life, but I refused! I'm the reason you're here," my mother says.

I put the bowls down and lean my hands against the counter with my head down. I shouldn't let her get to me, but I'm only human. Every day that goes by, a part of my soul is chipped off and forever lost. She's supposed to protect me from this sort of thing, not cause it. How can a mother be so cruel? I take a deep breath and continue. I turn the stove off. The soup needs more time, but I can't wait any longer, so I dish out our portions.

I place her bowl down on the coffee table. "I'm turning in early," I tell her before taking my dinner upstairs.

I put the bowl and glass of water down on my nightstand and flop myself down on my bed. I look at my phone, almost dialing Max's number, but then I think twice. She has enough to worry about, and calling upset would only amplify that. Besides, I don't want anyone feeling sorry for me. I keep this part of my life to myself. It's just easier this way.

CHAPTER THREE

66 Two ball, right corner pocket," Junior calls before sinking it in.

I take a big pull of my beer. "Damn!" I say as I spit some out. Junior laughs. "So, have you talked to Kyle lately?" I ask.

Junior calls out his next shot and misses. Finally! "No, not recently. You know how we are: oil and water. We just don't mix. I gave up a long time ago."

"Fifteen ball, middle pocket," I point with the cue stick. "Did your mom tell you about Max?"

He stops in his tracks. "No, what happened?" Junior asks, clearly worried. It's obvious that he holds a special spot for Max. It's nice to see. Even if he doesn't have a relationship with his brother Kyle, at least he will have one with his niece if Max has anything to say about it.

I sink the ball in. "I forgot to mention it to you at lunch, but she was having some early cramping. The doctor put her on bed rest. Kyle's a little freaked out," I explain. "You know, it's never too late to give him a call, even just to check up—"

His eyes glaze over, and I can see him shutting down. "That's definitely not happening. I'll give Max a call, though."

"You talk to Max on the regular?" I ask, sinking my last ball in.

Junior nods his head. "We're playing the best out of three," he says, taking another swig of his beer. "Yeah, Max and I talk a lot actually. Believe me, she has tried hard to get Kyle and I to see eye to eye, but there are just too many years of issues between us. Shit just can't get fixed overnight."

I call the eight ball and sink it. Junior swears under his breath. This game always starts out friendly and ends up competitive. "Do you even remember the issues after that many years of them? I mean, I know how stubborn Kyle can be, believe me, but you're both going to regret the time lost. I don't know what I would do without my brother in my life. I don't care what we've argued about; at the end of the day, those things don't matter. My brother does.

"Maybe there's no need to rehash the old stuff; just agree to move forward and start fresh. Fuck the rest of it. Put it all behind you guys," I tell him, giving him the best advice I can without taking sides or judging.

Junior stops the waitress and orders us another round.

He nods his head. "Maybe you're right. I don't know. It's definitely something to consider. Lord knows it would make everyone else happy as well," he admits. He smacks me on the back; nothing else needs to be said. He listened, and that's all that matters.

The rest of the week goes by routinely, and it's finally Thursday night—McGregor's night! I'm dying for a drink after this long, bland workday. The only highlight of my day was seeing Elise, and I'm pretty sure she hates me.

It's almost as though she trying purposely to avoid me at all costs, and I can't say that I blame her. I was a jerk, and when she tried to kiss me, I shut down. I was afraid if I felt her perfect, plush lips on mine, I would never be able to let go. She just deserves so much better. She's perfect, and I'm a mess.

I pull up to the bar and see all the regulars. Beth and her whole crew are here, including Carrie. Great. Junior and the other guys from work are here too. I walk in, and Matt and Wes start whistling and clapping, purposely trying to embarrass me and make a spectacle. I take a bow, showing no fear.

They already have a beer and a shot of Patrón ready for me, which I'm thankful for.

"Thanks, bro." I give Matt a pat on the back.

He holds up his shot, and we both throw them back. "Whoo! Damn that burns!" Matt gripes, chasing the shot with his beer. He turns to scope the bar scene. "Dude, why does Beth still hang out here?"

I shake my head. "I think she's hoping to catch Kyle here someday. Carrie told me the other day that she's still obsessed with him."

"Wow. That's some crazy shit! Is she ever going to move on? That girl needs some major help." Matt says.

"Didn't you fuck her, too?" Wes asks, jumping in.

I can't help but laugh. "Really funny. Why do you gotta bring that up though? I was just forgetting about all that," Matt responds with a tiny smirk creeping across his face. "She may look good, but she's not worth all the hassle. The sex wasn't that great either!" he admits.

We all burst out laughing—maybe a little too loud, because now we have onlookers, including Beth and Carrie. Out of the corner of my eye, I can see Beth stalking this way. I move down the bar to where Junior is parked to shoot the shit with him. I'm keeping away from that hot mess.

"Man, I think we need a new hangout, some new bodies to be around. These girls are all just used-up drama," I tell Junior, sitting down on the barstool next to him.

Junior puts his beer back down. "I agree. They are definitely not wife material, but it's clear they couldn't give two shits about that."

I look past Junior and see Wes and Matt getting mauled by Beth and Carrie. I shake my head. I signal Jenny over to get Junior and the guys another round. It looks like they're going to need it. I think tonight just might be the first time I leave a bar by myself. My dick doesn't even get a twinge around these girls, and believe me, that's a first!

"Speaking of wife material—what's up with Kinsey? How are you guys getting along as roommates?" I ask.

Junior rolls his eyes in a dramatic way. "We get along by staying away and ignoring each other. She's a freaking nut, man. Her sarcastic attitude is out of this world! And she's a flipping slob! She's leaves her junk all around the apartment," he explains, exasperated.

I can't help but laugh. "Who gives a fuck? She's hot as hell! Don't tell me you haven't even considered banging her?"

His face gets a little flush. Bingo! He definitely wants to tap that ass. Now, to get him to admit this would be a teeth-puller. "Definitely not, man! No effing way! I am steering clear of that. You never shit where you lie. Didn't anyone teach you that?" Junior asks, trying to deflect this back on me. Typical.

"Whatever you say, bro. I know that look when I see it. Kyle had the same look for Max, and look where he is now. Just saying," I say, shrugging my shoulders. I take another sip of my beer while he lets it sink in slowly, or maybe he's trying to come up with some defense. Either way, Kinsey is on his mind.

Junior stays for another beer and then heads home. I grab one more shot for me and the guys before I head out as well. I got my bro time in, and now it's time to hit the sack—alone.

I exit the bar, but before I can make it to my car, I realize Carrie is behind me.

"Hey, Jeff!" she calls. I stop and turn. "Round two?" she asks with a mischievous smirk smeared across her face.

I lean my head down and take a deep breath. Aww, man! I *really* don't want to be alone tonight, but I know leaving with Carrie will be a big mistake. I usually never make the same mistake twice. That's when feelings and messiness start to develop, and I am definitely not about that shit.

Carrie catwalks drunkenly up to me, giving me her best seductive eyes. She reaches out and grabs my junk unexpectedly. I jump; completely caught off guard. She's in rare form tonight. This may actually be fun. Darn! No, no, no.

"Not tonight, Carrie. I have to get up early tomorrow," I lie. I see the spark light up in her eyes as though I have just given her a challenge to overcome. "You know we were only a one-time deal anyways. I told you that."

She pokes her lip out and pouts. I have to admit, it's sort of cute. Maybe I can break my rule just one time? But then what? What's to say she won't want to spend the night or do this again and again? I can't take the chance. She's not the one. Bottom line.

"Aww, come on Jeffery. How about one for the road then?" she offers and begins to walk towards my car. Maybe she's on to something. If I don't bang her in bed, then there's no need to worry about her wanting to spend the night. I can get my rocks off and go home.

I grab her arm and direct us to her car.

I lie in bed, looking at the clock that now reads four. I can't sleep. My mind keeps drifting back to Elise, and I can't stop feeling guilty about what I've just done with Carrie. God I'm so *stupid!* I really have to gain control over myself. The whole act was so pointless. It was fun in the moment, but once it's all said and done, I just feel disgusting.

I came home and took a shower right away. I couldn't wait to wash her smell off of me. I could never forget how Elise smells. Her scent is so sweet and intoxicating that I now crave to wrap it around me and have it envelope me like a cocoon. I smell her every time I walk through the reception area at work and immediately feel my dick twitch. Her fragrance just does something to me; I can't explain it.

I'm dying to taste her. I can only imagine what she tastes like. Pure heaven, I'm sure. Someone else is probably doing what I should be doing to her right now. She should be safely wrapped up in my arms, not some dickhead's that probably doesn't cherish her the way she should be. Just the thought of her with someone else completely undoes me.

I throw my covers off of me and get up to turn my fan on. Kyle got me into the weird habit of sleeping with my fan on year-round. It was all the sleepovers we had as kids. I got that addiction from him while he got his player skills from me. Man, those were the days—the teenage years. Who would have ever thought Kyle would be the first one to get linked up?

I can't help but smile as my thoughts drift to Elise before my heavy eyelids slam shut.

CHAPTER FOUR

Elise

My muscles are screaming bloody murder as I slip out of bed. I didn't sleep much last night; I kept tossing and turning, reliving my own daily nightmare. My mind just wouldn't shut down. I just can't escape my life for one moment. I'm being haunted on a daily and nightly basis. My life at home is a living hell. I need to figure out how to get out of this mess. I need to figure out what to do with my mother. If I don't, I may end up just like her.

I get dressed, bypass the coffee this morning, and get the hell out of this house. As soon as I hit the fresh air and warm sun, my whole outlook on life changes. That house is like a vortex of misery, sucking anyone who enters it into the deep depths of hell.

The birds are chirping sweet melodies with not a care in the world. We coexist in the same universe but our worlds are so different. What I wouldn't give to have not a care in the world and the ability to fly far, far away.

It's quiet when I enter work. I'm usually not here this early, but at this point, I'd rather be here than home. I head to the kitchen. I am in dire need of some caffeine; it's screaming my name.

I hear the door open and slam shut behind me. When I look back to greet the person, I stop, completely caught off guard.

"Good morning, Elise. You're here early," Jeff says. My heart sinks as I gulp hard.

He walks by me to pour his cup of coffee, and I can feel my body sing with need: need for him, need for his arms to be wrapped around me, and need for his lips to be touching every aching part of me.

All air is constricted in my lungs as I hold my breath, almost unable to speak. But somehow I find the courage. "Yes, I'm working some overtime," I lie.

I busy myself with pouring the sugar and cream into my coffee, but I can still *feel* him behind me. Every nerve ending in my body can sense his presence and closeness. When I'm near him, my body just comes to life.

He sets his steaming cup of coffee next to mine, mimicking the same routine. It's weird, when I turn to reach for a stir stick, I swear I can hear him inhale the air next to me. Do I smell? I almost want to sniff myself just to check. My cheeks flush pink from embarrassment.

His aroma is refreshing but almost a little provocative. His delicious, tangy smell is alluring in the most sensual way. The smell screams sex and makes me wet in all the right places. *Crap!* I need to get away from him—and fast!

"Will you be working overtime tonight?" he asks.

I hear the door open and a group of cackling employees come through in rare morning form. The laughing chatter now swarms around us. I don't want anyone staring, making this more awkward than it already is, so I give him a weak smile and walk off without answering.

What does he care anyways? He gave up the right to ask me questions and know my business a long time ago when he stopped being my friend. Max was right; I need to cut my losses and keep it moving. Maybe this Kroy guy will turn out to be a good thing for me. Just what I need to get my mind off of Jeff and all the other craziness in my life, hopefully. I could use a good distraction.

I have to admit though, walking away and leaving him hanging gave me a little boost—like I've just gained a teeny tiny bit of power back. I can't help but smile at myself as I set my cup of coffee down on my desk. I have to text Max; she'll love hearing about this!

I throw her a quick text and set my phone aside on my desk to begin my daily routine. Not five minutes go by before my phone is lit up and vibrating across my desk.

It's Max. "Hey!" I whisper as an employee walks by. I buzz him in.

"No. Fucking. Way! Did you really leave him hanging like that?" she questions excitedly.

I giggle. "I totally did! I caught him staring at me through the reflection of the door as I walked off!"

Max screeches through the phone so loud I have to remove it from my ear. "I'm so proud of you! And don't you dare feel bad, Elise. He deserved it after the way he treated you. Didn't it feel good?" she asks.

I nod my head as if she can see me. "It felt really good! And I think you're right about getting my feet wet. I think I'm definitely ready to meet that guy, Kroy," I tell her.

I can hear her clapping her hands together. "Yay! Ok, I have a doctor's appointment later today to check if everything's okay. So if everything goes well, I'm hoping they take me off of bed rest. Then tomorrow, Kinsey and I are taking you to the spa for a makeover and shopping for something to wear at the shower next weekend, okay?"

I smile. "Yes, I could totally use some girl time!"

"Okay, I'll text you later to let you know what's going on."

We hang up. It's time for me to get back to work before Mr. Saunders walks in and catches me on my cellphone. The rest of the day goes by like normal. Nothing exciting or unusual happens, and as soon as five o'clock comes, I am dreading going home. Maybe I should just work some overtime, but I'm sure my mother hasn't eaten all day, and if I don't feed her, she will just feed herself with pills. One day I'm going to come home and find her dead on the couch. Somehow, someway, I have to get her help. We both can't go on living like this.

I decide to stop at the liquor store to grab a bottle of wine. Screw it. It's Friday night, and it's been a long week. I could use something to relax me. To my surprise, when I enter the house, my mother is downstairs on the couch watching TV. This is a very rare occasion, and I can't help but wonder if her boyfriend, Reggie, has just left.

"Mom, was Reggie just here?" I ask her.

She doesn't even bother to look my way. "Of course not, why would you think that?" she responds, annoyed.

I head to the kitchen and begin taking out the cheese, butter, and bread to make us grilled cheeses—something easy for tonight. "Oh, I don't know . . . maybe because you're out of your bed and down here," I reply.

We don't say another word to each other. I place her plate down in front of her and take mine up to my room with me. In order to get peace and tranquility, I have to seclude myself in the confines of my bedroom. It's sad, but it's better than the alternative—being in the company of misery.

I get a text from Max letting me know she will be able to go to the spa but that she still needs to take it easy and be off her feet as much as possible, so no shopping just yet. We have all next week to do that anyways. I'm just glad I get to spend some quality time with my girls.

My body's relaxed enough after my second glass of wine and some much-needed reality TV therapy; I am ready for bed. My mind unconsciously drifts to this morning's conversation with Jeff. He hasn't said more than two words to me in the past couple of months. I can't help but wonder why the change now? Was it because he felt obligated to speak to me since it was just him and I in the room? I don't like feeling like an obligation or taking pity from anyone. If I did, I would simply share my depressing life story with others.

I just wish there was some small part of him that maybe misses me, misses our friendship. I know we weren't friends for all that long, but he was the first male that ever gave me the time of day. I know I'm not the prettiest or have all that much going for me, but he didn't seem to care. He seemed to like me just as I am. I think that's why it hurt so much when he began to act as though I don't exist.

I'm exhausted. When I close my eyes, I envision those chestnut eyes staring back at me. This comforts me as I fall asleep.

My phone shrieks and my eyes snap open, sucking me from my peaceful sleep. Ugh! I look at the clock, and it says ten in the morning. What the hell? I pick up my phone, and I see Max's number across my screen.

"Hey, Max," I say. I sit up, hoping something's not wrong. "Is everything OK?"

"Everything's fine, girl! Are you ready?" Max asks.

My brows furrow. "Ready for what?"

She clicks her tongue. "Um, hello? It's spa day! I'll be there to get you in an hour. Kinsey is going to meet us there, so go get ready!" she insists.

I laugh. "Okay, see you then."

I jump in the shower. By the time I'm finished getting ready, Max is in the driveway and beeping the horn. She's become so impatient since pregnancy. I hurry and get my shoes on and then lock up behind me before she has a coronary.

I jump in the car, and she hands me a coffee. "Oh my God! I *so* need this! Thank you," I say while taking a big whiff of the steam pouring out of the cup.

She backs out of the driveway. "I figured so since I woke you up. Today is not the day to sleep your life away."

I take a much-needed sip, and it tastes like heaven. "So, what did the doctor have to say?" I ask.

She runs her hand through her hair. "They said I'm doing too much and I need to lessen my workload. Yeah, okay! I'm the boss; how the hell am I supposed to do that?"

Max is married to her work. It's been her comfort and security for years, and I can see it's hard for her to put it on the back burner while she just lies around the house. But she's going to be a mama soon, and I know when it comes down to it, Max will do whatever it takes to keep her baby safe, because that's what good mothers do.

I can see how stressed this is all making her. "Max, that's what Kinsey is for. And Kyle's mother, I'm sure, will also agree with the doctor. They will figure it out. So will you still be working from home?"

She nods her head. "Yeah, most likely until the baby is born. Kyle set up camp in the bedroom. It now looks like a full-blown office in there. Poor guy. I think he finally realized that he's not going to get any until this baby pops out. The doctor said no sex until further notice," she tells me while shaking her head.

I almost spit out my coffee. "Well, there are always other things besides sex that can be done. I'm sure you guys can get creative," I joke.

She rolls her eyes and laughs along with me. "Yes, you're definitely right about that one! He does love my BJs!"

I feel the heat creep across my face. This is a topic I am definitely not used to talking about. Max and Kinsey are professional sex talkers, but I lack the experience and the knowledge to feel comfortable about putting my two cents in. Of course, after spending enough time with them, I should be caught up real soon.

I groan. "That's just too much information for the morning. You can keep that to yourself," I gripe. We both laugh.

We pull up to the spa. The parking lot is pretty empty. I'm sure the rest of the world is still sleeping—like I should be. Kinsey pulls up right next to us. She is clearly a morning person. She is sparkling and energetic, and she makes me want to puke.

I hop out of the car while Max slides out carefully.

"Hey, girls! I am *so* ready for this spa day!" Kinsey blurts out, happily waiting for us at the back of the car.

I keep my sunglasses on, still not ready for the happy, gleaming sunshine. I continue to sip on my coffee as though it's my lifeline. "I better be able to take a nap in here," I say to Kinsey, grumpily.

"Aww! Do we have a Miss Grumpypants with us this morning?" Kinsey teases. God, I hate when she talks like this.

I open the door and watch Max waddle in. I wonder if she realizes she is waddling yet. "We sure do!" Max chimes in as I grumble something incoherent next to her.

I roll my eyes in exaggeration and take another sip of my lifeline. We walk into the spa.

"Good morning, girls! My name is Rachael, and I'll be your go-to girl for the day. Please follow me," she directs, her voice too chipper for this hour. It's frankly annoying.

Rachael is petite with an all-American-girl appearance. She and Kinsey will definitely hit it off, I am sure. She brings us down a small hallway that leads into a vacant room with a tranquil setting.

It smells divine with the floral and coco aromas. The lights are dimmed and the candles are lit and leave light dancing softly across the walls. Soft melodies surround us gently as the trickling waterfall on the back wall calms our energy into a humble silence.

Rachael hands us each a robe. "Okay, ladies. Change into these. We have some mimosas, fruit, and pastries laid out in the back room through there," she says, pointing behind us. "I'll be back in fifteen minutes to take you to your rooms to start your massages." She exits and closes the door behind her.

Aahh! This actually sounds like heaven. I just hope I don't end up falling asleep during my massage. I'm not too sure if I snore, but how embarrassing would that be?

"Hell yeah!" Kinsey shouts, heading for the room filled with goodies. "I might just get drunk before noon!"

Max and I can't help but laugh at her. Kinsey is just so out of control sometimes, and I love it. She's a breath of fresh air. I only wish I was as outgoing as she is. She doesn't put up with anything, and I know without a doubt she wouldn't allow herself to get sucked into the mess I'm in. If only I could separate from my mother and not feel guilt from doing it. I think the shame alone would rip me apart. I don't know which option is worse—living with her or living with a guilty conscience the rest of my life.

Max sucks me out of my vortex of self-pity. "Elise, is everything okay?" she asks, worried.

I almost don't want to look at her for fear that she may see the truth. I look down to my lap, fiddling with my fingers. "I just feel a little off-kilter today," I answer, telling the truth. I'm a mess after this whole week. I finally gather the courage to look up. Max is studying me intently. She gives me a kind smile, and immediately I feel safe. I'm with someone who really cares.

She reaches for my hand and gives me a squeeze. "You know you can always talk to me. I'm here for you if you need anything," Max tells me.

I give her a reassuring smile, but before I can say another word, Kinsey comes in. "Oh. My. *God!* You have to see the spread in there! This place is *amazing!* Do you see these danishes?" she asks us, holding up a huge apple danish with sugary glaze melting off the sides. My stomach is now growling. I think I just gained ten pounds by looking at it.

Max slides and bends out of her seat immediately. "Yup. Baby is hungry!" she proclaims while waddling to the other room.

Kinsey and I change out of our clothes and put the robes on. She hands me a mimosa. "You're not pregnant yet, so you're drinking with me. I can't be the only drunk one here," she says, giggling.

"Okay, but only so you're not the odd one out," I reply, joking.

Max comes waddling out of the room with a plate full of goodies, and Kinsey can't control herself. "Damn, girl! Are you packing twins in that belly?"

Max stops and glares at her. "Shut up, Kinsey!" Her mouth is fully stuffed with a donut.

I stifle my laugh, trying hard to contain it. Now the glare is on me. Not good to piss off a pregnant lady. Even I know this. I hold my hands up in surrender. We hear a knock at the door before Rachael enters.

"Are you girls ready?" she asks. She looks to Max who is fully dressed with donut crumbs hanging from her lips. I can see Rachael's amusement, and Max rolls her eyes. "How about you two come with me?" Rachael points to Kinsey and I. "And you can meet us down the hall once you've changed," she says to Max.

We get settled under the sheet on the massage table. The soft music is humming around us, the candles are flickering with the aroma of wet wood and a hint of lavender, and the built-in waterfall trickling down the wall is extremely hypnotizing. I feel like this is what heaven must be like. I close my eyes, saturating myself in this moment.

"So, Max told me about your run-in with Jeff—" Kinsey informs me, waiting for my reaction.

I keep my eyes closed, not wanting to give anything extra away. "Yeah, it was just me in the kitchen at work, so I think he just felt obligated to speak to me," I tell her. Pain stabs through my heart with this thought.

"Elise, any man would be lucky to have your attention. You are an amazing person and an extremely beautiful woman. I think there's more to it than just him not wanting to hang around you. I think he realized he just wasn't good enough for you. But if he gives up that easily, then he's not worth it."

"Just wait until you meet Kroy! He is one hot tamale, *and* he can cook a mean meal—he's a chef!" Kinsey says.

I open my eyes to look at her. "Then why aren't you with him?" I ask, confused.

Kinsey is beyond gorgeous. She can have any man she likes. Why not Kroy, if he's as great as she says?

She smacks her lips. "He may be hot, but he is just not my type and vice versa. He has never once hit on me since I've known him. We are completely in the friend zone!" she tells me, laughing. I can't help but laugh right along with her—it's contagious.

Hmm. I'm starting to wonder if she has a thing for Kyle's brother, Junior. I mean, they do live together, and being under the same roof day in and day out has to do something to them physically and emotionally. I mean, they're both hot as hell, and Kinsey is always complaining that she hasn't gotten laid in months. Of course, she'll never admit anything relating to Junior. Last time Max brought it up, she totally freaked on her.

"Okay, so I am ready to meet this Kroy guy, but tell me, Kinsey, who are you into lately?" I ask.

She narrows her eyes at me. "Don't even! We are *so* not turning this around on me!"

Gotcha! "Okay, fine. But one question— have you seen Junior in just a towel yet?" I question with a giggle. That's gotta be one hot sight!

Max walks in just as Kinsey is about to give it to me. "Uh-oh! What have I just walked into?" Max asks, looking between the both of us.

Kinsey huffs, and I roll my eyes. "Nothing much. I was just asking her about Junior."

Max lies down on the special pregnancy table. It has a cutout in the middle for the baby bump. "Oh my God! I've being dying to lie on my stomach! This is pure heaven!" Max moans. Kinsey and I laugh. Max's face looks as though she's just had a major orgasm. I am not looking forward to those baby bump days. I'm not too sure I'll even get a chance to have *those days* if I can't find a man. I'm gonna be the old, single woman forever. "Anyways, Kins, what's up with you and Junior? How's the whole roomie thing going?" Max adds.

Kinsey slams her forehead on the massage table. The three masseuses come over and begin while we're in the midst of our conversation.

"He's annoying as ever. I swear, he's never in a good mood and is always complaining about my messes. It's like living with a grumpy, old man!" Kinsey vents. I jump a bit as the masseuse pours the cold lotion on my upper back.

"Well, you can be a little bit messy. I remember our room in college. You had too many clothes, and they were everywhere!" Max reveals.

"Yeah, and who let you borrow them?" Kinsey huffs.

I lift my head up to quiet them down. "Girls, this is supposed to be a relaxing massage! And Kins, if I must be hooked up, then we need to find you a man as well. It's only fair."

The rest of the massage goes by without any bickering. Now on to the salon part of the day. They told me this would be a full-on makeover day, but I didn't think my hair was included. I allow Kinsey and Max to surprise me by deciding what to do with my hair. After hours of coloring, washing, and cutting, the hairdresser turns me around to face the mirror.

Immediately my hands go up as I gasp. Is this really me? It can't possibly be. The golden-blond highlights liven my hair up to a vibrant shine—no more dull and boring dirty blond. She added layers and angles that sweep around my face, making my hair look healthy and bouncy like a Suave commercial. I want to shake my head back and forth and replay it in slow motion. I've never seen my hair so alive before.

"Wow, Elise! You look amazing!" Max screeches, trying to jump up and down.

We all look back through the mirror. "I can't believe this is really me!" I say.

"Well, you better believe it! I can't wait to take you shopping this week!" Kinsey jumps in. "With this new look and your hot body, you're gonna kill 'em!"

I look at my phone, and I can't believe it's almost three o'clock. We have been here for hours. Poor Max; first it was her feet that ached, but since she's been forced to remain off them, her butt is now taking the brunt of it all.

Max and Kinsey take care of the bill. Before we leave, I just have to let them know how I'm feeling. Tears begin to fill my eyes. God, I don't want to cry! "You girls are amazing! I feel so lucky to have you both in my life. I just wanted to say thank you for the best day ever. I don't deserve friends like you," I tell them honestly. A tear creeps down my cheek.

"Aww, Elise! Yes you do!" Max and Kinsey both say at the same time while wrapping their arms around me for a group hug.

"We love you, girl!" Kinsey says. "Anything you need, we're here for you!"

Max wipes the tears from my cheeks. I feel so emotional and so loved at the moment. This is most definitely a new feeling for me. It's a feeling that I didn't realize how much I was missing out on until today.

CHAPTER FIVE

Jeff

Man, I can't stop thinking about Elise. I was so close to her Friday—it was killing me. The sensational vibe that courses through my body every time I am that close to her completely knocks me off of my feet. I am totally off balance when I'm near her, surrounded and completely submerged by her energy and her tantalizing smell.

She's a goddess, and she doesn't even know it. I think that's why I'm so drawn to her. It's refreshing to be in the presence of someone who is completely unaware of their effect on others. She's the light to my dark. I'm just not too sure how much longer I can stay away from her; it's a constant battle I have to fight.

I yawn loudly and stretch before I make my way out of my warm bed into the bathroom to do my normal Sunday morning ritual. It's only nine in the morning. I have to meet Kyle and my brother, Julian, at the gym in about thirty minutes. I need some major stress relief, and working out is the perfect outlet.

Kyle and Julian are already warming up as I walk in. Kyle looks extremely alert for a Sunday morning—it must be the lack of partying. I wish I could say the same, but lately, me, my beer, and my tequila are best of buds.

"What's up, man?" Kyle says, slapping me up. "You're looking a little rough this morning. Long night?" he asks.

I begin my stretches. "Yeah, you can say that."

"Damn, bro. Please don't tell me you brought Carrie home again," Kyle replies.

Julian jumps in from the treadmill. "No way! You know Jeff doesn't mess with the same girl twice," he responds through heavy breaths. These guys know me like the back of their hand.

"Nah, definitely not Carrie. I actually met up with the girls from work: Alison and Jadah and some of their girlfriends. They were a wild bunch of chicks," I exclaim. I jump on the treadmill next to Julian.

"Aww, man! Don't tell me you banged Alison!" Kyle says. "You're going to regret sleeping with someone you work with, believe me! Learn from my experiences, man," he tells me, shaking his head.

"Are you crazy? I didn't take any of them girls home. I went home solo. I look like shit because I couldn't sleep last night. I kept tossing and turning. My mind's been going crazy. I think I need a vacation," I say to Kyle.

They both stop mid-run. "Wait, *you* didn't smash last night?" Kyle questions.

"Nope."

"Yeah *fucking* right!" he responds.

Julian puts his two cents in again. "How about we take a guy's trip? We can go to Miami or even Vegas!" he says excitedly.

I just shake my head at him. My brother has completely lost it.

"Can't. I gotta be here in case of any emergencies with Max. She's now close to her third trimester, and anything can happen at this point," Kyle explains.

Julian pouts. "How is Max doing? Is she still on bed rest?" I ask.

"No, the doctor took her off Friday. She and Kinsey took Elise to the spa for the day yesterday. She can do normal stuff, but she just can't be on her feet for long periods of time. It's driving her crazy. She won't be going back to work until after the baby is born, though," Kyle answers.

Just the mention of Elise's name completely undoes me. I swear I flinch, and I'm hoping Kyle doesn't notice this small movement.

"Yeah, she is most definitely going to go crazy," I agree with a laugh. Kyle has a lot on his plate when it comes to Max. She can be very demanding at times, but somehow Kyle deals with that part of her very well. "How's your dad taking all of this?"

Kyle begins on the weight bench. "You know, he's actually coming around. He's stopped by the house a few times with Mom and had dinner with us. I think the idea of Max and the baby is growing on him. What about you, have you spoken to your father lately?"

I take a deep breath. "I talked with him before he left for London on a business trip. He asked me and Julian to come down to South Carolina for a week when he gets back. I guess he wants to introduce us to the woman he's been dating. He said it's getting pretty serious," I answer, sitting next to him on the bench.

"So, how do you both feel about that?" Kyle asks.

Julian shrugs. "I could care less. Mom and Dad have been split up for a long time now. Dad can't stay single and lonely forever, you know?"

He most definitely has a point, but I just don't see it that way. I barely see my father enough as it is, and now he wants me to share the time I do have with someone else? It's just not something I'm interested in or care to do.

"I feel as though I would be betraying my mom. She'll act like it doesn't bother her, but it will. She's still in love with him, though she'll never admit it. I know it's true. He broke her heart already. I don't want to be the next one to break it," I admit.

Man, this is getting really deep for a Sunday morning conversation. Kyle's the only one that knows my family issues. I don't talk about them with anyone else.

My mother left because my father couldn't put us first above his work. She was hoping that he would follow after us to try to win his family back, but he never did. He hasn't even been to New York once to visit his sons, he figured a substantial trust fund would make up for his absence, and now he wants me to travel down to South Carolina to meet this new important person in his life? I think he is out of his mind.

"Jeff, I don't think your mom will see it that way. She's always pushed for you and Julian to have a relationship with your dad. I think you should just talk to her before you make your decision," Kyle says. How did he become so wise? I think Max is most definitely rubbing off on my friend in the best sort of way.

We finish up our workouts and take off. I'm sweaty and in need of a major shower. Today is definitely a lounge-on-the-couch sort of day; I just wish I had someone to lounge with.

It's already Monday morning. I have no idea where the weekend went, but I'm glad it's over because now I can steal a glimpse of Elise, even if it's for a short moment. I see her through the glass doors as I make my way up the sidewalk. Her hair is different. It's lighter and feathers around her face just so. She looks angelic and delicate, mesmerizingly beautiful. She looks this way every moment of every day, but today she seems to have a special glow to her.

I crave to have my lips against hers, to have my fingers glide against her velvety soft skin, and to hear her small moans against my ears. I'm getting hard just thinking about it.

God, why did I freeze up when she was practically begging for me to touch her? She was right there in front of me, and all I had to do was reach out and reciprocate. I fucked up. I regret that decision every moment of each passing day.

I pull open the entrance door, and Elise looks up. We lock eyes for a moment. I swear time halts, and it's just her and me. Everything else around us fades into the darkness. My heart is pounding through my ears. She does things to me that no other girl has ever done, and she doesn't even try. I smile and she immediately disconnects from me, looking down, ripping us out of my moment of bliss. Damn! In just one instant, it's all gone.

I decide now is as good a time as any to give her more than a quick smile—to show her something more. "Good morning, Elise. Your hair looks beautiful," I add.

Her brows furrow together, confused. "Um, thank you," she replies, clearly unsure why I'm speaking to her.

I don't want to make her feel more uncomfortable, so I head into the office without another word.

The rest of the week goes by without a hitch. I made it a mission to say hello to Elise every time I passed by her. I think it threw her off, considering I haven't spoken more than two words to her in the last couple of months. I just can't stay away anymore. The pull is just too great. I'm thinking about asking her out for some coffee or maybe a drink or something. I'm just not too sure she will take my offer, considering how I treated her last time around. I wouldn't blame her, either. I got her to trust me, and then I just stomped all over it and threw it away. I won't be making that same mistake again—no flipping way.

Tuesday and Thursday night I went out to McGregor's with the guys. Unfortunately, I ended up leaving with a warm body on Thursday night, and I completely regretted it right after. I felt dirty and sleazy, considering I just met her hours before. I don't know what my deal is, because this wasn't my first rodeo, but it *was* my first time having feelings of guilt. I never thought this day would come.

I fall asleep with thoughts of Elise in my head. I just can't seem to get away from her no matter what I try. I am her bitch in every way possible, and she doesn't even know it. I'm just beginning to realize it myself.

It's finally Saturday morning, the day of Max's baby shower, and the day I will be in Elise's presence for more than five seconds. This is the day I'm going to make my move. I'm going to ask her to grab a drink with me after. This time I'm not walking away; it will have to be her that makes that move.

I pull up to Valencia's Restaurant, where the shower is being held. Max and Kyle decided to do a co-ed shower, which is fine with me as long as there is a bar. I walk up to the main entrance, and the first person I see is Kyle's father smoking a cigarette.

I reach out to shake his hand. "Hey, Mr. Saunders. How's it going?"

He gives my hand a firm shake. "Oh, you know, just out here to get some air. It's pretty crowded in there," he says. This is clearly not his thing.

"Okay, well I'm going in," I tell him. He slaps me on the back as I walk past him. Ready or not, here it goes—my first baby shower. This ought to be interesting.

I step in the room, and it's jam-packed. The place is swallowed by pinks and frilly lace—completely over the top. This definitely has Kinsey written all over it. I still can't believe my man is having a girl. Now, instead of being the guy that tries to steal a girl's virtue, he has to protect his daughter from that guy. Boy, is he going to have his work cut out for him. Karma's a bitch; let's just hope my future kid is a boy.

I scope the place out real quick to locate Kyle and Max. I see them in the far corner, surrounded by friends and family trying to cop a feel on Max's belly. Kyle looks content, like a proud papa. Once we make eye contact, I give him a quick nod and head over to the bar.

"Excuse me," I say to two beautiful brunettes sitting at the bar. I squeeze in between them. They both look my way and flash flirtatious, seductive smiles. I smirk back, trying to be on my best behavior. "How are you ladies this afternoon?"

"Good now that you're here," says the girl to my right.

The chick on the left giggles and then smacks her friend on the leg. "Samantha!" she scolds. She then turns to me. "I'm sorry, she can be a little bold sometimes. I'm Josie, and this is my friend, Samantha," she says. They both hold out their hands for me to shake.

I shake their hands but quickly take my hand back. "Nice to meet you both. Are you friends of Maxine's?"

The bartender comes over to take my drink order. I decide to keep it classy with a glass of merlot. Somehow, a beer seems out of place here. This is definitely not the bar scene.

"Yes, we all went to the same college together. How about you?" Josie asks, taking a sip of her pink drink.

The bartender places my merlot in front of me. I cash out and leave her a nice tip. "I've known Kyle since eighth grade. We go back a long time," I explain, rotating the stem of my wine glass.

Samantha rubs her leg against my hip. I freeze. This is not going down here at a freaking baby shower. I gotta keep myself in check. I step away from her an inch.

"So, did you come with anyone?" Samantha asks. I look in her direction while taking a sip of my wine. She's giving me a smile filled with promises. I stop immediately, completely dumbstruck when I see a blonde bombshell in my view. She looks freaking hot! Where the heck did my innocent, precious Elise go? This woman standing in my eyesight is a sex kitten waiting to get jumped. She has legs for days in that short, hot pink dress. I can picture those babies wrapped around me as I pump myself deep inside of her. Samantha must have noticed my hesitation and looks in the same direction. "Is that your girlfriend?" she asks, wide-eyed.

Her voice is distant, just noise in the background, as I take in the scene unfolding in front of me. Elise looks radiant, strikingly beautiful. I can't take my eyes off of her. She seems happy and so carefree. I haven't seen her this way since she was with me last. She has this amazing magnetic energy that just draws a person in, and I can see that's exactly what's happening with the douche she's talking to.

I know the guy. He's a friend of Junior's. When I see Junior, I'm gonna let him have it for this! We've talked enough for him to know I have a thing for Elise, and just because I've never said it straight out, he should have still gotten the picture.

I can't help but feel anger, heartbreak, and insane jealousy all at once. I shut my eyes for a moment and breathe while rubbing the bridge of my nose. I can't act like a jackass, but every muscle in my body is screaming for me to walk over there, grab her hand, and blow this joint. Just breathe, Jeff. Just breathe.

"No, she's just a good friend—for now. Listen, it was nice meeting you both," I tell them without another thought before walking towards my future.

I swerve in and out of the crowd. I watch as Kroy places his hand on the small of Elise's back and leans in closer to whisper something in her ear. My jaw locks as I hold back my erratic feelings. *Finally,* we lock eyes as she looks away from him, and I now have her undivided attention as I walk up to them.

I stop right in front of her, blocking him out of the way. "Hello, Elise," I greet her, pulling her to my side. I kiss her on the cheek and make sure to linger just a bit longer than normal.

She clears her throat before she speaks. She looks to Kroy and back to me again. "Jeff, this is—"

I jump in before she can finish. "Kroy." She looks a little confused, so I clarify for her, "We've known each other for a while now."

Kroy holds out his hand to me. "Nice to see you, Jeff. How are things going?" I can see him clearly sizing me up, preparing himself mentally for the tug-of-war fight for Elise's attention. Well, I'm game. Or I can just beat the shit out of him. I don't want him anywhere near her.

"Good. Things are going good," I answer back. Elise is just quietly observing. She takes a sip of her drink nervously. "I wasn't aware that you two knew each other—" I say.

She quickly jumps in before Kroy can respond. "We don't. We've only just met," she says so matter-of-factly.

I take a sip of my merlot while taking the sight of her in slowly. She squirms under my scrutiny. I have to control my thoughts—and the images of me taking her to the bathroom and bending her over the sink in that little pink dress—to myself before I go rock-hard in front of everyone here. That would make for interesting baby shower talk.

Kroy's eyes narrow as he's trying to figure me out. He's clearly wondering what my connection is to her. I can't help but puff out my chest and lift my chin, staking my claim. He smirks, now understanding my threat, and the game is on. He's not getting near her.

He turns all his attention to Elise as though I have miraculously disappeared. "What time should I pick you up tomorrow?" he asks her.

Ugh! I didn't just hear him say that! There is no way she can see this piece-of-crap scumbag! Everyone thinks he's all high and mighty—the all-around do-gooder, but not everyone knows what I know. I should have outed him when I had the chance, but I had too much at stake back then. I couldn't risk him doing the same to me.

See, years ago—during my high school years—I was a hot mess. The typical teenage boy who lacked a father figure, who was easily temperamental and despised the world and everyone in it. I did some unthinkable things back then, but nothing nearly as bad as Kroy.

Clearly, those years molded me into the fucked up man-whore I am today. The only thing my father taught me was that women are disposable. The only one who could get through to me during that low time was Kyle, and that is still the case.

I even blamed my mother for leaving my father. I told her it was her fault he wasn't there for us, but deep down I knew that was simply not the truth. If he wanted to be with us, he would have been there, plain and simple. I needed to take my anger out on someone, and unfortunately, I used her as a punching bag. I hurt her tremendously. I still haven't forgiven myself for that. I don't know if I ever will, but ever since then, I have made it a point to treat my mother with the utmost respect.

She made the decision to walk away from a life of unhappiness and had the courage to raise two boys all on her own. To me, she's the bravest person I've ever known.

But if she ever found out the things I did as a teenager with Kroy's help, it would ruin her. That's why I've always kept my mouth shut about it, and now it has come back to bite me in the ass.

"How about six?" she replies to him. He smiles, gloating. I want to pound his face in. "Actually, it might be easier if I just met you there. Text me the time and place," she tells him. I can't help but grin. He doesn't have her in the bag—yet. That means I still have a chance.

"Sure, I'll text you tomorrow. I'm gonna go find Junior," he tells her, giving her a leisurely kiss on the cheek. He turns to me with an irritated nod. "Jeff." He turns and walks away.

Now it's just Elise and I. I have so many things I want to say to her, but none of them seem to want to leave my mouth. The deadly silence is uncomfortable as she looks to me to start. I quickly take another sip of my wine. I probably should have eaten something before I began to down this.

"So—you and Kroy, huh?" I ask. Maybe I should have begun with something a little more subtle. I just couldn't resist though.

She furrows her brows and narrows her eyes accusingly, as if I have some nerve even asking. Maybe she is right, but I can't help it. "Yes, he asked me out on a date. Why is it you're all of a sudden so curious, when just the other day I didn't exist?"

Wow. Ouch, that definitely burned. I must have really hit a nerve. Never has she been this outspoken before, but I know I deserve it. She's only part right, though. I always knew she existed.

"I've always been curious—more than you know," I tell her. "And you've always existed to me—just so you know. I was hoping we could get to know each other again. Maybe go out for a drink after this—"

I allow my words to hang. I can't tell what she's thinking. She's not giving anything away. "Why would I want to do that?" she asks, squinting her eyes at me.

Boy, she's definitely not going to make this easy on me. "Because I miss you," I say honestly, giving her my best panty-dropper smile.

"You miss me? You're the one that stopped talking to me without even giving me a reason, Jeff."

I can tell she's angry with me. I grab her free hand and entwine it with mine so we're skin on skin. My whole body lights up with just this small amount of contact. This never happens to me. No woman has ever even fazed me, let alone drove me to my wits' end like she does.

I lower my gaze, making sure I have her undivided attention before I speak again. "I only did it for your benefit. I wanted to protect you."

"Protect me from what, Jeff? Why would I need protecting?" she asks.

In this moment, it feels as though everything surrounding us has dissipated into thin air. She's all I see, all I smell, and all I hear. It's just us, the way it should be. "From me. I wanted to protect you from me," I finally answer her honestly.

She slowly lifts her hand to my face and then strokes my cheek lightly with her thumb. I close my eyes, soaking in every moment of this. It's like heaven being touched by her. Nothing else compares. "Don't you understand that I was willing to take that risk? It was my choice, and I chose you. While you were trying to protect me, you also crushed me. You stole that choice away from me, and I just can't trust that won't happen again, friends or no friends. I'm sorry, Jeff," she says to me. She touches my face one last time before walking away.

I open my mouth to yell after Elise, but nothing comes out. My whole world crumbles in a matter of seconds. I watch her walk off into the crowd. I want to run after her, to make her listen to me, but at the moment, I'm completely speechless. I know there's nothing that could be said right now to change her mind. She completely rejected me.

I've never been rejected before. I was so confident up until this moment. So confident that I would be leaving here with her, hand in hand. None of this is anyone's fault but my own. I just have to keep telling myself that I was an ass to her, and she has every right to be scared. Regardless if I meant to or not, I messed with her head. I built up her trust in me and then just smashed it down. I was clearly an asshole. But I don't care what it takes; I got this! I'm going to do whatever I can to get her back into my life.

A loud, hard smack on my back tears me out of my thoughts. "What's up, man? Why do you look like a kid who just dropped his ice cream on the ground?" Kyle asks.

I rub the back of my head where a headache is forming and exhale loudly. "Dude, I screwed up *big* time," I tell him. Kyle looks a little confused. "I made the biggest mistake of my life when I pushed Elise away. What was I thinking, bro?" I question, not necessarily looking for a response.

I watch Elise from across the room. She leans down, speaking to Max's belly. For a split moment I wonder what she may look like carrying my child in her womb, but I immediately shake the thought away. I'm simply going crazy! Everyone else in the room seems oblivious to what just transpired a minute ago, but not me. I am completely consumed by my feelings of loss and regret—it's eating away at me bit by bit.

Kyle squeezes my shoulder. "It's never too late. Take Max and I as an example. I pushed her away, even left her, but it was our love for one another that brought us back together—and, let's not forget, my groveling!" he says, laughing. I can't help but crack a smile.

He's right. Max did take him back, but that was because of her love for him. Elise and I didn't spend a lot of time together, so there's no way she could love me. So why should she be willing to try again?

"Dude, you and Max are completely different. You two practically lived together. Elise and I just hung out a few times," I say. "Can you believe your brother? I mean, Kroy, for God's sake? What was he thinking?"

Kyle just shakes his head. "That wasn't my brother's doing for once. You can thank Max for that. She insisted on inviting him, and insisted he go up and speak with Elise. You know how she can be."

"Oh, I definitely know!" I reply with a laugh. "Unfortunately, I don't think she had to twist Kroy's arm. Did you look at Elise today? She's beautiful every day, but man, what the hell happened? She's my wet dream come true!" I tell him. I look around at all the other men stealing side-glances at her. "Every other guy's wet dream, too. I hate it. It's driving me nuts!"

Kyle can't help but laugh. He shakes hands with Jonathan as he walks by us. I think the guy still has a crush on Max, but Kyle just shrugs it off now. There's no need for him to get bent out of shape when she's walking around, carrying his child. I know, a little barbaric, but that's just how us guys think.

"If you want her, bro, don't give up on her. There's always going to be douches lurking around to steal your girl, but it's up to you to stop that from happening," he tells me. Kyle's face brightens, and I see Max is walking up towards us. He is head over heels for her. The twinkle in his eyes says it all.

"Jeff!" Max says, walking up and embracing me with a warm, welcoming hug. "I'm so glad you could make it!"

I give her a big squeeze. "Where else would I be?"

She pushes me out at arm's length. "Thank you for being here, really. Actually, Kyle and I have something to ask you—"

I look back and forth between the two. "Sure, ask me anything!" I encourage.

"We want you to be Penelope's godfather," Max says, dropping the bomb on me.

My mouth hangs open. This is *big*. This is *really* big! "Wait, are you guys serious?" I ask, making sure I didn't hear this wrong.

"Yeah, man. We're totally serious. There's no one else to consider but you. We've been through thick and thin together. You're like a brother to me," Kyle ensures.

Tears threaten to spill, and this man doesn't cry—ever. I embrace him with a happy hug. "Of course I will!" I turn away and blink excessively to keep the tears at bay. Max jumps up and down excitedly. "Wow. Stop jumping or that baby might fall out." Max smacks me. "I feel so honored, but what about Junior?"

"Maybe the next one," Kyle jokes.

"Who's the godmother?" I ask them.

Max slaps my arm again. "Kinsey of course!"

"Did I just hear my name?" Kinsey says from behind Max. She's always popping up out of nowhere.

Max squeezes Kinsey's arm. "We just asked Jeff to be the godfather, and he said yes!"

It's crazy how something can be so meaningful and exciting to so many people. It's just crazy that Kyle's having a baby—period.

"Oh good! Looks like Jeff and I are united now forever," Kinsey says to purposely antagonize me. I just roll my eyes. She brings out the worst in me. She's such a bitch.

"Yeah, I'm so looking forward to that," I reply sarcastically.

Mrs. Saunders, Kyle's mom, comes over to let us know lunch will be served now. Kyle and Max take off to make the announcement to the others in the room. Thank God! I am starving. Before I head to my table, I look for Elise.

"Looking for someone?" Kinsey asks with her annoying-ass voice. "She's looking pretty hot today, huh?" she asks, knowing exactly who I am searching for. I bite my tongue. I don't want to be rude at a baby shower.

I nod, agreeing. "Yeah, she's gorgeous," I admit.

"You should have claimed her while you had the chance, you know. She's an amazing person; you totally effed up. I am personally going to make sure that doesn't happen again, you understand?" she asks with a threatening tone. She's digging right under my skin, and she knows it.

I turn to look her directly in the eyes. I want to make sure she understands me clearly. "You're right, and I'm not going to make that mistake again. You're a good friend, but I'm what's good for her, and I intend on proving that to her." I walk away. The last thing I want to do is cause a scene.

CHAPTER SIX

Elise

I see him across the room, speaking with Kinsey. Lords knows what is being said. If I know Kinsey, she is threatening to rip his balls off or at least demanding that he stay away from me. I'm not too sure how I feel about that, but I know whatever is being said is out of love.

Kinsey is such a strong, ambitious woman. She knows what she wants, and she sure as hell knows how to get it. I just wish I was a quarter of the woman she is. Jeff would have never refused me in the car that night if I was. I know he just said he was trying to protect me, but part of me thinks that's straight bullshit. From what I've heard, he's never passed up an offer, and boy did I put myself out there.

Now he wants to be my friend again? It sure as hell didn't feel like we were just friends at the time, but that was probably all my imagination.

I could never speak to my mother about any of this, because she would tell me I deserve his rejection for thinking a man like him would want a nobody like me. It's times like these I crave a normal mother to receive advice from. Unfortunately, this is just not the case for me.

"Hey, we're ready to eat. Why don't you come sit over at my table?" Kroy asks.

"Okay."

The rest of the event goes off without a hitch: baby games, gifts, and one amazing pink, flowered cake. Kinsey and I planned the perfect event. I can only imagine what the wedding will be like.

I'm thanking God for the warmth, finally, as I walk outside. I swear, you would think we live in Alaska, because eight months out of the year it's winter here in Rochester. It just feels nice to finally walk outside with no jacket on, especially in the middle of summer when I should be sporting bikinis on the beach.

I say my goodbyes and help pack everything up with the girls. I have to admit it is hard, considering both Kroy and Jeff are there helping as well. I like Kroy. He seems genuine and attentive, but he's still not Jeff. At some point, I'm going to have to stop this obsession and just move on. But how do I do that when Jeff will always and forever be in my circle? How do I stop comparing him to others?

I press the button on my keychain to unlock my car. I hear two loud bleeps, but before I can enter, I hear someone calling my name behind me.

I turn around, and Jeff is now standing in front of me. "Hey, I just wanted to ask you one last time to have a drink with me. I know I caught you off guard earlier, but I really want us to be friends," Jeff insists, almost looking desperate.

"One last time? And if I say no?" I ask. I don't even know why I'm entertaining the idea. I should just say no and get into the car, but something's pulling me towards him.

"One last time tonight," he smirks, clarifying. "If you say no tonight, there's always tomorrow."

I can't help but crack a smile. He's good; he's *real* good! I shouldn't even be falling for his B.S., but I can't help it—just like the rest of his girls, I'm sure, couldn't help it.

"And if I say yes?" I question, making him work for it. This is definitely out of my comfort zone. I'm never this bold. It must be the hot pink dress and the new hair.

He steps closer to me so we are now nose to nose. Aww crap! The energy shifts to a warm serine hum that's vibrating in all the right places. "If you say yes, I *promise* you won't regret it," he tells me, sure as ever. He grabs my hand. His hot flesh against mine feels so right, and it does things to me that feel so foreign but *so* good.

I'm curious. He has definitely piqued my interest in more than one way. I'm getting spun into his web of seduction. If I stay here one moment longer, I'll never be able to let go. Not good. I need to stay in control. I have to protect myself and my heart.

I back up a step to gain some control and to get some distance to clear my head. My thoughts are consumed by him when I'm too close. "Jeff, you can have any girl in that restaurant. Why me?" I ask.

He takes another step forward. "Because none of them *are* you. I don't want those girls or any girl for that matter, unless she is you."

Man, he's better than I thought. How the hell do I get out of his hold? He reaches for me and slides his hand behind by neck and tangles his fingers into my hair, pulling just a tad to keep me still.

"Jeff—" I whisper, barely getting his name out.

He shushes me with his other finger against my lips. I gulp loudly. He slowly leans into me, his lips only inches away from mine. I close my eyes, preparing for my first kiss. It seems as though a decade has passed and still no kiss.

"Elise!" I hear a male's voice yell from behind Jeff. My eyes snap open, and Jeff releases his hold. It's Kroy, and he's walking towards us. I take a deep breath and straighten myself out. "I just wanted to make sure you made it into your car alright," Kroy explains as he looks between the both of us.

Jeff looks like he wants to rip Kroy's head off. He not only interrupted a moment, but he's purposely cock blocking him and is trying to piss all over his hydrant, so to speak. It's almost like a territorial standoff, and I'm the territory. I see Jeff's jaw muscles protrude as he grinds his teeth together. It's clear he's trying his hardest to hold his composure.

Kroy stands right beside us. "I'm okay. I was just leaving. Thanks," I say to him and Jeff. I turn and jump into my car. I quickly turn the key to ignite the engine and back out before I change my mind. I can see them both through the rearview mirror. They haven't moved as they continue to watch me pull off. This whole scenario is crazy. I've never had a man chase after me, let alone two.

I pull up my driveway, turn off the ignition, and just sit for a moment. The last person I want to see is my mother. I can see her through the blinds, sitting on the living room couch. This is one of those moments where I wish she was passed out upstairs in her bedroom.

I've had a great day and really don't want to ruin it with my mother's mouth. I don't want her misery to grab ahold of me tonight. But I have to go in at some point. It's now or never. I unbuckle my seatbelt, grab my keys and purse, and head up to the door.

The first thing I see when I walk in is liquor bottles and beer cans strewn about. What the hell has been going on all day?

"Look who decided to stroll in," my mother comments, sounding very snarky.

I take a deep breath before I speak. "Max's baby shower was today, Mom. I stayed late to help her."

I head into the kitchen to clean up. I snap my head around as I hear a creak coming from the stairs I've just passed. My gut drops. It's Reggie, my mother's boyfriend, who I've made clear isn't welcome here. I just can't believe her! She has no respect for my wishes.

I begin clearing the counter loudly of all the bottles and cans, slamming them into the trashcan. I feel a hand on my bottom as I bend over to grab a bottle from the floor. I gasp and immediately stiffen, every muscle in my body tenses with fright, and the glass liquor bottle slips out of my hand and shatters on the floor.

I back up to the other side of the kitchen. "Don't touch me! You need to leave! *Now!*" I screech. I feel so violated.

My mother stands up with her hands on her hips. "What the hell is going on?" she yells, looking back and forth between Reggie and I.

She's looking to me as if this is my fault. "He grabbed my butt, Mom! I told you I didn't want him here! He's disgusting and no good for you!" I scream.

Reggie holds up his hands in defense mode. "She's lying, baby. She backed up near me on purpose. Rubbed herself against me. I would never grab her ass. I love you," he lies. What a freaking sleaze.

I can't freaking believe him! I look back to my mom, and she is staring me down like this is all my fault. My heart breaks just a little more and gets just a little colder. "He's lying! You can't believe him. He's a disgusting perv, Mom." I just want her to take my side, to be my mom, to protect me.

She looks me up and down, clearly noticing my dress. "Look what you're wearing! You look like a fucking prostitute, like a whore. What the hell do you expect, Elise? You dress like that, and you're just asking for it!" my mother tells me.

My bottom lip quivers uncontrollably. My tears betray me as they spill down my cheeks. The pain in my chest is unbearable, ripping my insides apart. I wrap my arms around myself to quiet the pain, but it doesn't help; it's slicing through me piece by piece.

I begin to sob, trying so hard to hold it back. Reggie just smirks like the evil son of a bitch he is. "I can't believe you just said that to me! After all I've done for you! After all I've given up just to be here for you!" I cry out. I turn to Reggie. "I swear to God, if you touch me again, I will *kill* you! Do you understand me?"

I'm now hyperventilating. I can't breathe. Everything in this room is closing in on me, suffocating me. I have to get out of here. There's no love in this house, no way to grow with all this negative energy consuming me and trying to bring me down every time I enter.

I push through Reggie, grab my keys and purse, and run out the door. I hear my mother scream behind me, "Where the hell are you going?" I don't stop. I have to get out of here. I don't know where I'm going, but I can't stay here a minute longer.

I jump in my car and fumble to get the key in the ignition, because my hands are shaking uncontrollably, and screech backwards out of the driveway. Everything keeps replaying in my head as I try to figure how it got so bad so fast. I already know the answer though—Reggie. She chose him over me. This isn't the first time she's done this, but it's the first time I have been touched by one of her low-life boyfriends and gotten blamed for it.

She's my mother, for Christ's sake! She's supposed to protect me. I don't care how old I am; it's her job. She basically gave him approval to do it again. Why not? No one will believe me anyway.

Tears are streaming down my face, and it's hard for me to see clearly. I continue to wipe them, but they keep falling. I'm just driving aimlessly, trying to get as far away from home as I possibly can.

I can't go to Max's house and ruin the rest of her night. She's exhausted, and the last thing she needs is to be stressed out over my situation and go into early labor. Kinsey was ecstatic about a date she was going on tonight with a well-known, hot bar owner that she's just met. He was cooking dinner for them at her place. So I definitely don't want to go there and be the crazy friend who scares him away.

I have no one else to turn to. Just this fact alone makes me cry harder. I'm now sobbing uncontrollably, tears gushing down my face. Maybe I should just rent a room at the

Crowne Plaza for the rest of the weekend. Hide away until I can gain the strength to go back to that house. There's just no way I can go back right now or anytime soon.

With so much running through my mind, my concentration is all over the place, and the next thing I see is headlights coming directly at me. I must have been in a major daze, completely zoned out, because the loud noise of the horn and the screeching tires scare the hell out of me. I slam the brakes and jerk my wheel to the right. I drive off the road, into a gas station parking lot. Thank God for the gas station. If it wasn't here for me to turn into right at that moment, I would have ended up in a ditch on the side of the road or maybe something even worse.

My shaky hands slam the car into park, and I lean my head against the steering wheel. I try to calm my breathing. I need to gather myself together for a moment before I begin driving again. That was too close of a call. I shouldn't even be driving in this condition.

I hear a knock on my window. I have no idea how long I've been sitting here. I look up through my blurry, tear-soaked eyes, blink a couple of times, and I almost think my eyes are playing tricks on me. Jeff is leaning against the car, asking me if I'm okay.

I unlock the door, and he rips it open. He squats down to meet me at eye level. "Elise, holy shit! Are you okay? Do you know how close that was? You could have been killed!" he shouts at me.

I don't know what's going on with me, but I think I'm in shock. I continue to stare at him blankly. He puts his hands on my upper arms and gently shakes me. "Elise, look at me," he pleads.

When I finally look up at him, I can see the worry in his eyes, and that's all it takes for me to jump into his arms. I hold on tight while crying like a baby. He doesn't say a word. He just holds me, rubbing his hand up and down my back, trying his best to soothe me.

"Elise, what happened?" he says softly. "It's okay, I've got you. Please talk to me."

After what seems like forever, I finally sit up straight and push myself gently out of his hold. I wipe my cheeks and my nose with the back of my hand. I'm almost too embarrassed to look at him. Its twilight now, and dark is on the cusp. I still have no idea where I am going, and I really don't think I can drive after all of this. I'm way too shaky, and I can't seem to get it together.

Jeff is still squatting down on the balls of his feet; they must be killing him. "I'm sorry. I don't know what got into me. I didn't mean to pounce on you."

He stands up to stretch. "Elise, what the hell happened? You were on the other side of the road, driving head-on into traffic," Jeff tells me.

I shake my head. "I don't know. One minute I was driving and the next I saw headlights," I explain.

"You must have zoned out. Something had to have happened to cause that, and your face is swollen. It's clear you've been crying. Did I cause this?"

I just shake my head. I can't bring myself to say anything.

"Ok then, where were you headed?" he asks me.

I look back up at him. "I don't know," I tell him honestly.

His brows furrow with confusion. "What do you mean you don't know?"

I look back down to my fingers. "I ran out of my house. My mother's boyfriend grabbed me, and she blamed me for it," I confess. I've never admitted anything like this to anyone. This is definitely a first for me.

Jeff looks shocked, repulsed, and extremely angry. "Are you fucking serious, Elise? Did he hurt you?" He starts looking me over to see if there are any marks.

"No, I'm fine," I answer him, completely embarrassed.

He curses, exhaling loudly while kicking some gravel. "How can your mother blame you for him inappropriately touching you?"

I chuckle. "You don't know my mother. If you did, you would understand," I say. There's not much else to say without divulging my whole life story, and that's just not really something I'm ready to get into.

He's quiet. I look back up to him, and he's just studying me. My breath halts. He holds his hand out to me. "Come on. You're coming home with me."

"Wait, what?" I question. He can't be serious.

He grabs my hand and lifts me up out of my car. "I won't have you staying in a hotel in this condition. You're coming back to my house. You can stay in one of my guest rooms for as long as you need. I'll come back tomorrow morning to get your car. Grab your things," he demands. He shuts the car door once I'm finished.

I'm a little thrown off by his bossiness, but I have to admit, it's sort of a comfort knowing he cares. He's making me feel safe, which is what I need most right now. He opens his passenger door for me like a gentleman. This is no different from months ago when we were hanging out. He was so thoughtful and sweet then.

When he hops in the car, he immediately turns down the loud music he must have had bumping. He looks me over once to make sure everything is intact before driving off, and then he pulls out of the gas station. I stare out the passenger window, embracing the silence. It's not an awkward silence, but a comforting one. Just a minute ago, I panicked at the idea of staying at his house, alone with him, but now I feel comforted knowing I'll be somewhere with someone actually cares.

CHAPTER SEVEN

My knuckles are white, and my fingers are beginning to ache from squeezing the steering wheel so hard. I can't help it, but I have to tell myself to ease up a bit before she notices. The last thing I want to do is scare her after what she's been through tonight. I can't help but get infuriated, though, with the thoughts of that man touching her. What kind of man touches a woman without consent? A pathetic piece of shit, that's the kind.

If she wasn't by my side looking so fragile and broken, I would drive right to her house and beat the ever-living shit out of that coward! It wouldn't be the first time I've surrendered to my anger, but I could make sure it's my last. He deserves to be in prison and thrown to the wolves. I'm sure they could show him a thing or two about being manhandled unwantedly.

I peek at her over my shoulder. She's staring blankly out the window while twisting her fingers together. It must be a nervous habit. I can see the tear-stained path on her face, glistening from the last of the sunrays. I want to touch them and make them go away, but how do I do that without her trust? And how do I get her to trust me again?

I pull up the winding road, and the trees seem to birth my house. It's pretty massive, and from her wide-eyed reaction, I can see she is impressed.

Elise looks over at me with her eyebrows raised and mouth slightly open. "Jeff, is this your parent's house?" she asks in amazement. "I can't stay here with your parents. I don't want to intrude."

I press the button to the garage opener above my head, and the middle door begins to lift. I have four garage spaces, seven bedrooms, six bathrooms, a pool, and a hot tub overlooking Lake Ontario. I chuckle, "This is my house; and no, I do not live with my parents."

She looks more baffled than anything, but also a tiny bit nervous. "Wow. This is really impressive. How long have you lived here?" she asks.

I pull into the garage with ease and shut the car off. I press the button again to close us in, and the door begins to crank down behind us.

I remove the keys from the ignition and hop out. Elise walks around the front of the car and follows me to the door. "I've been here a little over three years now. I bought the house on my twenty-first birthday," I tell her while unlocking the door.

She follows close behind as I head into the house, flipping on the light switches as we go. We pass through the mudroom, walk down the hall, and finally make it to the kitchen. When I flip on the last of the kitchen switches, I hear her gasp.

I turn to face her. "What's wrong?" I ask, concerned.

She just shakes her head as she takes in her surroundings. The kitchen was built for a chef—literally. The prior owners ran a huge catering business, wrote cookbooks, had their own cooking show, and held a lot of influential parties here. This is a kitchen made for a king. So of course she is speechless. This was one of the selling points when I bought the house; it drew me in along with the amazing views.

"It's gorgeous, Jeff. Sorry, I just wasn't expecting this. I've never seen a kitchen like this in-person," she tells me.

I chuckle. "Well, make yourself at home while you're here. What's mine is yours," I say to her. She looks down towards the floor, uncertain. I grab ahold of her chin to lift her eyes to mine. "I mean it, okay?"

She nods her head. "Okay."

"Come on." I take her hand to lead her towards the stairs. We get to the top of the stairs, and I begin to show her the four unused bedrooms to pick from. But I save the best for last—the room closest to my bedroom. It's actually the second best room in the house with its own balcony overlooking the lake. The view is spectacular.

She walks in and spins as she looks around. This room is what I call the stone room. The huge stone fireplace stretches all the way up to the vaulted ceiling, and the wall behind the four-poster bed is laid out in extensive brickwork. It's very cozy in a medieval sort of way. My designer had fun with this project.

I pull open the french doors to the veranda. The cool night's breeze glides over me. Elise follows closely behind. There's no need to look back; I know she's there because every nerve ending in my body senses her presence. This feeling is just simply crazy.

The sun has already set beneath the horizon, and the night's world has now taken over. The moon and stars own the sky, reflecting their natural beauty on the water down below.

Elise and I stand side-by-side, resting over the top of the balcony's ledge, quietly taking in the view. After a moment of perfect silence, Elise finally speaks. "This is incredible, Jeff.

But I can't take this room. I'll stay in one of the smaller ones," she advises.

I can't help but crack a smile. She's so oblivious to material things. It's refreshing. "No, I want you here in this room. I won't accept no for an answer," I inform her. I want her close to me. Just knowing she's in the next room over does something to me. I want to close my eyes and picture her bare body laid over that four-poster bed. Man, the things I could do to her on that bed—I'm getting hard just thinking of the possibilities.

"Jeff—" she starts her rebuttal. I quickly place my pointer finger over her lips to quiet her.

"Shhh," I tell her. "Get yourself settled in, and then come downstairs. I'll cook us something to eat. Tomorrow we can go back to your house to get some of your things."

She looks confused. "Jeff, I only agreed to stay tonight. I have to go home. My mother's there, and she needs me," she tries to explain.

"Your mother needs *you*? What about when you needed her? You're not going back there. What happens the next time her boyfriend is there and wants to do more than just grab you?" I warn her. I just can't risk anything happening to her. I would never forgive myself if I let that happen. I grab her hands and entwine her fingers with mine. "Please, just stay here with me," I beg quietly.

She bites her bottom lip indecisively. "I'll think about it," she finally answers.

I release my breath and squeeze her hands before letting go. "Okay, that's better than a no," I say. "I'll be downstairs if you need me."

I leave her to herself. It's clear she needs a moment to clear her head and take everything in—all the events of the night. I probably shouldn't have pressed her so hard about staying here, but I couldn't help it. The thought of her going back there, vulnerable and unprotected with that dick still lurking around, freaks me the hell out.

I look through my refrigerator to see what I have to throw together. I just bought some chicken cutlets, sugar snap peas, and red potatoes. I whip up a quick seasoned mix and bread the chicken. I cut the potatoes in small chunks after marinating them in oil, salt, and pepper, and I toss them in the oven.

I look at my watch. It's been twenty minutes since I left her upstairs. I continue to maneuver around the kitchen gracefully, trying to busy my mind and thoughts. Should I go up there to see if she's okay? No, she just needs some time to do whatever it is women do. I'll stay right here.

The hissing and crackle grow louder with each piece of chicken placed in the hot oil. I hear the barstool scrape across the tile behind me.

"That smells amazing. What is it?" she asks. Her voice is a beautiful melody to my ears.

I put the top on the pan to allow the chicken to brown and grab the snap peas to put in the steamer. "My mom's special chicken and potatoes. You hungry?" I ask, facing her.

"Starving!"

"Me too. I really didn't eat that much at the baby shower," I admit.

"Neither did I," she giggles. "So, your mom taught you to cook?"

I grab two Coronas from the fridge. I take the tops off and hand one to her. "I liked hanging out with her while she cooked. I guess I just picked it up from watching. We had some of our best conversations in the kitchen. Being a single mom, she worked a lot, so that was the only time I really got to spend with her."

Her face softens. "That must have been hard on her, raising you and your brother by herself."

I turn to the stove and flip the chicken. "Yeah, my father didn't chip in much. He wasn't present in our lives at all growing up. She kept a good façade when we were younger. It wasn't until I was older that I realized how much she sheltered us from," I tell her.

I don't even know why I'm telling her any of this. I've never really talked to anyone about this except for Kyle. She's just easy to talk to. There's not a bad bone in her body; she's just purely genuine. Everything about her is so magnetizing. I'm completely drawn to her. I just want to absorb every part of her. I want to *know* every part of her, inside and out.

"She seems like an amazing woman. You're pretty lucky to have her. Not all moms are like that," she says.

I leave the chicken cooking just a bit longer but take out the potatoes to allow them to cool down. I grab my beer on the counter and take a long sip. "Yes, you're right. Not all moms are like her. It's pretty shitty how your mother treated you tonight. I'm sorry you had to experience that, because if anyone deserves a good mom, it's you. Me—I was a selfish kid. My mother deserved way better," I confess.

"What happened with your father? Why wasn't he around?" she asks.

The steamer turns off. I take the chicken off and dish out our meals. I take my seat next to hers.

"Wow, Jeff! This looks amazing!" she gushes.

I smile proudly. It's not every day I cook for a woman. The compliment feels sort of nice. "Thank you," I say shyly. We both dig in. I wait a moment, letting the food settle before I divulge any more. "So, you asked about my father—my father tried the family thing, but he wasn't too into it. He was really committed to his career. Work first, then family. That seemed to be his motto. It's not the most horrible thing in the world, but my mother was lonely and sick of raising us on her own. My mother could only take it for so long. She basically gave him an ultimatum: his job or us. We lost," I explain. It always hurts more saying it out loud, but I've learned over the years to push the pain back down.

"I'm sure that's something he regrets every day of his life. I think you're pretty incredible. I feel bad he missed out," she adds before taking a sip of her Corona.

I nod, not quite knowing how to respond. "Thank you," I say diffidently. "Yeah, he has a lot of guilt, but it's not my job to soothe him. He wants me and Julian to go down to South Carolina to meet his new girlfriend."

"Are you going to go?" she asks.

"No," I reply without hesitation.

She studies me before speaking again. She waits for me to explain, but there's nothing else to say about it. "Jeff, just make sure your decision is coming from the right place. You don't want to live with regret like your father is. You'll be no better than him."

I know deep down inside she is right, but I'm just not ready to admit that to her yet. I give her the best bullshit answer I can. "I'm just taking things one day at a time, worrying about today. I'll worry about tomorrow, tomorrow.

"Anyway, you told me before that you don't speak with your father because of him leaving your mother, but you never mentioned anything about your mother—" I leave the question open-ended, hoping she may fill me in on her own.

"There's not much to tell. She lost all ambition for life when he walked out on us. She's never been the same since," she explains while looking down at her plate, shifting her food around.

"What was your childhood like?" I ask.

She takes another bite of her chicken. I notice she hasn't drank too much of her beer. I make a mental note to find out what she likes to drink.

"We were a normal, happy family—at least that's what I thought as a kid. Now that I look back, I know that wasn't the case. My father was the provider while my mother stayed home. She took care of me and the house. She didn't know how to do anything else. She only knew how to be a wife and mother. She was so devastated when he left; she fell into a deep depression and has never recovered from it. I had to raise myself and become the provider for the both of us," she discloses.

"That had to be rough. I'm surprised you didn't end up like me as a teen—hating the world," I say with a chuckle. I down the rest of my beer.

"Oh, I hated the world! I just didn't express it outwardly; I kept everything bottled up. But what I deal with now is all my fault. I could have left and lived my life, but how was I supposed to do that knowing my mother would probably end up on the streets without me? She can't take care of herself. So I stayed," she tells me.

God, she is unbelievable. There are just no words for her. I am completely in awe of her! I can feel the energy shift, and I know it's time to change the subject. I don't want her hurting any more than she already is. I want to learn *everything* about her, but it doesn't have to be in one night. She's the light that makes my dull world bright. I can finally see ahead when I am in her presence. It's such a freeing and fucked up realization all wrapped up in one.

"Hey, can I show you something?" I ask.

She looks up at me curiously. "Sure."

I grab her hand, and she hops off the barstool to follow me. I take her through the living room, out the sliding glass door, around the balcony to the stairs that lead down to the pool, past the pool house, and down another flight of stairs leading to a small private beach.

The stars flood the sky, glittering through the darkness and creating a diamond-filled canopy. It's serene down here. The sound of the waves gently caressing the beach is calming, which I think we both need right about now.

"It's so beautiful down here," she tells me while looking up at the stars.

I created my own little sanctuary down here. I had a cabana built directly on the beach: soft pillows for nighttime stargazing and sheer curtains for the daytime sun. I love to come down here and de-stress. Of course, I did make it down here the other night in one of my drunken stupors. It was one of the first nights I denied free pussy. *Me*—actually turning it down! I never thought the day would come, but it has, and it totally knocked me off-kilter. The world was spinning, and all I could think of was Elise.

I lead her to the cabana and tie the curtains back so we can look at the stars. "Was this here when you bought the house?" she asks.

I lay back on the cushions, and she does the same. "No, my designer actually had it made for me. This part of the beach is very secluded and private, which means I can suntan nude down here and no one will ever see," I joke. I haven't done the nude tanning—yet. But I *am* dying to fuck down here.

Elise looks over at me, shocked. "Oh, that didn't cross my mind," she laughs. "And how many girls have you brought down here to charm, Mr. Ladies' Man?"

I chuckle. "Ladies' man, huh? You're actually the first to come down here. Is that so hard to believe?"

I roll to my side and lean my head on my hand so I can get a better view of her. Being this close to her on these soft, squishy cushions make me want to do naughty things to her.

She looks back up to the sky. "Well, yeah. Let's face it, the whole office is aware of your reputation with women—and with a house like this? Why wouldn't you wine and dine them right out of their pants?" she points out with a smirk.

I know she's joking with me, but I also know there's some truth behind it as well. I was always proud of my many conquests—shit, I'm a stud! But right at this moment, I'm feeling more ashamed than anything. It's true; I'm a male whore. "I've definitely played the field. I've had many dickhead moments, but bringing girls here was always a no-no. I like my privacy, and I don't like stalkers or girls just showing up here. So, unless it ended up as something serious, no one's been here. I keep my sex life and personal life separate," I explain.

She lets my words hang for a while. "Have you been in a lot of serious relationships?" she finally asks.

That's an easy question. "No."

She now turns on her side to face me. "Really? So you just fuck them and move on to the next?"

She slaps her hand over her mouth. "Whoa!" I laugh. That sounded hot coming out of her mouth. The way the word "fuck" just rolled off her tongue made me hard. I know; I'm a sick dude.

"I'm sorry! That just totally slipped out!" she apologizes, looking completely mortified.

I'm still laughing. "I like this side of you. So bad girl–ish," I tell her. "It's sexy."

She smacks me on the arm. "Don't get used to it. I don't know where that came from. You must be rubbing off on me already," she admits, giggling.

A chilly gust of wind howls over us, making Elise shiver slightly. I use this as an excuse to get closer to her by wrapping my arms around her and pulling her into my embrace. She immediately stiffens, but she slowly thaws out.

Her hair smells of lilac and honey, somehow the perfect mix. It's intoxicating and highly addicting as I inhale her sweet aroma. "Well, get used to it because being around me, you're gonna become a professional potty mouth shit talker!"

"Don't count on it," she jokes back.

I look down at her as she looks up at me, and for a moment, I get lost in her gaze. She takes my breath away, but before I know it, she disconnects from me. The moment is gone. I should have made my move to kiss her while I had her attention.

"You're so beautiful—"

CHAPTER EIGHT

Elise

He just told me I'm beautiful. The last thing I feel is beautiful. Especially when I'm next to someone as hot as him. I've seen the girls that have held his interest, and I most definitely don't compare. The women he "dates" are supermodel material; they don't look like me. I already got turned down from him once, and I will not put myself through that again. It was a completely mortifying moment that I will never live down.

The cool wind blows over us again and my shiver deepens. "Are you ready to go inside?" Jeff asks, rubbing my arm in an attempt to warm me up. The shivers are more from his touch than the cool air.

"Yeah, I should probably get to bed. It's been a long day," I tell him. He gives me a hand, and I can't help but feel all warm and tingly when his hand tangles with mine. I do my best to act nonchalant, like his touch and closeness don't bother me, but in reality I'm screaming inside.

I follow him up the stairs, past the pool, and up through the sliding glass doors to the living room. Jeff abruptly turns to me, stopping me dead in my tracks. He reaches for my face and slowly strokes my cheek with his thumb. My breath halts. I want so badly to lean into his touch, but if I allow myself to let go, I'm a goner.

I back up from his touch so I'm just beyond his reach. "Thanks for allowing me to stay here. Can you drop me off to my car in the morning?" I ask.

"I can have it here in the morning. My brother can bring me to get it for you, and then I can take you to your house to grab some clothes," he offers.

"Okay, as long as you agree to wait in the car," I bargain.

He smirks and holds up three fingers. "Scout's honor. I won't go in with you, but I will wait on the front step just in case you need me." God he looks so freaking adorable, how can I say no?

"Okay, deal," I say, holding out my hand in an attempt to be serious. He takes it with a chuckle. I hold my ground.

He starts walking towards the kitchen. "Do you want a drink before you turn in?" Yes! Yes! No, that's definitely a bad idea!

"No, thank you," I answer, heading towards the foyer for the stairs before he can talk me into it.

"I thought maybe we can hang out by the pool tomorrow? I think you could use some relaxation time, and I'll do some grilling for dinner," Jeff adds.

I turn back to face him head-on. "Jeff, I have a date with Kroy tomorrow. I told you that earlier."

He's busy pouring himself some Jack on the rocks, not facing me. His jawbone protrudes as if he's biting back his words. Once he gathers himself, he looks up at me. "You're still going on a date with him?" he asks, eyes now piercing into mine.

I shift in my stance. "Well yeah, why wouldn't I?" I question.

"He's not good for you, Elise."

"Why not?" I ask, crossing my arms.

Jeff takes a sip of his Jack. "Just trust me; he's not. What will you do if he doesn't take no for an answer? Who's going to be there to help you?"

"Listen Jeff, I'm a big girl. I can take care of my own self!" I growl back.

He glares at me. "You don't know what you're getting into. Please just drop the date. *Hell,* I'll take you on a date if you want to go so bad!"

"I'm going, and that's that!" I refuse to say anymore.

"Okay, got it. I'll leave you be about it. Just text me when you're back, and I'll let you in."

He doesn't say another word. He takes his drink and exits to the balcony, shutting me out as he closes the sliding glass door behind him. Man, he can be so difficult. This is a new side of him.

My eyes crack open. I feel groggy, but I slept amazingly well. I rub the sleep out of my eyes. Where *am* I? I look around and remember my nightmare—why I can't go home. I lean over and grab my cell phone from the side of the bed. Shoot! I can't believe I slept this long! It's almost ten o'clock!

I throw the sheet off me and jump out of bed. I go for the bedroom door but then pause. I can't go downstairs like this. I haven't even brushed my hair or my teeth yet. I make a quick stop to the bathroom; luckily for me, I have a private one connected to my room. I finish my morning duties and head downstairs.

My stomach growls as the morning hunger sets in. There's a breakfast spread in the kitchen: bagels, donuts, and fruit all laid out on the counter as I walk in. The smell of delicious coffee fills the air, saturating every breath I take. The only thing missing is Jeff. He's nowhere in sight.

I pile my plate with all the yumminess, but the coffee is what I really need. I'm in dire need of some wake-up juice. I hear the sliding glass door open in the living room. I look up, and my heart stops. My armpits begin to perspire. I have no idea where I'm supposed to look.

Jeff's hair is wild and crazy—just-rolled-out-of-bed sexy—enticing me to feel the strands between my fingers as he enters inside of me. The ripples and valleys on every inch of his amazingly toned body registers as panty-dropping status. I can't stop myself from drooling over those pajama bottoms barely covering his hips and just kissing the top of his buttocks. I think I may have just had an orgasm in my pants. Why is he not wearing a shirt? Is he doing this on purpose?

He must like to see me flustered like this. I can tell by the all-too-knowing smirk plastered on his face. It must be payback from last night. I rip my gaze away from his and concentrate on putting the cream and sugar in my coffee.

"Morning. I hope you slept okay," Jeff says. He reaches around me for the sugar, his naked chest grazing my back, and of course I immediately stiffen. He chuckles, knowing exactly the effect he has just caused.

I slide out of his way and take a seat on the barstool across from him. "I slept good. I woke up forgetting where I was, but other than that—it was fine."

"Your car is out front. You were sleeping, so I picked it up early this morning. What time did you want to head over and grab your things?"

"Whenever you're ready. I have to meet Kroy at three, so we have some time," I tell him, hitting him with that info on purpose. Two can play the "catch-you-off-guard game."

He does his best to look unaffected, but I can tell it's bothering him. I don't know if it's the simple fact that I'm going out on a date or the fact that I'm going out with Kroy on a date. There seemed to be some tension built-up between them yesterday, and I'm guessing it has more to do with that.

"Where are you meeting him?" he questions.

I finish chewing my bagel before answering. "Okay, well don't laugh—" I warn him. He looks at me, confused. "I'm meeting him at the zoo, and then we're going bowling."

His confusion quickly turns to laughter. He crumples over, holding onto the counter so he doesn't fall down. I can't help but laugh along with him, because his laughter is contagious. Honestly, I thought Kroy was joking when he first asked me. I didn't take Kroy as the zoo type. But after the initial shock wore off, I thought the idea was sweet.

Jeff can't control his laughter. "Wait—so you're telling me—" he says between breaths, "that he really asked you out on a date to the zoo?" He can barely get the last sentence out.

"Yes, he's taking me to the zoo. I haven't been to the zoo in years, so maybe it will be fun," I admit, taking a sip of my now-warm coffee.

Jeff settles down a bit. "If you really want to go to the zoo, I'll take you. We can go to the Buffalo zoo instead. Now *that* one is date-worthy. Just cancel with Kroy, and we can leave now," he says.

I know exactly what he's doing, and it's not going to work. "Thanks, but I don't want to take up any of your time. We tried that 'hanging out' stuff before, and it didn't go too well. So if you don't mind, can you please take me to grab my things?" I ask.

I refuse to fall for his shenanigans again. I would just be setting myself up for disaster.

Jeff finishes his coffee. "Okay, if you're ready, we can head out now," he offers.

He seems a little bummed but isn't giving me any attitude. He's not giving me a hard time, either, which I was secretly praying for.

I finish up my bagel and wash the plate off. "It's okay, just leave it there. We can clean it later," Jeff tells me.

We drive to my house in silence. No music, no random questioning—just pure silence. The silence leaves me alone with my thoughts. If I have a million things going through my mind, then Jeff has to have some thoughts as well.

I peek over at him; he seems tense and on edge. "Jeff, are you okay?" I ask.

"Yeah, I'm good."

He says nothing more for the remainder of the ride, and I decide to leave it that way. He pulls up to the house, and my heartbeat thumps and my muscles coil with tension. I almost feel as though I may faint, but something seems to be holding me together, and that something is—anger.

I'm angry at my mom for allowing that inexcusable behavior to go on, and for not believing me. She took his word over mine, her own fucking daughter. I'm afraid if I see her now, I may go somewhere I might not be able to return from. I despise every weak bone in her body. For a split second, I stop; I feel as though I am speaking about myself.

Sometimes I feel just as weak as her, because I didn't have the courage to leave. I stayed here to endure the abuse and complete loneliness, only to make sure my mom was taken care of. Or did I? Was that the real reason I stayed, or was it because I was simply scared to be on my own in the real world?

We finally pull up to the house. Every nerve in my body is tingling rapidly with a million emotions. I just pray that her boyfriend isn't here. I take a deep breath. Jeff grabs my hand. "Nothing's going to hurt you. I got you," he comforts me.

His words soothe me. "Thank you. I really appreciate it," I reply, and we both step out of the car. I turn to Jeff once we reach the front door. "Wait here."

He grabs my hand again before I unlock the door. "I mean it, Elise. Just yell if you need me," he advises sweetly.

I crack a smile shyly and head in. The house is dark and dreary. All curtains and blinds are drawn, and it smells like straight ass and cigarettes. I quietly tiptoe past the couch where my mother is laid out sleeping. I don't see Reggie anywhere in sight so far, so I can breathe a little easier.

My mother looks worn-down and un-showered. Her pill bottles and liquor bottles are strewn about the coffee table. I see a couple of empty beer cans, so I know her boyfriend has been here.

The kitchen looks a mess, but it doesn't look like anyone has cooked since I left. That's what worries me and keeps me here. If I'm not here to feed her, she'll just waste away.

I head upstairs and quickly pack some of my things.

"So, you're leaving me?" my mother questions, standing with her hand on her hip in my doorway.

I continue packing without looking up. "I'll be back. I just need some time away. I don't feel safe here with Reggie walking around, try-ing to feel me up," I tell her.

She snorts. "Now you're going to blame this all on him like you had nothing to do with it? Did you see what you were wearing? You looked like a cheap prostitute!"

I flinch at that comment. I just don't understand how she can say such hurtful things to me. It's just downright disgusting. The anger inside of me boils over. I just can't contain it anymore. I zip up my bag, throw it over my shoulder, and walk straight up to her.

"Like you have any right to speak. Look at you. You're a pathetic excuse for a human being and a mother! You should be ashamed of yourself!" I finish, pushing my way past her.

She follows me down the stairs, calling me names and spouting nasty remarks out of her mouth. I open the front door and run into Jeff. He catches me just as my breath hitches, and I try so hard to hold my tears back.

My mother takes one look at Jeff and snickers. "Oh, I see now. You're leaving me for a man. You're just like your father. Am I not good enough?" she screams. Jeff takes the bag from me and helps me into the car, but before he shuts the door, I hear my mother call out to me. "You're just a whore! He's gonna throw you out on your ass once he realizes how pathetic you are!" Jeff shuts the door and walks back over to my mother, anger rolling off of him like smoke. I see him confront her. She backs up, putting her hand on her chest, and then slams the door in his face.

Jeff gets into the car, reaches over to me, and pulls me into his chest. I can't hold back any longer; I begin sobbing. He holds me, rubbing his hand down my back in a comforting manner. He's being so sweet and gentle. I like this side of him. He's just a man who cares for a woman.

"I'm sorry you had to go through that," he whispers. "Are you ready to get out of here?"

I nod my head. I can't bring myself to speak. He releases me and backs out of the driveway. I feel like I need a nap. All the energy has been sucked out of me, and I'm exhausted and completely drained. The ride back to his house is quiet. I stare out the window, watching the world go by and wondering what has happened to mine. How the hell did I get here, and how do I fix it?

I think it's time that my mother goes into rehab and gets some therapy. I, on the other hand, need to grow some balls and take the bull by the horn. I am twenty-four years old, for Christ's sake! I need to begin my life. I'm just not too sure how to do this exactly.

We pull up to Jeff's house. He carries my bag to my room, but before he leaves, he breaks the silence. "Elise, you can stay here as long as you need. I think your mother needs some serious help, and I don't think you should go back until she gets some," he says, seeming genuinely concerned.

I know he's right, and I'm very thankful he is here at the moment. I couldn't do this alone. "You're right, I need to get her into re-hab. She's out of control, and I'm afraid of what's going to happen next. I'm just not sure where to start," I admit.

Jeff leans against the doorjamb. "I'll get some information together on some good inpa-tient rehabs around here for you. Believe me, I'm not proud of it, but I've had some friends who have had to go through it. Some did great, but others just weren't ready for it. She also has to want to get better, and if she's not ready, then she has a long road ahead of her. I just don't want her to drag you down with her," he says sweetly.

I take a seat on the bed. "Thank you for letting me stay here, Jeff. I really mean it," I say to him sincerely. "Nobody knows about my mother, so can we keep it that way?"

His face looks somber—surprised. "You're telling me you have been going through this all by yourself? You haven't even talked to Max or Kinsey about any of this?" he asks, completely taken aback.

I look down at my fingers, nervously. "I didn't want to burden anyone with this."

I hear him exhale loudly, and when I look back up, he is rubbing his temples with his eyes closed. "I don't want to scold you, but you know you are not a burden to them. I'm here for you as well. If you're not ready to confide in them, you can confide in me, okay?"

I nod. "Okay."

He smiles sweetly. "I mean it, Elise. Please let me in."

"Okay."

He nods, looking satisfied, and then exits the room.

I took a much-needed nap, and I'm feeling refreshed. I head downstairs after getting dressed. I kept it casual: a nice pair of jeans and a white tank top. We're going to the zoo, so no need to get too dressy.

I look around for Jeff to let him know I'm leaving, but he's nowhere in sight. I remember him on the balcony this morning, so I check there first.

He looks peaceful, in deep thought, as I slide the door open. "Hey, I just wanted to let you know I'm leaving. I shouldn't be too long," I tell him.

He turns and gives me a once-over. "You look nice," he says, turning his attention back to the water. He takes a sip of his drink. It looks to be some sort of bourbon or cognac.

"Thanks. I decided to keep it low-key today."

"I'm going out with the guys, so I'll leave a key in the mailbox for you to let yourself in in case I'm not back in time," he tells me.

Hmm, drinks now and drinks with the guys? That makes for a lethal combination. I haven't quite seen Jeff at his worst, but what I've gotten to experience wasn't always his best, either. "Maybe you shouldn't be drinking the heavy stuff yet if you plan on drinking later," I comment, hoping he will take it into consideration.

He just rolls his eyes. "Maybe you shouldn't be dating a complete stranger. You never know what's laying under the exterior. Why don't you just stay here?"

"I can't."

"Fine. Aren't you going to be late for your date then?" he questions sarcastically.

I know this is my queue to exit, so I shut the sliding glass door and leave without saying another word.

CHAPTER NINE

Jeff

I hear the glass door click shut, and I know she has left. *Damn!* I slam back the rest of my Jack. I enjoy the amber liquid as it burns its way down my insides, leaving everything in its wake numb. I definitely need some more. Tonight's gonna be a messy night. I don't give a fuck. I just want to feel nothing—be back to my happy, carefree, fuck-it self.

The problem is, no matter how hard I try, I can't get Elise out of my head! Every petite curve on her body; those beautiful, judgeless blue eyes; and the innocence that radiates off of her is so addicting in every way possible. My dick twitches at the thought of every piece of her wrapped around me. If I could just taste her, then maybe she wouldn't be running through my mind like this. Yeah right! Who the hell am I kidding?

This all changes the game for me. The old me from just a week ago no longer exists. It doesn't matter how much I drink or how many girls I sleep with, it will always be her. I just know it from deep down in my core. I want her in every sense of the way, and now she is going on a date with that dimwit.

She doesn't know what she's getting into with him, and I'm sure as hell not going to let her find out, either. I'll be watching over her whether she likes it or not.

I pick up my cell. "Hey, change of plans. We're going to the zoo."

CHAPTER TEN

"Hey!" I greet Kroy with a smile. He lifts me up in an embrace and gives me a tight squeeze.

"Hey, yourself," he says, putting me down. "Are you ready to go see some stinky animals?"

He tangles his hand with mine. His hands are big, almost giant-like compared to mine. We don't fit together like Jeff and I do. Jeff's hands fit flawlessly with mine, like there's no end or beginning. A perfect fit.

I nod my head with excitement. "Very much so! I haven't been here in a very long time. I think I only came here one time as a kid," I admit. He looks over at me in shock, as if my head just rolled off my body.

"Are you serious, Elise? Just one time?" he questions.

I'm beginning to feel a little self-conscious. I should have kept my mouth shut. "Yeah, my mom was a busy woman," I lie. "So, what about you? Did you come here a lot as a kid?"

We walk by the monkeys first. One is hanging on the metal cage, gazing out. He looks worn-down and tired, as though he's finally succumbed to his fate. Poor little guy. I know exactly how he feels.

"Yes, I definitely came here a lot as a kid," he responds.

I can't take my eyes off this monkey. "Do you have any siblings?" I ask.

He tugs on my hand gently, and I follow his lead. "I have an older sister and a younger sister. I've always been surrounded by girls growing up, and man, did they love the zoo," he chuckles.

"Wow, what was that like, growing up with sisters?"

Next stop is the elephants. "Let's just say there was a lot of Barbie's involved and me being their muse for hair and makeup. I hated it, but they would coerce me into it—threaten to run to my mom crying that I hit them. She always took their side over mine," Kroy reveals.

I squeeze his hand for comfort. "Aww, I'm sorry! That sounds terrible—but awesome at the same time, because I always wished for brothers or sisters. It was so lonely being an only child. What was your father like?"

Kroy scrunches his nose at the horrific shit aroma wafting through the air. "He was my best friend growing up. When he wasn't busy working, he would take me fishing—just the two of us. The girls would get jealous, but he would tell them it was 'grown man time,'" he laughs. I laugh along with him. "Holy crap, these elephant smell! Let's go look at the tigers."

I follow his lead again. "Your dad seems great. So tell me, how do you know Junior?"

We stop at the huge outdoor cage. The tigers are lying down, resting. They hardly move at all, except for the twitch of a tail. It's the only way I can tell they're alive. "We went to school together. We were both on the same football team in high school until he got injured and never played again. That's when Jeff ended up taking his place. He was really good, but he ended up in some trouble, which got him kicked off the team. No colleges would look at him after that," he explains.

I ponder that info for a moment. "Hmm, Junior playing football, huh? I can't really picture that," I tell him. "He's so uptight and serious. And what did Jeff do that was so bad?"

"Jeff had a bad temper. He didn't know how to control it, so he was kind of a loose cannon." Kroy chuckles. "But Junior hasn't always been so uptight; he can be real intense sometimes, but he's a good dude at heart. Man, that Kinsey chick really does a number on him though," he divulges.

I look at him questionably. "What do you mean?"

"Don't tell me you don't feel the sexual tension between them! He's got it bad for her, but he won't admit it," Kroy confesses.

I just let this information sink in for a moment. He could actually be on to something. "Kinsey is definitely one tough cookie. He drives her insane, and being roomies with him is making her go crazy," I say with a laugh. "She says he's a major neat freak, and he follows her around like a sergeant, making sure she picks up after herself." He bursts out laughing.

We head over to the underwater seal attraction. "I can totally picture that. Every time I ask him what's up between them, he gets all defensive. That's how I know. So tell me, what's up with you and Jeff?"

He just asked the question I was hoping to avoid. "Nothing really. We hung out for a short amount of time a couple of months ago, mostly in group settings, and then he just stopped talking to me completely. It was really strange. I just can't figure him out. His moods change like the weather. One day he's really warm and the other he's as cold as ice. You two went to school together, you said?"

The reflection from the water against the walls is almost a little romantic. It's so peaceful and desolate in this underground cabin. It's just him and I, and the two seals that keep passing by us. Is it wrong that I wish Jeff were here instead of Kroy? Ugh! I'm totally not being fair to Kroy whatsoever. I need to tuck Jeff deep away into the lands of "never gonna happen" or "I'll never find a man."

Kroy lets go of my hand for the first time. I can see the strain of his neck as his muscles tense up instantly and then quickly relax. "Yeah, he was two grades below us with Kyle though. We just never really clicked. He was always trying to go for the girls I dated. He liked my sloppy seconds, I guess. Or more like he just wanted to be me."

I look back to the seals as they pass. "They are so graceful. They glide around like there's not a care in the world," I whisper. I turn my attention back to Kroy as they disappear out of sight. "Maybe he just looked up to you. There's nothing wrong with that."

"You're right, there is nothing wrong with that, *but* when the man-whore of the school tries to go after every girl I date—that becomes a problem. It was almost like he was obsessed with trying to compete with me. That guy pretty much had sex with every girl in his path, probably most of this town too," he informs me. I don't know whether he is telling me this to stick it to Jeff or because it's the truth. Either way, what he's saying just doesn't feel right.

We walk through the whole zoo and stop to take a look at each animal exhibit. Kroy's kind, funny, and most definitely has a lot to say. He turns heads too. All the moms that walk by take a second glance. Most of them are probably wondering what he sees in me. He's clearly used to this attention, because he's completely oblivious to it.

I follow behind him as we exit the car to the bowling alley. He's comfortable to be around, so I'm looking forward to the rest of our date. He requests a lane in the far-right corner. You can definitely tell it's family Sunday. It's noisy and kids are scattered all over this place.

"I forgot it gets a little crazy in here on Sundays. You don't mind, do you?" he asks.

I finish tying my laces. "No, of course not! The action is nice."

He flashes that beautiful smile at me. I can't help but melt just a tiny bit. "You ready for me to kick some ass?" he teases. "Ladies first." He puts his hand out for me to grab as I lift myself up.

"Sure, I'm ready to beat your butt," I flirt. This is sort of fun. This is what I've missed out on when it comes to dating?

His eyes sparkle with excitement. "Ooh, I am definitely ready for that!" Kroy responds with a mischievous smirk. I feel the chemistry buzzing around us. It's wild and untamed, and I like it.

I pick up my ball and get ready to bowl my turn. But I'm interrupted by someone clearing their throat behind us. To my surprise, when I turn, I see Jeff standing below the stairs with another drink in his hand.

I furrow my brows in confusion. What the hell is he doing here? I look around, and he looks to be alone. "Um, hi. What are you doing here, Jeff?" I ask.

Kroy glares at him. "Yeah Jeff, since when do you bowl?"

"Actually, my man's girl works here. We're all sitting up there at the bar having some drinks," he replies. "Would you guys like a drink? I can have them sent over."

Yeah, right. Me drinking on a first date would not be good. I wouldn't even dare attempt that. "I'm fine, but thank you," I answer.

"We're good, man," Kroy tells him while staring him down, trying to get his point across.

Jeff nods his head, looking between the both of us. "Okay. Elise, I'll see you back at the home front," he says, taking the pin out of the grenade and leaving it with us to blow up. Not freaking cool. Now I'm pissed!

Once Jeff is out of earshot, Kroy turns to me. "The home front?"

I take a deep breath and exhale. "I'm sort of staying with him right now," I admit.

Kroy takes a seat at the scoreboard chair. "What do you mean you're *staying* with him?"

I take a seat across from him. "I'm having some problems at home with my mother, and Jeff offered me a place to stay until things cool down," I tell him honestly. I just hope he doesn't ask me any questions about my mother. What will I say? That she's a pill-popping alcoholic and she needs help? It was hard enough telling Jeff.

"I'm sorry to hear that. But staying with Jeff? Are you sure that's a good idea? It's clear that he wants you, and I don't want to have to compete with an old ghost."

Jeff wants me? If he only knew the truth. Me throwing myself at Jeff months ago would probably not go over well. "Kroy, he doesn't want me. He's just helping me out, that's it." I decide to be a little ballsy and sit on his lap.

"Well, that's more like it," Kroy says with a goofy smile on his face. I can't help but giggle, and when I glance over my shoulder, I can see Jeff staring at us from the bar. He looks wounded. But why? I just can't grasp him. I hate it.

Kroy tickles my side to grab my attention, and I screech. "Okay, okay! Enough!" I say with a giggle.

"Okay, before we bowl our next game, how about we plan another date?" he slips in.

He patiently waits for an answer. I look down, fiddling with my fingers. "Another date?" I ask him, looking up. He just nods his head. "Sure, I would love to. What do you have in mind?"

"I was thinking we do something more old school, like dinner and a movie."

I have to say that answer is extremely cute. I mean, why not? Why not see where this takes us? What else do I have to do? "Okay, tell me when and where, and I'll be there."

"Oh no! This time it's the real thing. That means I pick you up and the whole spiel! How about Friday? That way we don't have to cut it short with having to work the next day and all."

Almost as a reflex, I look over to see if Jeff is still watching, but he isn't. I can't see him anywhere. I wonder if he left. He didn't seem too happy about seeing me so close to Kroy, but I have a feeling he may not like seeing any girl with Kroy. Maybe Kroy was right about Jeff being in competition with him. God, I wish I could read guys. "Okay, I should be back at my house by then anyways. I will text you the address later on this week."

He pulls me into him, his head now leaning against my chest. Awkward! This is just too intimate for my comfort. I unwrap his hands from me and stand up to stretch. Thank goodness he doesn't press the issue. I'm sure my discomfort clearly shows, but he's being a pure gentleman about it.

We finish up our games and say our goodbyes. For a moment, I almost thought he was going to try and kiss me, but I made sure to keep my distance. I was happy when he respected it and just gave me a kiss on the cheek. I like him. I really do. I had a fun time. Kinsey and Max were right. It's time I start getting myself out here.

Hinder's "Better Than Me" comes on the radio as I head to Jeff's. Reminds me of his confession the day of the baby shower. I wonder if he's home yet. Wait—did I just say home? Geez Elise, get it together! And so what if he's there? Do I really want to talk with him about how my date went? No, definitely not.

I pull up in front of the house, and there's an unknown car in front. It looks pretty dark inside; he must not be home yet. I grab the key he stashed from the mailbox and head inside. The kitchen is dimly lit, just enough for me to find the hallway light. I trip and fall over something small lying at the bottom step, and I catch myself on the step in front of me. What the hell?

I flip on the switch to the stairs and see a black heel near my foot. I look up the stairs and see clothes scattered along each step, both men and women's clothing. I begin to feel sick.

Jeff said he never brought girls home with him. That was his number one rule. Please let it be that he allowed one of his rowdy friends use of the house for their drunken love fest.

I leave the clothes where they are, step around them, and head to my room. I hear a muffled noise from down the hallway. With each step closer to my room, it gets louder. I reach the handle to my door and jump when I hear a woman's loud moan coming from Jeff's room. My heart pumps furiously and echoes through my ears.

There it goes again. Only this time, it's followed by a man's grunt. Jeff's door is slightly ajar. Oddly, I'm drawn to it. I can't help it. I want to see who is in there. I *need* to know if it's Jeff, so I tiptoe over to his door and peek through the crack. God, what am I doing? This is the epitome of stalking, isn't it? It's dark, but the moonlight casts a slight glow, illuminating the room enough for me to see Jeff lying down on his bed with a naked girl on top of him.

My gut sinks. I slam my eyes closed quickly and cover my mouth so I won't make any noise. Tears begin to stream down my cheeks. I turn towards my room but the floor creeks, betraying me. I hear her whisper to him as I book down the hallway to the stairs, taking two at a time. I open the front door to leave. I pause before taking a step over the threshold. Where am I going to go exactly? Back to my house? No way. To Max or Kinsey's? Then I would have to explain all the gory details to them. I'm not ready for that. Maybe I should just go to a hotel like I originally planned.

I look behind me, up the stairs, wondering if someone might follow, but no one does. It's clear that he's way too occupied to have heard anything. I am completely and utterly alone. I wrap my arms around myself tightly for comfort. The only man I've ever felt anything for is now upstairs fucking God-knows who. How am I supposed to face him tomorrow?

I still hear muffled moans from upstairs. There's no way I am going back up there to listen to that. I already am on the verge of throwing up, and that would just solidify the deed. Maybe I should call Kroy.

CHAPTER ELEVEN

My head is pounding. I open my eyes, and it's pitch dark. I try to sit up. *Ugh!* My goddamn head feels like I just got out of the boxing ring with Mike Tyson. I sit on the edge on my bed with my head in my hands. Why the heck did I drink so much?

I hear a quiet moan from behind me. I immediately stiffen. Did I take Elise to bed? "Come back to bed and fuck me."

Aww no! That is not Elise's voice! I stand up quickly when her fingers graze my back. "What the fuck? How did you get here?" I screech. Instant panic takes over as I realize I have actually brought a girl to my home. What was I thinking? Then nausea hits. What time is it, and where is Elise?

"Um, I drove you home, and you asked me to come in, silly. Don't you remember jumping my bones in the car?" she tells me, sitting up and holding the sheets over her breasts.

I look at the clock, and it's quarter past three. I look around for our clothes, but they're nowhere in sight. "Where are your clothes?" I ask her.

She giggles. I cringe. "Well you couldn't wait. You were a little impatient getting me undressed, so I'm assuming they're still on the stairs." *No!* Elise had to have seen them. How am I going to explain this to her?

"Wait right here," I direct and head out into the hallway.

All the lights are off. I pass Elise's room, and her bedroom door is wide open. I quietly walk in to see if she's sleeping, but her bed has not been slept in. I rush over to the balcony, but she's not there either. Maybe she didn't come back at all. Maybe she stayed the night with Kroy. Who knows what he could have done to her. How could I be so stupid? My fists clench, my teeth lock down, and my jaw tightens. My body is consumed with pumping adrenaline at the thought of her with Kroy.

I storm down the stairs, grab all the clothes in my wake, and rush back to my room. I throw the mystery woman's clothes on the bed in front of her, and she looks to me, confused.

"You want me to leave?" she asks.

"Yeah, I need to work in the morning," I tell her. At least it's the truth.

She puts her shirt over her head to cover her naked body. "So do I. It's okay, we don't have to cuddle. We can just sleep or stay up the rest of the night if you want," she suggests with a seductive, irritating smirk.

I shake my head and hand over her shoes. "You have to go," I tell her, sternly this time, maybe a little too abruptly. She begins to sniffle as though she's going to cry. This is exactly what I always try to avoid. I soften a bit. "I'm sorry. I should have never asked you to come in. I just think it's best we call it a night. I'm not looking for anything serious."

She quickly jumps out of bed and puts on the rest of her clothes. She then turns to me with her arms crossed over her chest. "I always heard about what an asshole you are, but I never believed it until now. Thanks for the fuck," she growls and storms out of the room. It's not until I hear the front door slam shut that I release my breath. Man that was a little intense.

Now I need to figure out where Elise is. I grab my cell and dial her number, but it goes straight to voicemail. I quickly shoot her a text asking her where she is. I head downstairs to lock up. I peek out of the glass in the door to make sure my visitor is gone. I see Elise's car parked next to mine. Weird. Did she fall asleep in the car?

I rush out front to peek in her car, but it's empty. Maybe she's on the couch. I run through the house to the living room, and there is no sign of her. Where could she be? I feel the adrenaline rushing through my body as my heart palpitates. This is all my fault. She had to have heard me. Guilt begins to set in.

I notice the sliding glass door to the balcony is unlocked. She must be out there. I head over to the outdoor couches, but she's not here either. I begin to scream her name, panic surging through me. I rush downstairs, past the pool and towards the beach, still screaming her name. She has to be there. Thank God the moon is shining brightly tonight so I don't have to search through the darkness. The light is illuminating her sleeping face just enough for me to see her lying in the cabana.

She looks peaceful—beautiful. I could watch her like this all night long. A small strand of hair blows in her face. I can't help it; I remove it, my fingers lingering against her soft skin. She stirs and opens her eyes.

"Hey," I whisper. "What are you doing out here?" I ask. She startles me by sitting up abruptly and giving me the death stare. I immediately stagger back a little. "Elise, are you okay?"

She gets up and aggressively pushes past me. "I'm fine."

I stand here, frozen for a moment, and then it suddenly hits me. I run after her and gently grab hold of her upper arm to pull her back to me. "Listen, I'm sorry. I didn't mean for you to see any of that. It wasn't my intention," I try to explain.

She rips her arm from my grip and folds them over her chest. "I didn't just see the clothes on the stairs, Jeff. I heard it too!" She turns back around and begins taking the stairs two at a time to get away from me.

I follow. "Elise, wait! Please, let me explain—" I yell from behind her.

She stops without turning to face me when we get into the living room. "I don't need you to explain anything to me! It's none of my business. You're a single man. I'll be leaving in the morning," she growls.

My world comes crashing down on me. I can't lose her. I *won't* lose her. "Elise, will you please look at me? *Please?*" I beg again.

She slowly turns around, not looking at me. She looks at everything but me, clearly still upset. If she's this torn up, then she has to care, right? Finally, her eyes connect with mine, but they're glossed over like stone. She has shut me out, and I can now sense a wall in between us.

"Just answer me one question, Jeff—is she still here?"

I hang my head with shame. "I made her leave. None of this mattered. She doesn't matter. I was feeling sorry for myself, because you left on the date with Kroy. I'm in no way putting this on you, but I drank too much and completely fucked up. I'm so sorry, Elise. Please don't go—"

"I'm going to bed. I'm exhausted, and we have to work in a couple of hours. Goodnight, Jeff," she says, turning to head upstairs.

Freak! I royally messed this up. I got bent out of shape when I saw her flirting with Kroy. She seemed to like him, and when I saw her sitting on his lap, that confirmed it all. I just wanted to forget I ever saw that, so I drank even more. I remember now that the chick I hooked up with came with Erica, my man Johnny's girlfriend, and things just got a little out of hand. Apparently, she drove me home. If Kyle was with me, he would have never allowed this to happen. I miss my wingman. He would have stopped me from screwing up.

My head launches forward after getting smacked from behind. "What the hell, man?" I screech.

"Dude, lower your voice!" Kyle warns, snickering. "It's payback time," he says with a laugh.

I rub the back of my head. "Whatever, man. I already have a splitting headache."

I know I'm acting like a complete bitch, but I'm just not in the mood today.

Kyle hangs his arms over my cubicle. I'm getting déjà vu. "You look like dog crap. I heard you got hammered last night. Johnny told me you ended up leaving with Erica's friend, Lacey—"

I blow out a deep breath. "Yeah, I made a *big* mistake. I guess my drunk ass let her drive me home, and I freaking asked her inside," I admit. *God*, what is wrong with me sometimes?

Kyle's eyes go wide. "No way! Aww, what the hell Jeff? You barely know the chick. You better hope she's nothing like Beth!"

I put my head in my hands. "I know. Tell me about it. It didn't end very well when I had to kick her out."

Now it's his turn to let out a deep breath. "Well listen, it's over and done with now. Maybe you should chill out on the partying for a bit. You've been going pretty hard these last couple of weeks. Why don't you come over for dinner tonight? Max would love to see you."

There's no way I'm leaving Elise to fend for herself tonight, not after the mess I created. She was already gone this morning before I woke up and had the chance to apologize for the millionth time. I stopped at the reception desk to speak with her this morning, but I was quickly interrupted by a call from Mr. Saunders. She looked tired and worn-down, and I caused it all. I am a walking, living douche. There are no other words to describe me at the moment.

"Man, I would love to, but I'm a train wreck today. I need some sleep tonight," I explain, only telling him half the truth. If I told him about Elise staying with me, he wouldn't be able to keep the secret from Max, and then she would grill Elise to spill it. I can't risk it. I already fucked up last night. I need to do whatever I can to make it up to her so she doesn't leave.

"Okay, next time, bro," Kyle says. "Oh listen, now that I'm moving up in the company, I'm going to need a personal assistant. I'm forced to do interviewing, but I need you to apply. I need my wingman by my side. And since you really don't need the money, just think of it as you'll be my bitch for eight hours out of the day."

He smacks my head again and runs off before I can yell obscenities at him. I can't help but laugh and shake my head. I'm totally going to get him for that one.

The rest of the day goes by slowly and feels torturous. The minutes drag as the day is filled with a never-ending pile of work. All I want to do is see Elise. I just want to be in her good graces again. I like when she opens up and talks to me, telling me things that she's not told another soul. It makes me feel special and important in her world.

Finally, the time on my computer flips to five o'clock! I clock my butt out and head out of the security door to the reception area. I look for Elise, but she is nowhere in sight. What the heck? My enthusiasm is sucked right out of me and worry now poisons my veins. Maybe she decided to go back home? Or maybe she decided to stay with one of the girls instead?

I push my way through the glass doors with a vengeance. I'm going to find her, and I'm going to bring her back to my house, even if it's kicking and screaming—I don't care! I stomp all the way to my car and then stop. She's standing in front of me, leaning against my car. All irrational tendencies have now vacated my body.

"Elise?" I ask, wanting to ask a million different questions.

"So I realized that I haven't spoken with you all day, and I don't have a key to your house and wasn't sure if the key is still in the mailbox—so I figured I would wait for you here," she says.

I can't help but grin from ear to ear. Her brows furrow in wonder. "Do you want to follow me? We can drop your car off and then go grab a bite to eat somewhere. I'm gonna have to go shopping for some more things this week, too. Maybe you could come with me to pick out some things you like?" I ask, not sure if this is too much for her.

She gives me a shy smile. "How about we just start out with something to eat?"

I want to jump up and kick my feet together like a little schoolboy. "Sounds good."

She follows me back to my house. I continuously look up in my rearview mirror to make sure she's still there. Man, what the hell is wrong with me? This feeling is so foreign. Never before have I cared to this extent. I want to give her the world.

CHAPTER TWELVE

I think I've told myself 101 times already to get off at the nearest exit and
get far away from Jeff. How do I stop
myself from getting all wrapped up in him
when he won't stay away? I want so badly to
cover my heart and run in the other direction,
but I just can't. Am I risking a severed heart
over this burning desire that I just can't walk
away from? Yes. I know it will scorch me if I
touch it, but I just have to feel the flames for
myself. God, I am a hot freaking mess.

I can only imagine what Max and Kinsey would say. They would completely freak. If I told Max about the last couple of days, it might just induce labor. This is definitely not a good time to invoke her in my messed up, self-destructing journey.

We reach his house and pull up the driveway. This house is absolutely incredible. Every time I see it, it amazes me. The lights shine through the tall glass windows that contrast the rectangular perimeter just so, making the house look open and magnificent. I'm reminded of the penthouses and skyscrapers of New York City. It's all so neat, precise, and eerily cold—kind of like Jeff is, or was just last night. He and the house are a perfect fit.

I jump from the knock on my window, awakening me from my own thoughts. He opens the car door, and I turn off the ignition. After getting out, he shuts the door behind me like a gentleman. Now this is the side of him I know. It makes me all giddy inside, but then I remind myself what has happened in the last 24 hours, and I stop.

"What were you thinking about back there? You looked to be in deep thought," Jeff comments.

I follow him to the foyer. "I was just taking the view in. Your house is really something," I answer.

He cracks a little smile. "I suppose it is, huh? It was love at first sight," he says so directly. If I didn't know any better, I would have thought he was saying this about me. But I know better.

"I see. Well, let me freshen up and change into something more comfortable, and I'll meet you back down here," I tell him. I don't wait for his response. I head to my room—or more like the room I'm staying in. I really need to get a grip on reality. This will never be my house!

I shut the bedroom door and lock it behind me—not to stop him from entering but to stop myself from running back down there, grabbing his face, and shoving my tongue down his throat. I've never wanted anything so bad in my whole entire life. The smell of his sweet, tangy aftershave, the adorable dimples that appear with his dazzling smile, and those ungodly beautiful biceps of his—I would lick the sweat right off of them. But I have to remember what has been done. How can I even have these thoughts after last night? Who's to say it won't happen again? This whole thing is a mess.

Yeah, I am most definitely in trouble! I should have left when I had reason to, but I stayed. What the hell is wrong with me? I swear I've asked myself this a million times already, but seriously, what the freak is wrong with me?! I slam the back of my head against the door in defeat.

"Uh, is everything alright in there?" Jeff yells from the hallway. Shit! I didn't realize my head-slamming was that loud.

I quickly turn around and back up from the door like it's on fire. "Yup!" I yell back. "I just dropped something—"

I hear nothing but silence for a moment. *Shit!* Please don't open the door.

"Alrighty then, I'm heading downstairs—" he says loudly.

I smack my forehead with the palm of my hand, but I make sure to do it light enough so there's no slapping noise. I could only imagine what he might think then. I run to my overnight bag and quickly pick out something comfortable to wear. I am so over trying to impress him at the moment. Honestly, I'm exhausted from my lack of sleep last night. So sweatpants it is!

Jeff is waiting at the front door for me. Our eyes immediately lock, and the first thing he does is crack a mischievous smirk. I can only imagine what may be crossing his mind at the moment.

"What?" I ask, intrigued.

He shakes his head, grin still intact. "You. I like this side of you. It's kind of sexy."

I look down at my sweats. "Um, if you haven't noticed, I'm in sweats," I inform him, descending the rest of the stairs to meet him at the door.

The smirk's still there, but his eyes are now full of intensity. My heart jumps just a tad. I feel breathy and out of sorts. I want to look away from his intense gaze, but I can't. He is one beautiful man. Every inch of him screams perfection, and he knows it.

I moisten my dry lips and his gaze now drops, staring at them like he wants to eat me up. A flare of heat now surges through my body and covers every inch of my skin, my cheeks now rosy and pink. Why does my body react to him so?

Jeff moves a step closer, and we are now toe to toe. I want him to touch me so badly. My body is begging for him. I've craved him for months now, and he's only inches away. He reaches his hand up to my face and strokes my cheek softly with his thumb. I naturally turn my head into his touch, closing my eyes.

This feels so right, but then I remember last night. My brain shuts everything down and crashes to a halt. My eyes snap open just as he's leaning in for the kiss. I take a step back, out of his reach. He looks at me, confused and maybe a little hurt. Good. Now he knows how I felt.

"I'm sorry. I got a little carried away," I admit, cheeks now blazing with fire.

He's clearly bummed but recovers fast. "Don't apologize. Are you ready?" he asks, quickly changing the subject and opening the door for me to go first.

We pull up to an Italian restaurant. I look over to him and then to my sweatpants. "Um, I am definitely not dressed for this place!" I tell him, feeling completely insecure.

He chuckles. I don't know what is so freaking funny. He could have at least warned me before we left. "You look amazing. Who cares?" he says, shrugging his shoulders. I'm glad he's so confident, but that is definitely not me. Confidence has never been my forte.

Who cares? Is he serious? "Well, for starters—I care, and probably most of the employees and customers do as well!" This place definitely requires some heels.

"Fuck 'em! You look beautiful just the way you are," Jeff sweet-talks me. I want to believe him, but he told me that before, and when I finally got my confidence up, he rejected me. It's clear he was only telling me what I wanted to hear.

Regardless, I can't help my body's reaction. My breath hitches every time he looks at me. He's just so damn sexy, and he makes me feel things I never knew existed. I now tingle and throb in places I've never known or felt before. This is all so bizarre to me, and I don't know how to stop this tidal wave from happening.

"Okay, let's go in," I agree. I'm still completely uncomfortable with what I'm wearing, but I'm willing to say screw it, because I am starving!

Jeff gives me a huge smile, and I can't help but smile back. It's just so contagious. "Good girl," he tells me.

I just roll my eyes. What am I, a dog? We step inside, and my worst fear is answered: everyone who sees me stares and shakes their head. I just want to shrink into a tiny little person the size of a fly. Jeff must notice, because he wraps his arm around me and kisses the top of my head. "Hello, Jeffery. Will it just be the two of you?" the hostess asks, eyeing him up and down. I secretly roll my eyes in disgust. Does she have to be that freaking obvious?

He squeezes me even tighter, and I am grinning wide inside. "Elise, you look beautiful. Don't let any of these stick-up-their-ass-pricks bother you. Our dinner is going to cost the same as theirs, and I bet we'll tip better," he whispers, trying to make a joke to cut the tension.

The waitress brings us to a nice private booth, and I immediately relax. She gives Jeff one last seductive smile. Jeff doesn't give her any reaction, and she heads back to her station. That was a little awkward and annoying. "Have you been here before?" Jeff asks, sitting across from me.

"Once, when I was younger, with my mom and dad," I answer. "What about you? The hostess seemed to know you pretty well—" I bait.

He chuckles. "She's just some chick from school. I didn't really know her. She was a grade or two lower. One of my many fans, I guess," he teases and winks, but I know he's telling the truth. Everywhere I go with him there's always some girl drooling over him. I could never get used to it, and I sure as hell would never want to compete with it either. I already feel insecure enough.

"I see. Well your fans seem to follow you wherever you go," I tell him while looking over the menu intently.

"Hmm, do I sense a little hostility in your voice?"

I bring the menu down to look into his eyes. A young brunette passes our table, ogling him as she goes. I roll my eyes and Jeff smirks, not taking his eyes off of me. I have to admit, I'm just a little amazed he didn't peek. "Not at all. I'm just making an observation. And I'm also observing the fact that you seem to eat up that kind of attention. No surprise there," I say in the most sarcastic sort of way. I'm not fooled; he wanted to look. Hell, everyone knows that peripheral vision can be more effective any-ways! I whip the menu back up for a much-needed wall against his adorable grin. If I stare too long, I'll get sucked into his over-the-top, engrossing charm.

"The only attention I want at the moment is yours," he says so bluntly.

I shake my head, brushing it off. Just breathe, Elise. Just breathe. Once I feel the wall back up and sturdy, I put the menu down and face the danger. He is all types of "yellow tape" and "beware signs." He's the walking cliché of the juicehead jock heartbreaker. He's what I've always steered clear of—not like I ever had to try too hard, though.

I was quiet and kept to myself during my school years. I remember having a couple of friends back then, but once my parents split up, I wouldn't dare bring anyone to my house or go to anyone else's house for that matter. My mother once picked me up from my friend's house and came in to meet her parents. She was embarrassing, and I was completely mortified because she was acting out of line and completely off. It was clear to everyone that she was on something. I never made that mistake again. From that point on, my only friend was myself.

I learned later in life that my mother was high as a kite on Xanax back then. She took it for anxiety and clearly overused it. That was the gateway and the beginning of her pill addiction—and the end of any sort of social life for me.

Jeff squeezes my hand that's lying on top of the table. "Hey, where'd you go?" he asks gently. I gulp and shake my thoughts off. "You completely zoned out on me."

"Sorry, I just had some quick thoughts of my mother," I tell him honestly. I'm sick of keeping it all in.

The skin between his eyebrows crease. "Are you worried about going back?" he asks.

The waitress comes to our table. We order our drinks. I wait until she leaves to speak. "I'm worried she hasn't eaten anything. She never eats unless I make it for her. Her normal intake would include pills and alcohol—that's all. But I've always been there to make sure she's eaten," I explain. The more I say my thoughts out loud, the more worried I become.

"Elise, she's a grown woman. You can't take care of her forever. But I know she's your mother, and she's lucky to have you. Do you want to stop there after dinner and check on her?"

God, he can be so damn sweet when he wants to be. But am I ready to go back and face her yet? Face her betrayal? I'm just not too sure. "Can I think about it?"

Jeff's smile softens a bit. "Of course! I'll be right by your side when you're ready!" he insists. "So since we're on the subject, I've been meaning to ask you—I'm guessing your mother doesn't work; do you pay all the bills in the house?"

This time *my* brows furrow. I'm not sure how I feel about him getting so personal. But I know I've been staying with him in *his* personal space, so I should probably give him some slack. "Yes, I pay all the bills. My father left her the house. She almost lost it a couple of times from being backed up on the mortgage when I was younger, but someone bailed her out. She never told me who it was, but if they hadn't helped, we would have been out on the streets. I started working under-the-table jobs when I was fourteen. Once I was able to legally work, I got a job and started taking over the bills," I divulge.

Jeff runs his hand through his hair. "Man, I am in complete awe of you! How did you even manage graduating?"

I huff. "Beats the hell out of me! Every extra moment I had, I studied: between classes, between jobs, or when I got home from work. I didn't really have a lot of friends, so it was easy to put all my extra energy into my work. I've always thought about going back to school—"

The waitress comes to set down our drinks and take our food order. She focuses completely on Jeff as if I'm nonexistent. But Jeff, being the gentleman he is today, allows me to put in my order first. He gives me a sexy wink and my cheeks heat up. I order the Chicken Angelo, and he orders the linguine with clams in red sauce.

"So tell me—what is it you want to go back for?" he asks.

I take a sip of my iced tea. "Well, since I've worked for Saunders for these last two years, I was thinking maybe publishing. I love a good book, and being able to make someone else's dream come true would be pretty neat!"

Jeff frowns. "But what about your own dreams? Would this career choice be one of them?"

I look down, fidgeting with my fingers. I hadn't really asked myself that question. I'm always worried about everyone else's needs.

"Maybe not a dream I've had since I was a little girl, but it would definitely be something I would enjoy. Does that count?" I question, feeling slightly lost at the moment.

This time he smiles and picks up his straw wrapper, rolling it into a little ball. "It counts if it makes you happy," he tells me. I give him the "don't you dare" look. He pushes the ball into his straw and blows. I try to block my face, but it doesn't help. He still hit me directly on my forehead. Oh it's on! This means war!

After a couple of spitballs and a sore stomach, we settle down to eat our food. I take a big whiff, and it smells delicious! Yum! My stomach growls with impatience. I take the first bite and close my eyes as it melts in my mouth. I can't help it; it tastes like heaven.

When I open my eyes back up, Jeff is staring with a satisfied grin. "You are so beautiful," he states. My cheeks flare pink.

I look back down to my hands. "You're not so bad yourself," I say quietly, slightly embarrassed.

"Elise, look at me," he says softly. I look up. "Don't hide—embrace it. You're a stunning woman. Any man would be lucky to have you. I'm just so glad you're here with me today," he says brightly. He then smirks and says, "So you think I'm hot, huh?"

God, he is so hung up on himself! I roll my eyes and take another bite of my food. Delicious. "I would tell you yes, but your head might combust."

Now he's got a huge shit-eating grin on his face. "I knew it!"

I giggle. "I wish you would do that more often," Jeff comments. "It's flipping adorable." Unfortunately, I haven't had much to laugh at lately, but I'm finding this time with Jeff to be easy and fun. We don't have to work at it.

My phone buzzes in my purse. I quickly dig through it and see Max's picture pop up. *Shoot!* I silently shush Jeff to warn him of the call. "Hey, Max!" I answer.

"Um, hello there stranger. Where have you been lately? I haven't really heard from you since the shower," she says.

I take a deep breath. "I know. I'm sorry. I've been a little busy. How are you feeling?"

"Oh between the swollen ankles and the swollen vajay—I've been just dandy," she jokes with just a hint of sarcasm.

I almost spit my drink out. "Whoa, Max! I could live without that visual!" Jeff looks at me with one eyebrow up, curiously.

Max laughs. "Honestly Elise, I'm fucking going insane! I am in need of a major girl's night! A night with no baby talk!"

I laugh. She is definitely not the sit-around-and-do-nothing type. "Okay, okay! Let's plan one. What about Wednesday night? We can call Kinsey. She can grab the non-alcoholic drinks, and I will grab us a greasy pizza. How does that sound?"

I hear her moan. "Yum. Yes, that sounds perfect," she says. "How did your date with Kroy go?"

I look up at Jeff who is now staring at me. "Um, it went good," I mumble. I don't want to go into any more detail. I wish I could tell her Jeff was listening, but that probably wouldn't go over very well.

"O-kay. That's being pretty evasive. Did you like him? Do you have another date?" she grills. If I don't answer her now, this questioning will go on and on until I do.

I knew this line of questioning was coming. I should have gotten off the phone sooner. "Yes and yes. Listen, I gotta go. I'll give you a call tomorrow after work, okay?"

"Okay, fine! And tomorrow you're spilling all the dirty details. I won't accept no for an answer!" she warns.

I laugh. I know this is not just a threat. "Okay, you got it, boss!"

We hang up. Jeff smirks. "What?" I ask. I take a big bite of my Chicken Angelo.

"Let me guess—she asked you about your date?" Jeff questions. How the freak does he know?

I'm not too sure I want to open this can of worms, but eff it. "She did," I answer, finally. "She wanted to know if I will be seeing him again."

"And will you?" he wonders. The waitress comes by to see how we're doing. Jeff quickly tells her everything's fine and dismisses her. I think she gets the point and walks away.

I square my shoulders and look him straight-on. "Yes. He asked me on another date, and I said yes."

He puts his fork down and closes his eyes, pinching the bridge of his nose. "Elise, I really don't think that's a good idea," he tells me.

Now I'm getting pissed! He doesn't want me, but he doesn't want anyone else to have me either? This is complete bullshit! "Jeff, just stop it!" I screech quietly. "I don't care what you think! He's a nice guy, and he *likes* me. You made it clear to me that we are nothing, so let me be!" I can't finish this dinner. He's so confusing. I've lost my appetite. I push my plate away.

He must sense my aggravation, because he doesn't say another word. He calls the waitress over and has her box up the food. She leaves the check and gives him a wink. I'm surprised she didn't leave him her number. Do girls really act like this? It seems a little desperate, if you ask me.

When we get in the car, before we pull off, Jeff has something to say. "Thank you for coming to dinner with me. I know this wasn't a date, but I'd really like to take you on one if you'd let me—"

I cross my arms. "I thought we tried that already. You backed out, remember?" I remind him.

I see the recognition in his face. "I told you, I only did that because I thought I was protecting you. But I can't stay away any longer. I don't want to share you. I want you to be mine and only mine."

Wow. I am at a loss for words. Unfortunately, I think he only wants me because someone else does too. The feeling will get old and will wear off real quick. "You could have had me, Jeff. You had me at hello—" Before I can say another word, he grabs my face and smashes his lips to mine.

Everything inside me awakens with just the touch of his lips against mine. His hands are rough, tugging on the back of my hair, but his delivery is soft as he coaxes my mouth open with his tongue. My taste buds explode with the exquisite jolt of wine and Jeff. I've pictured this moment a million times, but nothing beats having the real thing. I moan slightly, and Jeff grabs a hold of my hair even tighter—it seems to turn him on even more. I almost feel sexy and womanly.

My fingers glide over his face and down to his chest. I grip his shirt and pull him against me. God, he tastes so good. Our kiss turns deep and needy, full of passion. He's taking my breath away. This is how I've always hoped my first kiss would be, and *boy*—Jeff has not disappointed me. He gets an A+ in delivery.

I feel like the girls do in the movies, all full of butterflies and jumbled nerves. But what they don't talk about is the tingling sensation that creeps through every limb and convenes all in one spot between the legs. I squeeze my thighs tightly together to ease the aching pressure.

Jeff eases back to look me in the eyes. He rubs his thumb over my bottom lip. His touch is so endearing and intimate that I almost melt right here in my panties. "I've been thinking about this moment for a very long time—" Jeff whispers. "You're so fucking beautiful. Are you ready to go home?"

CHAPTER THIRTEEN

Jeff

ww, man! My dick is hard as a rock. How is this possible with only just a kiss? I glance over at her as I drive; the wind's blowing through her hair and the sun casts a bronze light on her flawless skin—she looks so mesmerizingly beautiful. How could I *not* want her? She's a goddess, and I want her to be mine. How do I convince her of this?

Every move I make consists of thoughts of her. I can't get her out of my head, no matter what I am doing or how hard I try. She's it for me. She's the one. Now I just need to get her to believe it.

We pull up to the house; twilight is upon us. I head for the kitchen to grab a bottle of white wine and two glasses, and I nudge my head for her to follow me out to the deck. "Come have a drink with me?" I ask her.

"Okay." She follows me out without a defiant word.

I set the wine and the glasses down on a small table between two cushy lounge chairs. The view of the sunset against the water is always a spectacular sight to see, no matter how many times I've seen it.

I'm hoping she might enjoy this so much that she may never want to leave. Would it be too soon if I gave her a key to my house? Damn, Jeff, what the hell are you thinking? I'm getting way too ahead of myself, and honestly, I'm shocking myself.

I open the wine with a corkscrew and pour us both a glass. I hand over hers. "Thank you. This view is just amazing. I don't think I would ever grow tired of it," Elise says. I hope she doesn't. I wish she would just stay here with me forever.

"I'm glad you like it. I swear if you listen hard enough you can hear the sun descend behind the horizon. It's a magical sound," I tell her.

Yup, she is now looking at me like I'm crazy. I can't help but laugh. As long as she's smiling, that's all that matters. "You don't believe me, do you?" I ask, chuckling.

She looks back towards the water. "Well, this is definitely the first time I am hearing about this. Do you think we might be able to experience it tonight?" It's clear she is trying to hold back a laugh.

She giggles. I like this fun, playful side of her. Not only is she mildly flirting—I think—she is also mildly turning me on. She really has no idea of the effect she has on me. Another glass of this wine, and I'm going to want to pounce on her like a rabid dog.

I finally got a taste of those lips, and I am insatiably addicted. "Maybe. I'm much more interested in kissing those lips than watching the sunset though—"

Before she can respond, the doorbell rings. Weird. I wasn't expecting anyone. *Shit!* What if it's Kyle? "You might want to stay here until I see who it is. It could be Kyle or even my brother, but they usually call before coming over," I tell her before I head inside. I leave her looking unsettled. Honestly, I could give two shits if either of them found out, but I know Elise doesn't feel the same way.

I walk through the living room, down the hall towards the foyer, and open the door. What the—? This is not what I expected whatsoever! "Hey there, *bad* boy." Lacey grins seductively as she runs her pointer finger down my chest. Fuck. Fuck. FUCK! This is *not* happening to me. I recoil against her touch.

"Aren't you going to let me in?" she asks, waiting for me to move aside.

I don't budge at all from the doorway. She is out of her freaking mind. "What are you doing here, Lacey?" I growl. I just need to get her out of here before Elise sees her.

"I thought I would stop to see if you are okay. You drank a lot last night, so I was thinking a comfort bang might make you feel better and, you know, take the edge off," she answers. She just puts it all out there. No bullshitting. If I wasn't so stuck on the girl inside, I might take her up on her offer. After all—who the hell says no to free sex with a hot chick? Definitely not the old me, but I don't want to be that guy anymore. She just caught me on a self-loathing-asshole night.

I made a mistake, and I royally messed up. I'm not making that mistake again. I don't want to lose Elise. No freaking way! I look behind me, hesitantly, for a split second. "Listen Lacey, I told you last night I wasn't interested. You can't just show up at my house—"

"Do you have another girl with you? Is that it, Jeff? You've already moved on to the next available screw?" Lacey questions with venom.

Now I'm getting pissed. First she shows up to my home uninvited, and now she's *questioning* me? This chick has completely lost her mind! "What I have going on is *none* of your *damn* business! You need to leave. And please—don't come back here. Do you understand?" This time I have raised my voice, completely unaware of the decimal level I have increased it to.

"Jeff, is everything okay?" I hear a small voice from behind me. I close my eyes in defeat. I am completely and totally fucked.

"Listen honey, he's just going to bang you and then kick your ass out!" Lacey screams to Elise. This chick is freaking nuts. "Don't get too comfortable, because he'll come back to me once he's done with you!" The worst part is I barely know this girl!

I'm about to open my mouth to shut hers, but I feel a nudge from behind me. Elise peeks her head over to look at Lacey. "Actually, he doesn't *bang* me. I'm not *that* easy. I live here, and considering he doesn't usually screw the same girl twice, I don't think we'll be seeing each other again," she states before walking back down the hall towards the living room.

I can't help but crack a small smile while watching Lacey's mouth drop open. It's priceless. I didn't think Elise had it in her, but damn, that was hot!

"Well, I hope you two are happy together, and just a word of advice—he'll eventually get tired of you," she yells. Then she turns to me, "She's clearly too good for you." Lacey turns around to stomp off.

My gut drops because deep down, I know she's right. Elise *is* too good for me. I don't deserve her, and she definitely doesn't deserve to be with someone as botched as me. I'm a foul guy, but goddamnit, I am willing to change everything I am to be with her.

I watch Lacey pull off, and then I head back to the balcony. I study Elise through the sliding glass door as she watches the last moments of the sunset. She fascinates me. I wish I knew what she was thinking. Then again, after what just went down, I might not want to know. Who could blame her if she doesn't want any part of me?

I take a deep breath and slide open the door. She takes a sip of her wine, but doesn't acknowledge the fact that I'm back. She may not even want to talk to me, and who could blame her? This is supposed to be her sanctuary, her time away from the crazies, and here I am bringing them straight to the house.

I take a sip of my wine, hoping to gain some alcohol courage before I speak. "I'm sorry you had to witness that," I tell her. "That's usually why I don't bring girls home."

She still hasn't said a word, and now I'm getting worried. Finally, after what seems like forever—she speaks. "You don't need to apologize. We're not together, Jeff. This is your house. You can have whoever you want here. I'm not the girl for you. You would get bored of me. You're better off with a girl like her," she says.

I run my hand through my hair in frustration. "I don't want a girl like her!" I raise my voice. I get off my chair and face her. "I want you."

Elise chuckles to herself. "Jeff, you just don't understand. I'm not experienced. I *don't* do the things those other girls will do. I'm a fucking virgin, Jeff! I've never even had sex before! You were my first kiss, for God's sake!" she screeches, tears filling her eyes.

My mouth drops open. Wait, what did she just say? This can't possibly be true. No effing way. I finally find my voice. "There is no way that *I* was your first kiss. Please tell me you're joking with me—"

Elise looks down towards her hands, embarrassed, cheeks now a light pink. A tear escapes her eyes, and this is when it hits me. She's not joking at all. She's letting me in, and I have just laughed in her face. "Man, I'm a dick! You're really being serious, aren't you?"

"Yes," she answers, still looking down.

I lift her chin so she has no choice but to face me. "How is that possible? You're amazing and your lips are so kissably soft," I say, rubbing my thumb over her bottom lip. "How did I get so lucky? This is the most beautiful thing I have ever heard." To know only my lips have touched hers is hot as hell. She's mine in every sense of the word.

"I've never had the urge to get close to anyone until you came along," she speaks softly. "No one's ever seen me before. It's like I've never existed until now."

She's more than I ever could have imagined. "I see you, Elise. I see all of you. I've never had the urge to change until you came along—" I confess to her. I'm in heaven. "Please, just give me a chance? I don't think I can bare another man touching these lips. I want to be your first for *everything*. Let me show you how good we can be together. I promise, once you're mine, you will be mine forever," I beg. I'm not going to take no for an answer.

She hesitates for a moment. "But I promised Kroy I would see him on Friday. What am I supposed to tell him?" she asks, dropping a bomb and completely bursting my happy bubble.

I look her dead in the eyes, because I've never wanted anything more. I couldn't bear seeing her with that scumbag again. "Tell him you will be with me."

It feels like a century has gone by while waiting for her answer. Finally, I hear the magic word, "Okay."

Wait—hold on—did she just say okay? My grin grows from ear to ear. I am one happy man. I don't even wait for it to sink in. I move in, gently stroke my finger down her cheek, and touch my lips softly to hers. She feels incredible.

There's no urgency at the moment, no one to compete with any longer. It's just her and me—no one else. She doesn't pull away. She embraces my kiss with a small moan. My dick twitches.

She's greedy, and she wants more. I coax her mouth open with my tongue, and she matches me stroke for stroke. She tastes incredible. I've never relished in anything as divine as her before. Where has she been all this time?

I run my fingers through her hair and tug ever so lightly so she reveals her neck to me. I place small feather-light kisses down her jaw to her ear and then gently sink my teeth onto her earlobe. She gasps and then moans. I am now hard as a rock.

"You have to stop doing that," I whisper to her. "Or I'll steal your virginity and make love to you right here on this chair—"

She giggles. "I can't help it. You make me feel *so* good," she divulges. *Damn,* if she only knew just how good I could make her feel, she'd never want to leave my side.

I continue my assault as she melts in my arms, but I pull back before we can get any more heated. I want more, but not yet. She deserves to be swept off her feet and ravaged in the most romantic sort of way. I've never done romance, never had to. Girls just peeled their panties off when it came down to sex. But for Elise, I am willing to try anything.

"It's late. We should call it a night before we get carried away," I inform her. She's breathy and she whines. Her brows furrow together in confusion, and I know she thinks I am denying her. I run my finger over the wrinkles between her eyes to smooth them out. I don't like this look on her. "Believe me, I would love to get carried away with you, but it's not the right time. You're way more than just a fuck. Hardcore sex is all I know, but with you I want more," I come clean to her.

Her eyes twinkle, and she's no longer worried. "Will you sleep with me tonight?" she asks, begging me with those naïve eyes.

Whoa! Does she realize that this would be torture for me? Sleeping next to her without being able to touch her is something I don't know how to do. She's stepping into dangerous territory. "I don't think that's the best idea," I break it to her. Not unless she wants her virtue stolen.

"Please? I don't want to be alone tonight. I've been alone for the last twenty-five years. I need someone—I need *you*," she states so matter-of-factly. How the hell am I supposed to say no to that?

Fuck it. I stand up, grab her hand, and lead her up to her bedroom. My palms are sweating as we head up the stairs. Never have I been so nervous to bring a girl in my bed. She stands on the other side of the bed, just watching me as I remove my shirt and pants and leave only my boxers on. No words are said between us, but the sexual tension is whirling thick around us. She slowly removes her sweatpants and hangs them over the end of the bed, but she leaves her T-shirt on. She is so sexy. Her legs look amazing naked. I would love to get my hands and tongue all over them.

I pull down the covers, still not removing my eyes from hers, and she does the same. I climb in first and pat the empty space beside me for her to come. She immediately climbs over and slides under the covers. She hasn't even touched me yet, and I want to come in my boxers. How the hell am I supposed to sleep with her body wrapped with mine?

I lie on my side and tell her to turn with her back to me. I wrap my arm around her stomach and pull her close to me. She smells so good that my mouth is watering. Be good Jeff, be good! I close my eyes and try to picture something horrible so my dick doesn't poke her in the back, but it's too late. Elise giggles.

"*Shoot!* Sorry," I apologize and move my hips back so I am no longer touching her with my hard manly parts. The more I try to keep my thoughts clean, the more dirty they become.

I close my eyes and sniff her hair. Her aroma reminds me of sweet vanilla cookies and fresh fabric softener. She turns her head slightly towards me. "Did you just sniff my hair?"

I laugh. I'm caught red-handed. There's no way I'm getting out of this one. "Yes, you caught me. I totally did," I admit. "I love your scent. Is that weird?"

She giggles. "Maybe just a little bit, but I'm honored. Smell all you want," she says, leaning her head back into mine.

I chuckle, squeezing her to me a little tighter while taking a huge whiff of her hair—tangling myself all in it. Her aroma, the warmth of her skin, and our breaths in sync lull me into a deep, deep sleep.

212

CHAPTER FOURTEEN

My eyes crack open. It's almost six thirty in the morning, and the sun is just starting to spill its rays above the horizon and into my bedroom. I have arms and legs tangled around me, caging me in. Jeff's face is nuzzled closely into my neck. If I make any sudden movements, he will wake up.

Thoughts of my mother come front and center. What am I going to do? I can't stay here forever. If I actually confront her with an intervention, there's no promise that she will go through with rehab. Then I'm left at square one.

Jeff's right; I need to start living my life for me and not for anyone else. I just have to find a way to stop the guilt from paralyzing me and finally take my life back. My mother has her claws deep inside of me, and I need her to release me. But the question is—will she?

Jeff stirs beside me as I try to sneak out of his grip. I look over to him, and his gaze is now on me. "Good morning," Jeff says, eyes twinkling. "Did you sleep okay?"

He releases me, and I stretch. My back cracks. "I did, thank you." I sit up for a moment and stretch again. "And thanks for sleeping with me. I know this is not really your thing, but you made me feel safe," I confess to him.

Who knew that Jeff would be able to give me this sort of comfort? "You're very welcome," he smiles brightly. "I haven't slept this well in a very long time. What time is it?"

"Six thirty."

"How about I go put some coffee on?" he asks.

"Okay, that sounds good. I'm going to get in the shower."

He reaches up to my face and brings me down for a sweet kiss. My body responds immediately; my heartbeat pitter-patters against my chest as a jolt shoots straight between my legs, electrifying every nerve ending in my body.

The thoughts running through my head are full of filth, and I'm liking it. I ready for him to do some dirty, naughty things to me. This urge is so foreign to me, but I'm craving the connection. I'm ready for anything he is willing to give me. Now how do I convince him that I'm not some porcelain doll that can be broken easily?

He told me he's willing to change for me. The big question is—is this something he really wants or just something he thinks he wants? All of these thoughts whip through my mind.

I deepen the kiss and decide to make a dangerously brave move—I roll the top half of my body onto his chest and completely take the lead. My bare legs tangle with his. Every inch of my skin touching his ignites into a burning blaze. My T-shirt inches up as Jeff pulls at the curve of my lower back, drawing me in me tight. I am bare against him, just my panties between us.

My heart is pounding against my chest. I know I am making an impact on him because I can *feel* him beneath me—all hard and stiff. I can't help but smile, knowing that I am affecting him so.

"You are so beautiful," he whispers between kisses. I almost want to believe him—*almost*. Instead, I thrust my tongue deep inside the cavity of his mouth, releasing all my turned-on inhibition through a single kiss.

I hear a deep groan from Jeff as he tangles his fingers through my hair, keeping me in place. His kisses are turning needful and passionate, such a heady mix to my inexperienced self. I'm loving every moment of this and soaking in everything I possibly can. If I'm going to keep his attention, then I will need to take mental notes on what he likes.

Is it bad that in just a matter of minutes I have contemplated losing my virginity? Shouldn't I wait until I know he feels the same as I do? I've never been in love before. How will I know when it's real?

I run my hands down Jeff's swollen chest. His skin is smooth and soft—no chest hair. I wonder if he shaves it. I feel him shiver beneath me from my touch. Just as I swing my leg over and straddle him, he pulls back and holds me in place so I am unable to move.

"Elise, *please,* we have to stop," he begs. He lifts me off of him and sits up. "I don't want to lose control with you."

I sit up and wrap my arms around him from behind. My hands are against his chest. "Why not?" I ask. "Please don't stop. I want you—I want this," I tell him, voice cracking with a desperate need. My libido feels disappointed and a little cheated at the moment.

He unwraps my arms and stands up, shaking his head. "You don't know what you're asking for," he says, staring out the glass door with his hands on his hips. His back is so lean and muscular; my mouth waters.

"I know exactly—"

He turns abruptly and puts both hands on his bed, locking me between them. "Be careful of what you ask for, because next time, I'm going to take what's mine. You are mine, Elise. I hope you're ready for this, because I am dying to get inside of you," he warns. He turns around and walks off towards his bedroom.

I release my breath. Wow, that was pretty intense. I could feel the sexual tension radiate off of him in huge waves. I'm disappointed, but also a little grateful. I was so caught up in the moment that I didn't have time to think; I just reacted off of my body's desires. I can't help myself when I'm around him. These feelings are so confusing. How do I stay in control when the throbbing between my legs just won't stop?

I decide now is a good time to escape back to my bathroom before he returns in just a towel. I won't be able to stop from throwing my body on him at that point. I shut the bathroom door and lean my head against it to catch my breath for a moment. I need to get some common sense back in order. It's amazing how fast that flies out the window when lust gets in the way.

The brisk aroma of coffee wafts under my nose from downstairs. I am in dire need of this. Jeff is sitting down at the breakfast bar, eating a bowl of cereal, as I walk up behind him. He already has a coffee mug set out for me. He melts my heart.

I'm pouring the french vanilla creamer in my coffee when I feel hands wrap around me. This contact feels so good. He leans down and kisses the nape of my neck, which immediately sends a jolt straight between my legs. Within seconds, I am all hot and bothered. How the heck does he do this to me?

I lean my body into him. "You smell *so* good," I tell him.

"Why thank you."

"What are you wearing?"

He turns me around. I leave the coffee on the counter. He lifts my chin up and places a feather-light kiss on my lips. My eyes close as I savor the moment. This is way better than coffee.

"I have on a splash of Ed Hardy," he answers finally. He takes a long whiff of my hair. "But I could smell *you* all day long. We should probably get going before we're late. How about we take just one car?"

"Do you think that's a good idea?" I ask after taking a sip of my coffee.

He grabs his keys off the counter. "Are you worried about what everyone will say?"

"I'm worried what Kyle may say to Maxine. I'm going over there Wednesday night for a girl's night, and I really don't feel like being put on the spot," I say. "You know how she can get."

Jeff chuckles. "Okay, good point. Do you want to go to lunch?"

I follow behind him out the door. "Can't. I have a lunch date with Kinsey."

"Yeah, I'm definitely not getting near that lunch," Jeff informs. He knows exactly what would go down if he were to join us. Kinsey still isn't his biggest fan.

Jeff decides to change the subject. "Elise, are you on birth control?" *Whoa!* Where the hell did that question come from?

"Are you serious?"

"Yes."

My cheeks heat up. I'm immediately uncomfortable, but I know I need to get over this if I am going to have sex—or even have an adult conversation about sex. "No, I'm not. I've never had a reason to be."

I open my car door and try to mentally prepare for the questions that may follow. "Do you have a woman doctor?" he asks.

I roll my eyes. "Yes, of course!"

He chuckles and then walks towards me, getting so close that I can feel his breath against my face. He leans in to my ear. "Good. I want you to make an appointment for birth control as soon as possible. I don't want any barriers with you," he explains, his breath tickling my ear.

My mouth drops open. "What about you?"

He smiles. "I have an appointment after work today, and I'll have the paperwork for you to look at when I get home. My blood test shouldn't take any more than a couple of days," he informs me, walking away. "I left the key for you in the mailbox, by the way. Keep it on you; it's yours."

I shake my head while he drives off. Nice way to drop that bomb on me. He doesn't give me the chance to reject his kind offer.

"Wait—hold on—you haven't had sex before? Like *ever*?" Kinsey questions, voice high-pitched and eyes bugged. "Does Max know this?"

Shoot! Max is going to kill me since I told Kinsey first. Oh well. "No, I didn't tell her yet either. Please don't repeat this—" I beg. I'm holding my seat, waiting for the backlash. I feel like a child whose mother is going to scold her.

Kinsey looks to be in thought, which is making me more nervous by the minute. I release my breath as the creases in her face subside. "I'm not mad at you," she finally says. "I just hope you know that you can talk to me about anything. I won't judge, Elise. I promise."

After I take a sip of my pop, I smile in relief. I don't know why I was so worried about telling her this important part of myself. "I know. I just wasn't ready to talk about it yet, I guess." I shrug my shoulders.

She lowers her voice as a group of teens walk by our table. "So why the interest now?" Kinsey asks, completely delighted.

Here it goes. It's now or never. "I think I'm seeing someone."

Her brows lift into a high arch. "*And?*"

She waits for me, impatiently. "*And* he makes me feel things I've never felt before. I don't really know how to explain it," I divulge honestly. I'm almost expecting her to laugh at me, but she doesn't.

"Of course you don't, and that's okay, Elise. Does he make your heart pound and your hands sweaty?"

"Yes!" I answer immediately.

She giggles. "And do you have this uncontrollable urge to jump his bones and ride him like a pony?"

We both laugh out loud this time. "Um yes! Totally! Is that bad?"

We get a couple of eyes-rolls from the teenyboppers' table next to us, and for a moment, I think Kinsey is going to bitch-slap them. "No. That's called being horny. If a man is doing it for ya, that's a good thing," she responds with a wink. "But Elise, don't rush into anything. You've waited this long, so make it worth it. And make sure the guy is worth it too. This memory will stick with you for the rest of your life, and believe me when I tell you, if I could redo the whole thing with a new guy, I totally would."

"You should have seen his face when I told him—" I add.

Her mouth drops. "What? You freaking told him? No, no, no!" she says, shaking her head back and forth. "Please tell me you're joking?"

I cringe at her reaction. It's clear I didn't make the right choice, but how the heck am I supposed to know what to say and what not to say? "I'm not joking. I told him last night."

Kinsey takes a long sip of her drink. "What did he say when you told him?"

I look around to make sure no one is eavesdropping, because what I'm about to tell her is more embarrassing than revealing my virginity card.

"I told him I was the wrong girl for him because of my lack of experience and the fact that he was also my first kiss."

She almost spits out her pop, choking. "Wow! Okay, whoa! You are killing me with surprises today. What did he say when you said that?"

I crack a small smile at the memory. "He said that it was the most beautiful thing he has ever heard," I recollect. My heart twinges with emotion.

Kinsey nods, taking this all in. "You said this all happened last night? Were you two on a date?"

"No, not really. We were just hanging out." If I told her the whole truth and all its dirty details, we would never make it back to work.

"I really like him, Kinsey—a lot!"

I see an evil thought forming in her eye. "When can I meet him?"

I look at my phone, and we have about ten minutes to race back to work. "Soon—I hope. We better get going. I don't want Mr. Saunders on my ass. He scares the crap out of me sometimes!" I admit. Kinsey just laughs. I don't think there's a thing on earth she's afraid of. Somehow she has Mr. Saunders and every other man wrapped around her finger. He just adores Kinsey, and it drives Junior out of his mind.

"Until tomorrow," Kinsey replies with a wink.

CHAPTER FIFTEEN

Here we go. I can't believe Kyle talked me into this. I know this interview is just for show, because I pretty much already have the job, but I still hate this sort of thing.

"Good afternoon, Jeffery. Please, have a seat," Mrs. Saunders advises.

I've known her for a very long time now. She's basically like a second mother to me. She's always been very straightforward but in a kind, non-aggressive way. I'd have to say that

Max holds the same qualities as Mrs. Saunders. Well done, Kyle.

I take my seat on the other side of the conference table. "Hey, Mrs. Saunders. How's it going?"

She smiles. "Fine, thanks. I'm afraid Mr. Saunders had a meeting to attend to, so it's just Kyle and I here for the interview."

Kyle knows how uncomfortable I am, and yet he's sitting across from me with a goofy-ass smirk. I want to slap it off of him. Next time I see him out of work, he has one coming.

"Okay, sounds good to me," I reply.

"So, tell me Jeff, I already am well aware of your work ethic and background—why a personal assistant?" Mrs. Saunders asks. Man, she cuts right to the chase, huh?

I give Kyle a "fuck you" look. "I honestly would have never considered it. My first thought was to turn it down when Kyle mentioned it, but he reminded me a personal assistant is the driver behind the man. I clearly know him very well—well enough that we can finish each other's sentences, and that can be very handy in this sort of business. Basically, Kyle knows I won't let him down. Never have."

Mrs. Saunders seems impressed with that answer. She nods her head and smiles, trying to keep neutral, but she forgets that I know her very well also. The interview continues for another ten minutes or so before they send me on my way.

I feel good about how it went. There really wasn't much pressure, considering I really don't need this job or any job for that matter. Elise is my only reason to stay here. A thought flashes through my mind: Maybe Elise would be more suitable for this position than me. She did express she may want to get into the literary profession, and what better way than to learn it directly from a professional in the field?

I think tomorrow night might be the perfect time to discuss this with Kyle. After all, it's ladies night, which means Kyle gets kicked out on his rear and is forbidden to enter his house until they have completely been sedated with gossip.

Kyle catches up with me at my desk. "It's ladies night tomorrow at my house. Wanna go out for a drink and catch up?"

"Yeah man, let's do it. McGregor's?"

Kyle seems hesitant. "I don't know, man. I really don't want to run into Beth." Beth was his stage-five clinger from last year. She was a former coworker who ended up getting fired after making an attempt to out Maxine and Kyle to his mother. Let's just say Mrs. Saunders didn't take that very well.

"Ah! You know she only goes on Mondays and Thursdays. She won't be expecting you to show up on a Wednesday," I point out.

He considers this for a moment. "Yeah, maybe you're right. I could go for a beer and some wings! It will be a nice break from being Max's bitch," he admits with a laugh. "No bro, you don't understand—this is on a whole new level." He runs his hand over his head, stressed.

Poor guy. I don't think I'll ever be ready for this, but what guy is?

"Dude, just wait until the baby's here. You're going to end up her bitch too!" I chuckle. Shoot! He almost looks as though he might pass out. "You okay, man?"

"Yeah, just ready for this 'man time,'" he smacks the back of my head. "Later!"

"Whatever, asshole!" I say quietly. Of course I get a couple of eye-rolls from my coworkers, so I guess I wasn't that quiet.

It's been an hour, and I'm finally through with the doctor. I should get my results back within the week. I'm ready to see Elise. I just hope all this preparation doesn't scare her away. I have to remind myself to take it slow with her, even though she's been the one jumping my bones. I just don't want her to regret any fast decisions down the road. I want her to want this just as much as I do.

I pull up my driveway and see Elise's car parked in her spot. Just knowing she is home waiting for me feels nice and surprisingly comforting. I enter the front door and get hit with a delicious aroma. My stomach instantly responds with a growl.

I quietly walk towards the kitchen. I see Elise slicing and dicing some vegetables. I lean against the doorframe to watch. She's beautiful. I smile. She looks to be on a mission, but most of all, she looks at home. I could get used to this.

I clear my throat, and she looks up. "Hey! I hope you don't mind me using your kitchen; I thought you might be hungry when you got back. I'm starving!"

I walk over to the stool and take a seat in front of her. "You can use whatever you like, especially if you're feeding me," I say with a wink. She looks mighty fine in the kitchen. I would love to take her right here on the counter.

"How was your lunch with Kinsey?" I ask, studying her every movement.

Her cheeks turn pink. She answers without looking at me. "Good. Informational. You know how Kinsey can be," she responds with a shrug.

It's clear they were discussing something off limits, so I won't pressure her into telling me. "So you're going to Max's tomorrow night?"

"Yup. I'm going there straight after work."

She dumps the vegetables into the steamer and turns the timer knob. "I'm going to take Kyle out for a bit. Max exiles Kyle from the house on girl's nights."

She giggles. "Yes, I know. Poor Kyle," she says, giggling again. "Max said if she has to deal with a huge stomach and swollen feet, then Kyle has to deal with her and her mood swings. I would say that's a pretty fair deal."

I would say she's definitely right. I nod in confirmation. "So, what's on the menu for tonight?"

She checks the oven and then grabs the white wine out of the refrigerator. "Some baked chicken and baked potatoes," she answers, holding up the bottle. "Wine?"

"Yes, please. It smells delicious in here. Where did you learn to cook?" I only ask because from what she told me of her mom, I'm sure she wasn't Betty Crocker. But I could be wrong.

"Well, before my father left, my mother was a great cook."

Damn, I am wrong.

"I watched her many nights, cooking dinner for my father. She was very meticulous on how everything had to look. The table and the meal had to be laid out perfect for my father when he got home from work. If not, he would throw a fit," she explains, pouring the wine and handing me my glass.

My gut sinks. It sounds like her mother was a victim of abuse long before her addiction problems. "That sounds pretty sad," I comment. I'm starting to realize that Elise is an amazingly strong woman. Her shyness is only her armor to shield anyone from getting in. "I'm sorry you had to witness that behavior. It sounds like those memories have left a lasting effect on both you and your mom. I just wish she could have been strong enough for you like you were for her. I'm glad you're here, Elise. I really am."

I mean it. If she's here, then I can protect her. This overwhelming feeling of alpha-male protectiveness surges over me. I don't want anyone to ever hurt her again—including her mom. I'm going to do whatever I can to make sure she doesn't shed another tear of sadness.

"Me too, Jeff, but I still can't stay here for-ever. Oh, and the key thing—that was a smooth move, by the way," she informs with a playful grin. Damn, she caught on to me. I give her a quick wink.

I take a sip of my wine. "I'm glad you thought so," I say with a smirk.

The stove timer goes off. Elise checks the food and grabs a potholder to take the dishes out of the oven. The chicken is sizzling and the potatoes are steaming. It all looks so delicious. I can't remember the last time a woman cooked for me. I was never interested in playing house before Elise either.

She loads our plates, hands me mine, and comes around to join me with hers. I feel like we should be enjoying this in the dining room by candlelight, but I'm sure that would be too much. Just sitting next to her and enjoying this meal is good enough for me. Man, I could defi-nitely get used to this.

I take my first bite, and my eyes immediately roll back as I groan. "Mmm, this tastes unbe-lievable! Damn girl, you can cook!" I say, stuff-ing my mouth.

She giggles. I love hearing that sound, so carefree and young. She shouldn't have all these burdens on her at such a young age. She should be giggling like this all the time. "Why, thank you! I'm glad you like it. I owe you. You have been so kind to me."

Oh no! I'm not doing her a favor. I'm doing this because I care for her, and she needs to know that. "You owe me nothing, Elise. You're here because I want you here. Like I said before, you can stay as long as you want. As a matter of fact, I want you to stay here permanently. I know this may sound nuts, but I have crazy feelings for you. My life seems so much brighter with you in it. You don't have to make a decision right now, but please think about it. You can still help your mom from a distance," I express, completely dropping a bomb on her. I'm just nervous about what her response may be.

The minutes pass by as her silence surrounds us. I won't say another word until she says something—anything.

"Jeff, have you ever been in a relationship?" she asks.

Unexpected. But, I'm glad she wants to talk. "No, nothing serious."

"If I stay here, what happens with us? What do you want from me?" she asks without touching her food.

I put my fork down and grab her hand so it's tightly entwined with mine. "I don't have all those answers. I've never wanted to commit to anyone until you came along. You make me think about my future. You make me want more. Does that make any sense?"

She smiles that beautiful smile I love. "Okay, we can try for more. I guess it will be the blind leading the blind, huh?" she jokes.

I laugh and bring her hand up to my lips, kissing each knuckle. "Yes, I suppose you're right. So, how do you feel about breaking the news to our close friends?" I'm praying she won't freak out on me.

"I'm okay with it, but are you sure you can handle the interrogation from the girls? You know that's to follow, right?"

She is most definitely right, but I know all they want is for her to be happy. They're just going to have to get used to the fact that I want to be responsible for her happiness. I feel like a giddy schoolboy. I can't stop grinning like an ass. I've gotten her to say yes!

"I can withstand anything as long as I know you're by my side. This is all new to me, so please be patient with me. We can figure things out together as they come up." I reach for her face and slide my thumb down her soft cheek. She turns in to my hand and closes her eyes, seeming to savor every moment of my touch. She is just stunning. My chest tightens, and a foreign feeling comes over me. I am one lucky man.

"You are so beautiful," I add.

She opens her eyes, unattached and glossed over. What the hell just happened? "Thank you," she says, but it's clear she doesn't believe my words. It pains me to see that this alluring creature has so much self-doubt.

I take back my hand to give her some space. We finish dinner and move out to the back deck with refilled wineglasses in hand. We've sort of retreated into a quiet comfort. It's nice. Usually, I'm filling in the silence with sex. If a girl can't hold a conversation, sex is the next best thing. But with Elise, I'm okay with just being.

I break the silence. "So, does this mean that you're okay with carpooling to work?"

She laughs. "Yes, I think that would be appropriate." She agrees—thank fucking God! The sooner everyone knows she's mine, the better.

"So, tell me, do you have a bucket list?" I ask while staring out towards the mesmerizing water. The sun is beginning to descend, leaving the sky swirled with reds and oranges.

"I do actually!"

"Oh yeah?" I chuckle. "Tell me one."

She pauses a moment as if to decide what words to use next. "To lose my virginity," she replies.

My breath catches and my head snaps towards her, looking for any sign of silliness, but there's none. She's dead serious as she looks intensely into my eyes, almost begging for me to make a move. My dick automatically goes stiff. Wow! I can only behave for so long. I want so badly to be buried deep inside her. I want to be the only man who's ever buried deep inside her.

I stand up, not giving a crap that my rod has pitched a tent, and grab Elise's hand. I lift her out of her chair. I can't deny her or myself any longer. She wants this, and so do I. We're both two consenting adults. The hell with it.

We leave everything where it is. I lead her up the stairs and to my bedroom. Glad I changed my sheets this morning! But she stops me before we cross the threshold. "Let's go in this room—" she suggests. I completely understand why. It wasn't that long ago I was shacked up with another girl in my bed, and the worst part was that Elise saw me. I quietly shake that from my mind. I'm such a jerk.

I lead her into her room and quickly push her back up against the wall. I have to taste her. I can't wait another moment. I want to claim every part of her. My left hand is against the wall. I grab her chin with my right hand so I am looking into her beautiful, picturesque, sky-blue eyes. "Are you sure you're ready for this?" I ask one last time.

"Yes," she answers, all breathy and sexy as hell.

I rub my hard bulge up against her, and she releases a soft moan that goes straight to my cock. Man, I feel like I'm going to combust. "You keep doing that, and I'm going to bury myself deep inside of you right here," I growl between kisses.

She runs her hands through the back of my hair and tugs. I bite down on her bottom lip and pull in reaction. This woman just does it for me. I've done this a million times before, but it has never felt *this* arousing. Her lips are electrifying, and her scent is unbelievably intoxicating. I am drunk in love. I can only imagine how she will smell and taste once I have my tongue in between her legs.

I grab a hold of her tank top and slowly lift it up over her head, only separating us for a moment. Her skin is so velvety soft; I could touch her for hours and never get tired of it. She's a goddess! I've never seen anything or anybody so perfect.

I coax her mouth back open with my tongue—playing and dancing into a provocative rhythm. I reach my hand around to the clasp of her bra and unhook it. I slide my fingers under the straps, slowly letting it fall to the floor. She freezes for a moment, and I know it's her self-preservation. I don't want her to feel uncomfortable and self-conscious. She has to know that she is absolutely stunning.

"Don't shy away from me, Elise. I've been dreaming of this moment for a very long time. You're everything I pictured and more," I whisper to her. I palm her breasts in my hand while laying a trail of kisses down her jawline to the nape of her neck. I hear her erratic breathing in my ear, and I am loving every minute of it! I tug her right nipple gently with my thumb and forefinger, and she immediately bucks up, pushing her chest out for me to examine closer.

My tongue trails a line from her neck to her chest and over the peaks of her breast. I slip a taut nipple into my mouth. She instantly calls out in ecstasy as she digs her nails into the back of my head. "That's my girl—just let go, beautiful," I encourage her. I'm now bursting at the seams.

I switch to her other breast, taking her in my mouth, getting the same glorifying reaction. I slowly tease and nibble on her erect nipple. She's like heaven in my mouth. I release her, and in one swift movement I have her in my arms, heading for the bed.

I lay her down on top of the bed, hair fanned out around her, and her perfect tits begging to be played with again. I smile as I climb on top of her. I have to make her nice and ready for me. I need her begging for me. This ought to be fun.

I take her breasts into my mouth, swirling my tongue around her nipple, then make my way up to her lips. I plunge my tongue deep into her mouth with her following my lead. My right hand slides down her tummy, into her yoga pants, and under her panties where I find her nice and soaking wet. This is hot as fucking hell, and the thought that no man has ever touched this makes me want to combust right here in my pants.

I run my fingers over her clit and through her slick folds. She immediately screams out.

This isn't the controlled Elise I've known. This is a sexual demon who is ready for some more.

My head is against her forehead. I want to see her come apart with her first orgasm. I make my way back up to her little nub, rubbing my thumb in slow clockwise circles while dipping my fingers deep inside her. Her nails dig into my back as she thrust her hips greedily towards me. I kiss her neck, nibble on her ear, and then crash my lips into hers. She moans into my mouth, and I almost want to come undone.

I make my way down to her chest and suck a nipple, hard and rough, while continuing my rhythmic assault between my thumb and my forefingers. I find the rough spot tucked away deep inside her, and the moment I stroke it, she clenches around my fingers like a vise grip. Waves and waves of pure ecstasy come over her as she screams my name. It's like music to my ears.

Before she has the chance to come down, I get up, slide her pants and her tiny pink underwear off and kneel in between her legs. The sight of her pretty pussy, glistening wet from my own doing, is like no other. But before she can get shy on me, I bend down and lick from her ass all the way up to her clit in one slow, precise movement, lingering over her swollen bud. She bucks up from my touch on her sensitive parts. I just had to taste her—she tastes just like my dreams, only better.

I now have her panting and ready for more. I sit up between her legs, remove my shirt, grab the condom from my back pocket, and kick off my pants. She looks down at my cock with wide, curious eyes. I smirk in response. That's right, this dick is going to be burrowed deep inside you in just one moment. I lock my eyes with hers as I roll the condom on. She looks sedated and apprehensive all in one. I lean over her, rock-hard, at her entrance. I begin to kiss her slowly. It's time for me to be gentle and easy on her. This is the moment she's going to remember her entire life, and I want to make sure it's a moment she smiles at when she thinks of it.

"Are you sure you're ready for this, Elise?" I ask between kisses.

"Yes, please, Jeff. I need you," she begs, voice raspy from screaming. This is all I need to hear.

I slowly push into her and all her muscles instantly tighten up as she digs her nails into my upper arms. *Fuck*, she feels so damn tight! I stay still for a moment, kissing her, waiting for her to accommodate my width and length. "Are you okay?" I ask, worried.

She nods, and I continue to forge ahead. My eyes roll back into my head in pure bliss. She feels amazing! I've never felt anything like it. My first time doesn't even compare. This is also a first for me. "Take a deep breath, Elise, because I'm going to rip through you. It may hurt for just a moment," I warn her. I start to kiss her to keep her mind off of the pain as I rip through her in one swift movement. She screams out, her body tightening and locking around me, so I stop to allow her time to adjust from my invasion.

I'm buried deep inside her where I've been dreaming of being for a long time now. "I'm okay," she whispers. I lay kisses on every inch of her face before I begin to move. I slowly withdraw and then move forward again and again, gently. She wraps her legs around my waist, meeting me thrust for thrust. "Yeah, beautiful, that's right. Just like that," I encourage her.

With each pump, I go deeper and deeper, increasing my speed. "Man, you feel amazing, Elise," I whisper. I then lean down, taking her erect nipple into my mouth, and she yells out beneath me. Her pussy begins to quicken and quiver around me. Whoa! If she moans like that again, I am going to explode! She cries out as I pump one last time into her, and we both come undone together, tidal wave after tidal wave until all that's left are the aftershocks from this catastrophic earthquake.

I slip out of her slowly, she winces, and I remove the condom before throwing it on the floor. "Are you sore?" I ask her.

"Just a little," she answers.

I head into the bathroom and come out with a warm, wet washcloth. "I'm just going to clean the blood off of you," I tell her. She looks a little mortified as I clean the red stains from between her thighs. "Don't be shy with me now," I tease. She rolls her eyes and giggles.

I get rid of the washcloth and lie down on my side next to her. I kiss the top of her head and bring her into me. I could stay like this forever. I've always hated after-sex affection, but with her, I couldn't think of anything better.

CHAPTER SIXTEEN

Elise

I can't believe this has actually happened! I *finally* feel like a woman. Eeek!
I want to jump around and call my girlfriends. Jeff's arms are wrapped tightly around
me as he snores faintly. I carefully stretch, trying not to wake him. I wince; muscles I didn't
even know existed are pretty sore. I think I
could really benefit from a nice, hot shower.

I slip out of Jeff's grip and tiptoe towards
the dresser to grab some clean underwear. I
close the door to the bathroom behind me and

turn on the shower to get it nice and hot. I undress, place the towel next to the shower, and step in. The hot water beats on my back, immediately loosening up my muscles. It feels heavenly. I close my eyes to absorb the tranquility.

I stand in place for a moment, replaying the last couple of hours in my head. I smile to myself. My cheeks even blush at the thoughts. His body, his touch—everything was just perfect. Hands wrap around my stomach, ripping me from my thoughts as I grab for the shampoo. I jump at the interruption.

Jeff chuckles. "Sorry, didn't mean to scare you, sexy," he whispers in my ear. He kisses my shoulder and neck. I shiver. "I couldn't let you take a shower—alone—naked," he jokes. I smirk, enjoying his playfulness.

I turn around and wrap my arms loosely around his neck. "I'm glad you're here. I was just thinking about you," I tell him, seductively.

"Oh yeah?"

I reach up and bring my lips to his. This time, it's me coercing his mouth open so I can devour him. He groans as our tongues tangle into one another. I rub my mound against his hard shaft while he lays kisses down my neck, all the way to my chest.

I moan and arch my back as he takes my breast into his mouth. He makes me feel sexy and wanted, things that I've never felt before. I take the initiative to reach down and grab him, stroking his whole length. I still can't believe this was inside of me just hours ago. "Turn around," he orders.

I hesitate for a moment but then comply. I know whatever he has in store for me is going to feel amazingly good. I trust him 100 percent. "Put your hands on the wall," he barks.

I do as he asks. He kisses my shoulders and trails down the middle of my back. I shiver with each sweet, soft touch. Every nerve ending in my body is electrified. I feel his fingers slip between my folds from the rear. I'm sore, but that is completely gone once he reaches my clit. He teases and gently circles his fingers, bringing my breathing to an all-time high. I grind my bottom as he plays.

I hear a rip from a wrapper, and then he is at my entrance, waiting. Where the hell did that condom come from? Who cares? I'm now in desperate need. My fire is blazing, and I need him to put it out. He cups my breasts and tweaks both my nipples. I yell out, and I back my ass into him, quietly begging for whatever he has to give.

"Are you ready for me?" he asks in a scratchy, hoarse whisper. God, he is so sexy.

I can't think of anything that I want more than him inside of me right at this moment. "Yes, please. I need you—now," I demand. Who is this woman saying such things? I'm surprising myself.

In the next moment, he is sliding slowly inside of me. I hear him grunt and feel him tighten his grip on my hips. I smile, knowing that I affect him this much. I'm still slightly sore, but it doesn't last long as Jeff's whole self is now buried deep inside of me. I feel full and stretched, but he waits, allowing my body to get accustomed to him once again.

"Does it hurt?" he asks, concerned.

It's so sweet that he is truly worried. Instead of answering, I push back into him so he inches a little deeper. He hisses and nips my shoulder with his teeth. Every inch of my body is alive and in desperate need of his contact.

He slowly pulls back, and then in one quick movement, he's deep inside of me. He hits what I assume is my spot, dead-on. I scream out in pleasure and shock holding my own against him. He pumps over and over and then reaches around to cup my breasts, tweaking and playing with my nipples again. It sends a jolt straight between my legs. I feel the heat consume my body as my insides begin to convulse around him. I can't hold back any longer. I let go, allowing every emotion and feeling to tumble down. Jeff follows my lead, grunting my name and crashing right behind me.

"Damn, Elise, you just feel too good. You're going to be the death of me," he growls, still inside of me.

I giggle. He slips out of me and grabs the soap, beginning to lather me up. He washes every inch of me while I wash my hair. Then he washes himself.

He steps out after wrapping a towel around his lower half and then holds one out for me. Is it weird that I'm now slightly embarrassed to be naked under his watchful gaze? Jeff's being attentive and sweet. I'm enjoying this side of him, but what happens after this? I'm in unchartered territory, and I do have to keep in mind that he is as well. He may have had multiple sex partners, but not one relationship. So this is new for the both of us. It feels nice to be a first in one area of his life.

"I don't think I'm ever going to get enough of you," Jeff admits while wrapping his arms around me as we gaze at each other in the mirror.

I smile shyly, looking down towards my fingers. He lifts my chin so I have no choice but to look at him dead-on. "Don't shy away from me, Elise. You are truly the most captivating woman I have ever known."

Is this man for real? Somebody pinch me, I must be in a dream. He turns me around and leans down for a soft kiss. This kiss is full of emotion and passion, like nothing I've ever experienced or even knew existed before, except in movies or books. My body immediately melts to his. I may be sore, but I'm ready to go again.

"You're not so bad yourself," I reply. He kisses the top of my nose.

"If you keep doing this, we might never get to bed."

We both laugh. He's totally right. I have a long day tomorrow with work in the morning and gossip at night. I have to prepare myself for the interrogation I'm going to receive once I spill the beans about Jeff.

Jeff leads me to bed and climbs in next to me. He grabs my waist and pulls me to him, my back to his chest, and snuggles his face into the side of my neck. These last couple of hours with him completely took my mind off my mother and the issues that still lay ahead. I feel relaxed, safe, and completely at peace at the moment. I haven't felt this way in a very long time—if ever.

Jeff kisses my neck, which rockets warmth straight down to my woman parts. "Did you make a doctor's appointment yet?" he asks.

Thank God my back is to him because I can feel my cheeks change to a crimson red from his question. I'm not used to having to share this information with a male. "Yes. I have an appointment Friday for the birth control," I respond, a little mortified.

"Have you thought about which way you want to go?"

Okay, now this is getting a little out of hand. I turn around so I can see his face. "Can you not? I'm going to get on something, but it is my choice which birth control I choose to take, okay?" I snap.

He chuckles and kisses my cheek. "Okay boss, you got it."

I yawn. Jeff reaches for the lamp behind him to shut it off and then wraps himself around me a little tighter. "Good night, beautiful."

I smile. "Good night."

My alarm shrieks, ripping me out of a deep sleep. Ugh! It's already time to get ready for work. I feel like I haven't slept in days. My muscles ache, and the more I try to move, the more Jeff tangles himself around me.

"Hey," I whisper, lightly shaking him awake. "It's time to get up."

He groans, not wanting to move. Thank God we showered last night. It won't take too much time for me to get ready. I slip out of Jeff's grip and head to the bathroom while he closes his eyes for a little longer.

By the time I finish up, Jeff is up and has already left the room. I feel a little disappointment as I look at the empty bed. I head downstairs, and the smell of coffee swarms my nose. I am in need of a *huge* cup! It's nice to share this consuming need of coffee with someone else.

"Good morning," Jeff says as I enter the kitchen.

I smile shyly, taking a seat at the counter. "Good morning."

He holds up a cup. "Coffee?" he asks.

"Yes, please!"

He chuckles, pouring me a cup. "You don't look like you got enough sleep last night. Did something keep you up?" he questions, teasing.

I roll my eyes. "You know exactly what kept me up," I say, my right eyebrow raised.

He walks around the counter to hand me my coffee cup. He bends down to deliver a deep kiss. I'm almost breathless once he's done. There's nothing else to say.

"Yes, I think I do know exactly what kept you up," he responds, smiling.

I shake my head. What the hell am I going to do with him? I'm a mess around him. I can't seem to control my emotions or my body's reactions when in his presence.

"You ready?" he asks.

We pull up to work—together. My nerves are getting the best of me. I see Kinsey already parked and exiting her car. Oh no! Here we go. She looks directly at us. I'm not ready for this. I don't think I'll ever be ready for her interrogation. So screw it. I take a deep breath.

Jeff turns off the ignition and looks over to me. "I guess there's no backing out now, huh?"

I shrug my shoulders; the cat is out of the bag. "Yup, you're definitely right about that," I answer as I watch Kinsey walk towards our car.

I get out to greet her. She has her arms crossed with a wicked grin spread across her face. I know that grin all too well. It's her "I can't wait to tell Maxine" grin. She's lucky I have already planned on telling them the deal, so I grin back at her.

"Hey there, guys! What's going on here?" Kinsey questions, curiosity definitely piqued.

"Hey Kins!" Jeff greets. "We're just heading in," he says with a smile, knowing that's not what she meant.

We walk and she follows. "Is your car broken down or something?" she asks me.

"No. Jeff just offered to bring me," I answer, being completely evasive. I know it's killing her.

"And why would he do that when you have your own car?" Kinsey asks, now getting annoyed.

"Because she stayed at my house last night," Jeff answers bluntly. Kinsey's eyes bug out of their sockets. If she were chewing gum, she would have choked. Way to go Jeff! Now I will not be getting any sort of work done today. She's going to be blowing me up through every type of media possible.

She now squints at me disapprovingly. "Tell me you two are fucking joking? Please!"

We make it to safety—the entrance foyer—where she can no longer raise her voice. I just shake my head. I can't seem to find my words at the moment. Jeff throws up the peace sign and leaves me alone with her. Oh he is in so much trouble for this! He drops the bomb and just leaves. Not cool, Jeff. Not cool!

Kinsey turns her venomous wrath on me. "Are you fucking out of your mind, Elise? This isn't some starter thing. You are playing with the big boys when it comes to Jeff. Didn't you learn the first time?" she squeaks. "My God, he freaking left you heartbroken. I can't bear to see him do that again to you." She's suddenly enlightened by something. "Shit, Elise, he wasn't the one you were talking about yesterday, was he?"

Yup, she has put it together. I just nod, still unable to speak.

An employee enters the front door, and Kinsey pauses her questioning for the moment. I telepathically beg the employee to stay. "Please don't tell me you gave up your virginity to him, Elise!" She puts her hand up to stop anything that might come out of my mouth. "Never mind. Don't tell me. I don't think I can handle the truth this early in the morning."

Now she's being dramatic. I wouldn't expect anything less from her. Thankfully, another employee walks into the foyer and walks through the security door. "Let's talk about this tonight. I was planning on telling you and Max everything then—okay?"

She's silently contemplating her response. "Okay, but there is no backing out." She points her finger at me, "If you don't show, Max and I are coming to find you!" she threatens before walking into work.

I blow out a long, deep breath. Man, that was stressful as hell! Forget the wine, I need to grab some liquor for tonight! It's going to be a long night, that's for sure!

I log into my computer, and the first thing I see is an email from Jeff.

"Yikes! That was a little intense. You OK?"

Is he really asking me this? He knows damn well that he left me adrift in the sea with a hungry shark.

"I see you can't handle the heat. Thanks for leaving me hanging, but I'm ok. I think I need to stop and grab an extra bottle of wine tonight. I'm going to need it!"

I start my normal daily duties as I wait for his response.

I look up and see Mrs. Saunders entering. I look at the time on the bottom of my computer screen, and it reads eight thirty. She is never here this late. I hope it's not because of Max.

"Good morning, Elise," Mrs. Saunders greets.

I smile. "Morning Mrs. Saunders. Is everything okay with Max?" I ask. Jeff's next email comes through.

She laughs. "Yes, dear. I had an appointment early this morning. Max is fine and irritable—poor thing. She does not handle confinement very well."

I laugh along with her because *boy* is she right! Max is going stir crazy, and Kyle is getting the brunt of the misery.

"I can only imagine! But your son is doing an amazing job at keeping her happy," I tell her, which is completely the truth. He is so patient and attentive to all her needs. It's actually pretty adorable to watch.

She softens a bit. "Thank you, dear. He's going to be a great dad. Could you email me the contact matrix for the Bailey Lit Agency? I don't think I have the most up-to-date one."

"Yes, no problem," I respond before she heads into the office. She may be sweet and motherly, but she is all about her business. I email her the info before I respond to Jeff.

"I don't think that's a good idea if you're driving. Did you want me to be your DD? I can drop you off there..."

I roll my eyes and smirk as I write out my next email.

"Thanks for the offer, but I am a big girl who can handle her booze and knows when to stop. Maybe I should be asking you the same? Let's face it, you don't have the greatest track record on making smart decisions when drinking. We wouldn't want another girl to end up in your bed tonight, now would we?"

My grin is from ear to ear as I press send. Another response comes in immediately.

"Ouch! That burned. Ok, maybe you have a point, but I still don't want you driving after drinking. I have to pick up Kyle and drop him back home anyways, so it wouldn't be out of my way and it's a win-win for the both of us . . . just say yes. Please? I promise to make it worth your while tonight. *Wink, wink*"

I instinctively squeeze my legs together tightly to contain the throb between them. Man, he does not play fairly! I can't stop thinking about last night. Details flash through my mind, projecting images of our first collaboration. My skin immediately flares. Crap! Not good. Getting all hot and bothered while working the front desk is not going to happen.

"Ok, but only because you are asking nicely—I will agree—just this one time. Now shouldn't you be working?" I respond by email.

I should be working as well. I can't help checking my email for his response. In record time, there is another manila envelope on the bottom-right side of my screen. I click on it.

"You just made me a very happy man. I will be working now, so I would appreciate it if you left me alone so I can do my job . . . "

I shake my head with a grin. He is just too much. I decide not to respond, because I have some work to do as well.

I worked through lunch today. I didn't feel like getting grilled by Kinsey for an hour straight. I would rather save that for tonight when I have a glass of wine in hand. Jeff and I head back to his house. I get a text from Max.

"Hey, girl! Kinsey texted me earlier mentioning you had some important information to divulge to us! This waiting is KILLING me! Get over here ASAP!"

I chuckle out loud. Jeff looks over at me, clearly entertained. "Whatcha laughing about?" he asks.

We pull up to the house. "Just Max. Kinsey informed her I have something big to reveal, and she's freaking out," I tell him, shaking my head.

"You have a long night ahead of you," he teases.

As we're getting out of the car, my phone dings—another text message. I roll my eyes. Now what does Max want? I open the text, and it's not Max. It's Kroy. Damn! My reaction must be noticeable, because Jeff asks if everything's okay.

I'm torn. Should I keep this to myself or just be honest? Is honestly really the best policy when it comes to jealousy? It doesn't help that Jeff has a personal vendetta against Kroy, either. I have to make a decision—and fast!

I follow him into the kitchen. "Kroy just texted me," I tell him, taking the honesty route.

He stops and turns to face me. Oh no—he looks pissed. I've never seen this side of him. I have to admit, it's a little scary. I almost want to huddle down so I'm smaller and more fragile-looking. I don't think I can handle him yelling at me. Yup, it's clear I should have just kept the text to myself or maybe even changed the subject.

"Did you tell him we are together and to lose your number?" he questions, clearly irritated. He throws his keys on the table.

The truth is—I didn't have the heart. Kroy was so sweet to me, and I already told him I would see him this weekend. I just don't have it in me to let him down. I guess I was just trying to avoid the situation all around, hoping that maybe he just wouldn't call back.

"No," I respond, looking down at my hands nervously.

I hear his footsteps in front of me. He reaches for my chin, forcing me to look up at him. "Elise, I don't want to share you. You are mine. If you can't tell him that, then I will."

This intense energy engulfs my body. I don't know what has come over me—but in this moment—I don't care. I throw all my inhibitions aside and just go for it.

I run my fingers through his hair and pull him towards me, crushing my lips against his. He seems to be in shock for a moment but quickly gathers his thoughts together and returns my urgency. I coax his mouth open with my tongue. I feel invigorated and sexy with him following my lead. I never knew it was possible for me to feel this way.

Jeff's tongue dances with mine—a slow tango. I pour everything I have into this kiss. I direct his hand to my breast. I *need* his touch—I crave his touch. This is such a foreign feeling for me, but I love it. He wants me just as much as I want him. I feel his need against me. There's no hiding it.

He trails his hand down to the hem of my shirt and lifts it up over my head. My chest heaves as he stares down at me, drinking me in. Normally I would shy away from someone looking so intently, but in this moment, there is no self-doubt.

"Damn—you are unbelievably gorgeous! I am a lucky man," he tells me. I melt. God, what did I do to deserve him?

I drop down on my knees and reach for the button on his pants. I yank hard, and it comes undone. I unzip his zipper and then pull his pants and boxers down to his ankles. He's completely erect in front of me. I grab a hold of him tightly—he hisses as I stroke him.

Our eyes lock. His are full of wonder and excitement and mine are filled with mischief. I lift my right brow as I slowly take him into my mouth without breaking eye contact. He groans while closing his eyes and lifting his head back. He's enjoying it, and this is confirmation that I am doing a good job.

I've learned bits and pieces from the completely crude conversations Max and Kinsey have had about how to pleasure a man. It's really not rocket science. I just take him into my mouth deep and hard while sucking slightly on the way back out. He bucks up, groaning louder while gently holding my hair away from my face for me. The girls told me guys like to watch.

I swirl my tongue around his tip while watching him watch me. I then take him in my mouth again and again. He rocks himself into me gently, following my rhythm.

"Damn, Elise. You're going to make me come!" he hisses out. He gently but quickly removes himself from my mouth, stands me up and bends down to pick me up so my legs wrap around him. "I'm going to have you on this kitchen counter," he tells me as he sets me down.

He reaches around me and removes my bra. It falls down my arms to the floor. My nipples are hard. He takes one into his mouth, sucking hard and grazing it between his teeth. I moan, releasing an electrified energy through my body. He then unbuttons my pants and directs me to lift up as he removes them and my underwear in one swift movement. I sit completely bare in front of him now.

He stands in front of me, gazing at me with drunken eyes. I squeeze my thighs together to dull the throb between my legs. My body is ready. I don't think I can hold on another moment, but before I can beg for him, he falls down to his knees and spreads my legs. I am now open wide and vulnerable, the cool air skimming over me and adding fuel to the fire.

My breathing is now quickened and erratic as I anticipate his touch. He blows gently over my swollen, wet skin. I arch my back and throw my head back. I feel a light, warm touch against my bud, and I scream out as he circles it with his tongue. He works me up and leaves me panting for more.

His tongue drifts down my moist slit, enters my opening, and then slides over my ass. I suck in my breath, caught off guard by how good this actually feels. My body is tense with anticipation but consumed by desire. He takes his time as he works his way back up, now circling my clit with his tongue again, driving me wild, while entering two fingers into my drenched passage of pleasure. I can't help it; I moan loud.

My body heats with blazing flames, scorching me from the inside out. I feel my insides begin to clench, but before I can tip over the edge of pure bliss, he removes his hands and mouth from my body. I whimper. "I want to feel you come all over my dick," he whispers in my ear.

I hear a foil rip open, and before I know it, he pushes inside of me with one deep thrust. I scream out in a twinge of pain that quickly turns to pleasure. He stops, giving me time to adjust and stretch from his width and length.

He waits for me to give him the okay. "Are you alright?" he checks.

I nod. He continues his thrust, pulling my knees up so he can dive deeper. I never imagined this could feel so good. He kisses me with urgency and raw emotion—tangling his tongue with mine, allowing me to taste my own juices. There's something sexy and arousing about this.

I feel my insides begin to quiver, tightening around him as he continues his exertion until he too calls my name out with one last groan while I tumble down the cliff of intense ecstasy.

He leans his forehead against mine. We are both a breathless mess.

He kisses my forehead before he pulls out of me. "Damn sexy, you have me hooked. How am I ever going to get enough of you?" he asks as he removes his condom, throwing it into the garbage. He comes back over to lift me off the counter.

Jeff bends down to kiss me sweetly on the lips. We're both still completely nude, and since we're not in the moment any longer, embarrassment creeps up on me. I wrap my arms around my chest and look for my clothes. He must notice my apprehension. It's clear he has no qualms about being completely naked. He acts as though this is an everyday, normal thing, and maybe it is for him but most definitely not for me.

He grabs my hand and leads me toward the stairs. "Come on, we need a shower before we leave." He doesn't give me a chance to dwell on my self-consciousness. He tears me away from my thoughts and leads me up to his bathroom.

He turns the shower on hot. I can't help staring at Jeff's ass. It's such a beautiful sight. I think I might have drooled a bit. The steam begins to cloud my view and saturate the room. He turns to me with a huge, mischievous grin. I can't help but smile back—his smile is contagious.

He holds his hand out to me. "Ready?"

I nod and put my hand in his. I get in first. I hiss from the heat of the water pounding down on my chest but quickly adjust. Jeff gets in behind me and turns me to face him. He grabs the soap and begins lathering me up. I bite my bottom lip, trying to decide whether or not to ask him what his deal is about Kroy. I just don't want to start World War Three by bringing it up.

"Jeff, can I ask you something?" I finally decide to just go for it. If we're going to have a fair chance, we need to be able to talk to each other.

"Sure. You can ask me anything, Elise," he distracts me by rubbing his soapy hands over my chest. My nipples are now sharp enough to slice glass. Damn this feels so good!

"What's your deal with Kroy? You said that you've known each other for a long time, so I'm guessing there's history with you two—"

Jeff removes his hands from me to re-lather. "We most definitely have a past together, but you may not want to hear about it."

Hmm . . . this doesn't sound too good, but I still want to know. "Tell me. I won't judge. I promise."

"Okay, turn around," he demands. I do as he says. He begins to wash my back. "Kroy was an alright dude. We played football together. We both loved the ladies, and we both had our pick of them, because of who we were and who we knew.

"It was Kroy's senior year, after a game. We were at an after-party, outside. I had to take a piss, and I heard some weird noise. I followed a trail through the woods behind the house—" I wait a moment for him to continue, but I hear nothing. I turn around to face him. He looks to be in deep thought.

"He was on top of this girl, and she was screaming. I blacked out and beat him to a

274

pulp. He ended up in the hospital, and his family pressed charges on me. I went to jail, and my mom bailed me out. We ended up settling out of court. They dropped the charges as long as I kept my mouth shut," he finishes.

I'm frozen, trying to comprehend all of this. This can't be real. Kroy was so sweet and attentive. I *liked* him. How can this be? "What happened to the girl?" I ask.

"Kroy's family is very rich. They have their connections. Nothing new. It's the typical rich boy's story. They paid her family off so she wouldn't talk," he runs his hand through his wet hair. The shower is beating down on us both as we stand here in silence.

What if that would have happened to me? Why the hell didn't Jeff insist that I stay away from him? He could have told me. He could have at least warned me! I grab the shampoo and wash my hair as fast as I can. I am fuming with anger right now. I need to get out of this damn shower.

"Elise—" Jeff calls quietly. My back is now to him. He tries to reach for me, and I freeze up. "Elise, don't do this to me. This is why I didn't want to tell you. I knew you would hate me. I was young. I fucked up. I can't change what I did! I got into a lot of stupid trouble when I was younger, and because of that, I had to take his deal. If they didn't drop the charges, I would have had a record that would have followed me my whole life, because of what I did to him that night," he explains, raising his voice.

I snap my body around, making sure to cover my chest. "I'm not upset at *your* actions that night; they were well justified. What I am pissed about is you not stepping up and telling me this before I left with him! God Jeff, what if that had happened to me? Did you even consider that for a moment?" I yell back. I hop out of the shower and grab a towel to cover my naked, wet body. Being angry in the nude is not ideal for me.

He follows me out, on a mission to explain his actions. "Are you fucking kidding me, Elise?! I asked you not to leave with him. I told you I didn't think it was a good idea, but you didn't want to listen regardless! If I would have broken out with this, you would have thought I was making shit up just so you wouldn't go out with him!"

I walk out to his bedroom, and he follows. "If he would have hurt you, I would have killed him. Do you understand that? And he knows that. Why do you think I was there at the bowling alley? I followed you to the zoo for Christ's sake!" he finishes, taking a seat on the bench at the foot of his bed. He lays his head in his hands, clearly upset.

I can't leave Jeff like this and the truth is— I believe him. I walk over to him. He looks up at me, clearly relieved that I didn't walk out. He grabs my hips and pulls me close. He lays his head against my lower abdomen. I have to admit, his stalker-ish ways are kind of sexy.

"I will never let anything happen to you. I'm sorry. You were right. I should have tried harder to stop you. I shouldn't have let you go—period. I guess I was just worried about telling you what part I had in it all," he admits.

I squat down in front of him, shifting my towel. "You did nothing wrong, Jeff. I applaud you for what you did. Imagine how worse it could have gotten if you didn't stop it. You're a hero in my eyes."

He is now smirking with a sparkle in his eyes. "So you think I'm a hero?"

Oh brother! I roll my eyes and try to get up. He grabs my hips and pulls me down on his lap, tickling my sides. I screech with a high-pitched laugh. "Wait—no! *Stop*—" I yell in between laughs. I wiggle and squirm right out of my towel, and I can immediately feel his excitement. "Oh no!" I shake my head back and forth smiling. "We have to finish getting dressed. Max is going to kill me if I'm late," I tell him while pulling my towel back up.

Jeff hangs his head and pouts. "Can't you just tell her it's my fault that we're late?"

I quickly slip out of his grip and rewrap my towel. "Um, most definitely not!" I try hard to sound stern, but it comes out more jokingly. "I'm going to get ready. I'll meet you downstairs."

CHAPTER SEVENTEEN

Jeff

G od, that woman drives me wild. Everything about her is so entic- ing, and she doesn't even realize it. She has a hidden sex appeal, and with every moment I spend with her, more is uncovered. She is the epitome of a jewel of the Nile. I am absolutely crazy about her, and truthfully, it's scaring the shit out of me.

I finish getting myself dressed and head downstairs to wait for Elise. I've only been down here for about ten minutes before I hear her descend. I love that she's not like the other girls I've dated. She has no need for the false persona that makeup provides. She wears very little, and she's stunning just the way she is.

I grab my keys and head out of the kitchen to meet her in the foyer. She just simply takes my breath away. I give her a quick kiss on the cheek and open the door for her.

We pull up to Kyle and Maxine's house, and I immediately feel a ping of jealousy that the girls are taking Elise from me for the night. God, what the heck is wrong with me? This just isn't me. What is she doing to me?

Elise opens her car door and begins to lean out. I put my hand on her wrist to pull her back. She gives me a seductive glance, and I swear my dick twitches. "What?" she giggles.

"Are you ready for this?" I ask.

"I hope so," she tells me honestly. I see a small amount of trepidation in her eyes.

I pull her closer to me. "I know these girls can be hard, and I know they mean well, but I want you to remember one thing—you're changing me. I don't know how, I don't know why, but you just are."

I grab her chin and pull her in for a kiss. I want her to feel what I'm saying, not just hear it. I can see the serene look in her eyes when we disconnect, and I know I've done my job—to leave her wanting more. I can't risk anyone changing her mind about us.

We head up to the door, and Max has her hands on her pregnant hips, waiting. Now it's time to be scared, especially since all her attention is on me. I hear a snicker from behind her, and I can only assume its Kinsey laughing. She knows exactly what's coming. Of course she wants to watch.

I greet Maxine first with a kiss to her cheek. "Well hello, beautiful. You look like you're ready to pop!" *Shoot*, did that just come out of my mouth?

She smacks me on the chest. "Thanks, asshole," she replies. She looks to Elise and greets her with a smile and open arms. "Hey girl! I've missed you!"

"I've missed you, too!" Elise responds back. I don't even know how they're hugging with that huge belly in the way.

I walk ahead of them, running right into Kinsey. I was hoping to completely avoid her. "What the fuck are you smirking at?" she blurts out.

I shake my head, expecting nothing less. She is just ruthless. I feel sorry for the man who snags her up. It won't take long before he throws her back.

"I'm just remembering the kiss I had a moment ago. Don't hate," I tease as I walk past her to reach the back deck.

She looks absolutely disgusted. Exactly what I was going for. "Yeah, and I'm sure you'll be locking lips with the next bimbo that sticks her tits in your face tonight!" she snarls back.

I pretend I don't hear her and exit to the back deck. I refuse to let her get to me. I'm floating on cloud nine, and there's nothing and no one that can pull me down.

Kyle is lying back in his lounge chair with a drink in hand. I walk over to slap him up. "What's up, man? You ready to get out of here?

You know if we stay too long they're gonna hang us over the fire pit by our ankles," I remind him.

He chuckles but gets himself up and out of the chair, because he knows I'm right. "Yeah, man. Let's get out of here before Max makes me run to the store for some strawberries or some shit."

"For real, bro?" I ask. He can't be serious.

He shakes his head and then downs his drink. "Dude, no joke. I make runs to the store at three in the morning sometimes. She gets me every time by telling me the baby wants it. You don't understand; I have to keep her happy. She pulls the 'you did this to me' card, and she won't stop until she gets what she wants. Pregnant women are cold, heartless killers when they're craving something. The best thing to do is to give in. Believe me; I learned the hard way," Kyle explains.

Wow! What happened to all the lace and pretty pink frilly things? Seems to be all sweat and hard work now. This is definitely store-away info to remember for the future.

Man—did that really just go through my mind? This girl has done a number on me, and I can't even blame her, because she's not even trying!

I follow Kyle through the sliding glass door into the kitchen where all the girls are. They stop talking as soon as we enter. Damn, this is *definitely* not a good sign. It's time to put on the charm.

"Do you ladies need anything before we head out?" I ask.

Elise smiles, but the other two clearly want to rip me to pieces. Kyle heads over to give Max and her belly a kiss. I decide to walk over to Elise and kiss her goodbye on the cheek.

"Where are you two headed?" Max questions.

"You know exactly where they're going—McGregor's, am I right boys?" Kinsey throws her unwanted two cents in.

Kyle quickly looks to me for the answer. "We may stop there to grab some chicken wings and a beer or two. I know Jenny will hook us up," I respond. Looking to Kyle, I ask, "Ready?"

Max gives Kyle the death look. I don't waste any more time. I head to the front door. Kyle follows suit shortly. Once we exit the front door, we know we're in the safe zone. I climb in the car, start the engine, and back up, putting some distance between us and them. I just pray they don't taint Elise with any doubts.

"Bro, that was pretty brutal!"

Kyle blows out a deep breath. "Honestly, I can't wait for Kinsey to get a man. She needs to get laid and maybe she'll ease up some!" Kyle suggests. "She always gets Max going. I love her to death, but sometimes she can be too much, man."

I jump on the expressway. We just missed five o'clock traffic, so the roads are pretty clear now. "Yeah, I can only imagine what they're saying to Elise."

He shifts his whole body to face me. "Yeah, bro—what the hell is the deal? You two are hanging out again?" he asks.

I totally forgot I haven't mentioned it to him. I guess I've been so wrapped up in Elise this week that I forgot. "Yeah, she's having problems with her mom, so I'm letting her stay at my place. Honestly bro, I can't get enough of her. She's all I think about. I want to spend all my time with her. She is just so addicting," I confess to him, putting it all out there.

Kyle whistles. "I think somebody's got it bad," he sings.

We pull up to McGregor's. "I don't know what I've got. This is all foreign to me, but I know I don't want it to stop, whatever it is."

Kyle puts his hand on my shoulder before we step out of the car. "I'm happy for you, man. I think you're finally growing up. I think Elise is the perfect girl for you. Now don't fuck it up!" he teases.

I laugh. He knows me too well. We head into the bar and make our first stop to see Jenny. "Hey, boys! What will it be tonight?" she greets us, already pulling out two Heinekens.

"How about two shots of Patrón?" I answer.

We take a seat on the stools as she sets the beer in front of us. We clink our bottles together and take a nice long pull. "Ah!"

"Coming right up, boys!" Jenny informs.

The bar is crowded with regulars, but it's nothing crazy. I enjoy it like this. I can listen to the music, talk, and still hear the TV over the buzz. I look around a bit, take in my surroundings. It's more of a sausage fest up in here—not that I'm complaining any. If it was a week ago, I may have been disappointed or even started calling a random girl to meet me. But now? All I care about is getting to Elise and going home with her.

"So tell me, how much does Max know?"

"What? About you and Elise?" Kyle asks.

"Yeah."

He shrugs his shoulders. "I don't think much. Kinsey filled her in on this morning's run-in with you two, but I think that's about it."

Jenny sets the shots in front of us and has one for herself. We hold them up. "Salute," we all say and throw them back. A chill runs over my skin as the fire licks my insides. Such a heady but perfect mix.

"Thanks, boys!" Jenny yells as she heads down the bar to another customer.

I grab the food menu. I'm starving! "Did she have anything to say to you about it?" I ask as I look over the menu.

I hold out a menu for Kyle, but he declines. "I'm doing the wings," he answers. "She just said the usual she'll-kill-you-if-you-hurt-her-again crap."

I put the menu down. I'm doing some wings too and maybe some mozz sticks. "Have you talked to your brother lately?" I ask. I'm ready and waiting for his comment on this subject.

"Really, bro? You already know the answer o that," he says with disgust.

I decide to continue this conversation, but first we put our food order in. "I guess Kinsey is driving him insane—"

He takes a swig of beer before responding. "I bet she is. Junior is OCD about things being a certain way, and from what Max tells me about living with Kinsey, she is the polar

opposite!" he laughs. "To tell you the truth—
I'm loving every minute of it. Let him live in
hell just as I did growing up with him."

"Ouch!" I comment, laughing. "Honestly, I guarantee they'll be banging any day
now."

Kyle almost spits out his beer. "On that
note, I need another shot!"

He calls Jenny over and orders us two more.

CHAPTER EIGHTEEN

"Alrighty, girl. They're gone. Now spill it!" Maxine demands. Her arms are crossed over her gigantic boobs.

I look to Kinsey. "How much did you tell her?"

She smirks. "Oh, just that you two came to work this morning in the same car . . . "

"That's it?" I question, shocked.

"What else was she supposed to tell me?" Max asks, irritated.

Okay, here it goes. I'm just going to lay it all out for them. "So this is the deal—my mother and I got into it, and I needed a place to stay. Somehow Jeff came to the rescue at the perfect time and offered me one of his guestrooms. I've been staying there since Saturday night. He wants me to stay and gave me a key to the house already. Oh, and we fucked. He took my virginity, and it was so good that I am now completely addicted. That about covers it."

I stop speaking, and I hear nothing but silence. I think I can hear crickets. Is this for real? Have I made my friends speechless for the first time ever? They are gaping at me with their mouths hung open. I almost want to take a picture to savor the moment.

I wave my hand in front of them. "Um, hello?" I say.

"Holy shit, Elise! You were a virgin? Why didn't you ever tell us?" Max asks before slapping her hand over her mouth. "Oh my *God*! All those things we've talked about in front of you!"

I know where this is going, and I want to save her from the guilt. "Max, it was fine—really! If anything, you both helped me prepare for the big night. Jeff was amazingly patient and sweet about the whole thing," I explain.

"Oh, wait until I see that dimwit!" Kinsey growls. "I am going to kill him! How could he be so careless? Elise, he didn't deserve that gift from you, especially after what he put you through before."

Max is now waddling back in forth. "Man, I so wish I could drink right about now. This definitely calls for some hard liquor," she states.

I have to make them understand that it was I who pushed him into doing it. "Listen, I know you both just want to protect me, and I love you for that, but this was my choice. Jeff told me no multiple times and offered to wait, but I seduced him. I am completely okay with my decision, and I know you don't want to see me with Jeff, but I'm falling for him. I don't know how to stop it either," I admit.

They both run up to give me a hug. Max leans back to look at me as she plays with my hair. "You know, Jeff really isn't a bad guy. He's a lot like Kyle, and it sounds like he may be falling for you too. But just promise me something: if he goes back on his Romeo shit, you will walk away for good this time."

"I promise."

"Time for some wine!" Kinsey shouts. "And some sparkling grape juice for the prego!" We all laugh. Thank God the mood has changed.

Max orders the pizza, and we take our drinks into the living room to get comfortable. Max's couches are huge and fluffy, made out of a suede or microfiber material. I could do some serious sleep damage on these!

"Okay, Sneaky Susan. Tell us—why Jeff's house and not one of ours?" Kinsey asks. It's a fair question. A question that I asked myself many times, but I always ended up with the same answer—I like being close to Jeff.

"Honestly? At first I didn't want to intrude on you both. Especially after your long day with the baby shower and all," I tell Maxine. I turn to Kinsey, "And you were going on a date with that chef. You were so excited about that. I was upset with my mother, and I ended up running into Jeff. And now, I sort of like staying at his house, though I know I need to get back to my normal life. I'll probably go back home this weekend," I tell them, a little sad.

"But, didn't he ask you to stay?" Max asks.

I take a sip of my wine. Yum. It tastes *so* good! Liquid courage. "Yeah, he asked me to stay, but for how long, I don't know. I can't move in with him after only a week, and honestly, I don't think that's what he was asking."

Kinsey jumps in. "To be honest, Jeff never deals with the same girl more than once. This is a first for him. I give him a hard time because it's fun, but Max is right—he's a good man at heart, and I think you may be changing him. Us women do that to men, but I want you to be careful. Just because you may be good for him doesn't mean he is good for you."

"Kinsey's right. Just go with your gut, girl. It will never steer you wrong," Max states.

My gut is telling me to stay. To spend as much time together until our time is up. He's the light to my everyday darkness. I've been walking blindly for so long. Now I see what could be, and the colors are magical. I don't want to go back to the dull emptiness.

"I think that's what I'm doing. For once, I'm doing something for me. I've been chained to my mom for so long, and I'm sick of being dragged down. I'm sick of living for someone else! I just want to experience this. I'm living in the here and now—I'm living for the moment. Is that so wrong?" I ask them.

Max looks teary-eyed. She immediately waddles over to my couch with her big belly. "Of course that's not wrong! You deserve to be happy. I support any decision you make, Elise. If Jeff is what you want, then I'm okay with it! I like this new you," she tells me with a smile.

Kinsey also agrees. This is why I love my friends. I'm so lucky to have them in my life. They're my support system. I don't know how I would have made it through this year without them.

"Thank you, girls. You are amazing!" I tell them. "Now how about some more wine?"

"Ugh! I can't wait to pop this baby out so I can have a glass. I'm going to need that shit on tap after this baby is born!" Max jokes.

"So, is Kyle ready for this?" I wonder.

Her energy glows, and her smile is addicting. "More than I am. He's been unbelievable. I'm so irritable and cranky, but he never complains. I think deep down inside he is nervous as hell. I mean, we're having a girl, for Christ's sake! He and Jeff devoured girls, and now he is going to spend a lifetime keeping guys like them away. Do you see the irony?" Max laughs.

Man, I never thought of it that way. She is so right, though. Kyle is in for the ride of his life. I guess this is karma coming back to him. I wonder how Jeff would feel if he were in the same situation.

"He is definitely getting what's coming to him!" Kinsey adds. We all laugh.

There's just one more question that needs to be asked. "Kinsey, what's up with you and Junior?" I question, putting her on the spot.

If looks could kill, I would be dead. "Um, absolutely nothing! He's annoying as hell! I don't know why I agreed to room with him in the first place."

Max jumps in. "I moved out, and you needed someone to pay half the rent, remember?"

Kinsey rolls her eyes and says, "Oh yeah, I forgot. *Someone* went and got herself knocked up!" I giggle. Watching this go down is fun. "He's so anal about everything. That's why his ass doesn't have a girl!"

"Who cares? He's freaking hot as hell, and it seems as though he has your panties all in a bunch. Don't tell me you haven't thought about tapping that ass?" Max throws out there.

Kinsey's eyes bug out. "You must be out of your pregnant mind! There is no way I am having sex with him! He is hot as hell, I'll give you that, but he's got to be so boring in bed."

"Oh, so that *has* crossed your mind then?" I tease. She's about to blow a gasket!

"Okay, if you two don't stop, I'm taking off!" Kinsey says. "This is uncalled for. I didn't come here to talk about that boring douche!"

Max and I can't stop laughing. It's very rare that we can stoke this kind of reaction out of Kinsey. It's clearly a sensitive subject. Why? I can only guess—Junior must be invoking something deep inside her, and she doesn't like it one bit.

Max is laughing so hard she might push that baby right out of her. I hold up my hands. "Okay, okay, no more. We promise!" I tell her to calm her.

The pizza *finally* arrives. After three glasses of wine and no food, I am buzzed and starving! Eight o'clock creeps up on us fast, and the guys walk through the door. We're in the living room, giggling like drunken hyenas.

Jeff comes straight towards me, grabs my hand to lift me off the couch, and waves goodbye as he runs off with me. I blow the girls a kiss as they yell goodbye.

"Jeff!" I pull back to slow him down.

He snaps his body around so I am now trapped against the car door. He puts his finger to my lips. "Shh." He slowly leans down, touching his lips to mine. He coerces my mouth open with his tongue. He tastes of smooth liquor and sweet sexiness. My body unconsciously melts into his. I can't seem to get close enough.

I'm intoxicated by him. Everything about him puts me in a drunken state. I moan softly as his tongue dances and glides with mine. He knows just what to do, and I'm loving every moment of it.

He begins to pull away, and I whine in protest. "I missed you," he whispers.

I crack a smile, trying not to look overly satisfied. "I've missed you, too," I reply.

"Come on, let's go home."

He says the word "home" so easily, like it's just an everyday thing. "Okay."

We pull up to the house. I follow him as he walks through the house, leaving it pitch dark. He opens the sliding glass door to the balcony, and I follow. The moon hangs bright in the sky, casting a glow across our faces.

Jeff stops me dead in my tracks for a wild, passionate kiss. It completely takes my breath away. I think I'm falling for this man, and I don't know how to stop. I may be in deep trouble.

He pulls away just long enough to say something. "You taste so divine. Come here, I want you to straddle my face so I can taste every inch of you," he says so matter-of-factly.

Holy crap! Did he really just say that? I'm dripping wet just thinking about it. He grabs my hand and brings me over to the couch. He begins to strip me of my clothing, slowly and gently, taking his sweet, tantalizing time. He kisses me at the nape of my neck and leaves a chill that jolts down my spine. I dig my nails into the top of his arms, dying to get closer to him. I can't seem to get enough.

He unsnaps my bra, freeing my taut nipples. They are begging to be put in his mouth. He slides his hand down my pants, under my underwear, and into the depths of my wetness as he takes my breast into his mouth. I gasp loudly, throwing my head back in pure bliss.

His fingers are magical. He knows exactly where to place them to drive me wild. He gently circles my swollen bud while diving deep into me. I can't help but scream, rocking my hips against his hand. Heat swarms my body, but before I can fall any farther, he removes his hand from me and rips my pants down, leaving me completely bare.

He quickly removes his clothing, sits back on the couch, and pulls me towards him so I am now straddling him. His dick is at full attention under me, and my hands are now on the back of the couch so we are face-to-face. "I want you to stand up and then kneel down over my face," he directs. He must see the uncertainty I am feeling. "Don't be shy, Elise. I want to taste that pretty pussy of yours. I want to smell your arousal. I want you to come all over my face." I feel like I'm in a porno, but I have to admit— this is hot as hell. And scary as hell.

He directs me over him and then takes a deep breath in through his nose. "God, you smell like heaven," he says. I feel my cheeks turn pink with heat. Thank God it is dark, or he would be able to see my inexperience and embarrassment tattooed on my face.

He kisses the insides of my thighs, teasing and licking my sensitive skin. Goosebumps flood my body. I'm getting impatient until *finally* he strokes his tongue against my clit.

God, it feels unbelievable! Such a new and foreign feeling. My eyes roll back as I scream out and begin to grind my hips against his tongue as he licks and sucks on my dripping arousal.

At this point, I could care less that I am smothering his face with my most intimate parts; I'm ready to let go of all my inhibitions. I'm allowing my libido to take full control. He slides a finger inside of me, and then a second, reaching my most sensitive spot. I hiss in return, and in less than two minutes, he has me convulsing around him, moaning and screaming his name.

I'm completely spent. He brings my body down to straddle him again; his excitement lies against his stomach between us. My body is shaking from the stellar orgasm. I lay my head down on his chest and listen to the pitter-patter of his heartbeat. I can't move yet.

He kisses my temple and rubs my back up and down my spine. I look around at the blanket of stars above as the warm breeze caresses our naked skin. For a moment, I forgot we were outside. It's like all my surroundings disappear when I am with him, as well as my rationality.

"Are you ready for round two?" he whispers.

I smirk and then look up at him. His intense gaze of desire is all I need to get the juices flowing. "Most definitely," I respond.

"Sit up for a moment," he directs again. I hear the rip of foil. After he rolls the condom on the head of his steel rod, he waits at my slick entrance. "Now slowly sit back. This may feel a little uncomfortable for a moment, because I'll be so deep, but take your time. I won't move until you're ready," he instructs.

I begin to take him in as I push down. It feels slightly painful, but I take it slow so I can stretch to his size. "That's right, beautiful. Just like that," Jeff approves. "Damn, you feel so fucking good."

I am now filled to the hilt with Jeff; I feel overwhelmed in the most wonderful sort of way. He leans down, smashing his lips to mine while grabbing my hips and moving me over him. Every pump forward and every thrust back brings us both closer to release.

"Come for me, beautiful. I don't know how much longer I can last—" he spits out. He reaches between us and slides his finger over my clit. I plunge over the edge at full speed and he follows. Our bodies drip with sweat as we sit here, still connected.

I lift off of him and he hisses. "*Shit!*"

"You okay?" I ask, teasing.

"I am more than okay," he answers.

I grab our clothes as he walks to the kitchen to dispose of the condom. "Come on, let's go take another quick shower before bed."

CHAPTER NINETEEN

"What's up, bro?" Kyle asks after I walk into his office and take a seat in the chair in front of him.

"I completely forgot to speak to you last night about this, but I think you should interview Elise for the position of your personal assistant. I think she would accommodate you perfectly, and she is interested in learning the business as well as moving up in the company," I explain to him.

He takes a moment to ponder this before responding. "Are you sure this is something she wants to do?"

I nod. "I think she would be amazing at it!" I tell him with excitement. He grins. "*And* I'm not just saying that because I like her. You know she is a hard worker, and taking her away from your dad would piss him off. So it's a two-for-one," I say with a smirk.

"You're such a dick! But, I *love* it!" Kyle hisses.

I chuckle. "I knew you would like that one."

"Listen, if you think she and I would work well together, then I'll give her a try. I value your opinion; you know that. But she requires an interview just like everyone else."

I stand up and slap him up. "Thanks, man. I really appreciate this. Can we just keep this talk between us, though?"

"No problem, bro."

I feel good walking out of his office. I think this is exactly what Elise needs. She needs to feel valued and important. With this move, she'll be able to get a real good look at the business and decide if this is the path she truly wants to be on. There's no point in me taking the position, because I don't see myself here much longer. I only came here for her, and now that my prayers are beginning to be answered, it's time to start thinking about my future—what do I want to do with the rest of my life?

I shoot Elise an email asking her to lunch, and she accepts. I want to run down the aisles, high-fiving everyone as if I just scored. I stop at the reception desk and wait for her to finish with a phone call before she clocks out.

After another minute or so, she is finally finished, and we head out to my car. "So tell me, you have this amazingly over-the-top house, why a Buick? Why don't you drive a car like Kyle's? Isn't that the 'guy' thing to do?" she asks.

Huh. I guess it never really crossed my mind. "I'm not really into the whole car thing like Kyle or other guys might be. Cars just get me from one place to another. I don't live in it, so why spend a ridiculous amount of money on it?" I answer.

"Makes sense. I like that about you. Even though you acquired your trust fund, you're still down to earth—you didn't allow it to get to your head," she states.

I think I actually may be blushing. I glance over at her shyly with a smile. "Thanks."

We head off to the café that her and Max like to go to. She opens up a little more about her childhood and then discloses that her father has asked to see her. He comes into town next weekend for business and is leaving that Saturday night open for her.

I find it pretty comical that I too am going through the same dilemma, but I don't think now is the time to bring that up again.

"Would you feel more comfortable if I went with you?" I ask.

She hesitates for a moment. "I'm still undecided if I'm actually going or not. What am I benefitting from it?" she asks, not really looking for an answer, as she looks away into the distance.

I grab her hand and bring her attention back to me. "If anything, it might bring you some closure so you can move on and heal from this all. Oh, and I got some information from a friend on a couple facilities close by that might be a good fit for your mother," I tell her. I watch as her eyes glaze over, almost as though she's shutting me out.

I grab her hand, immediately entangling it with mine. I need her to *feel* our connection. "I'm here for you, Elise. I know you're not used to leaning on anyone, but you can lean on me. I'm here for you for as long as you need. We're going to get your mother some help, and while she's doing that, I want you to stay with me. I don't want you to go back to that house alone."

She's thinking things through. I see the wheels turning in her head. I'm just nervous she may be talking herself out of my offer. "Are you sure? If my mother goes to rehab, I'll have the house to myself—"

I interrupt her before she can say anymore. "That doesn't mean a thing. What if she gave her boyfriend a key? And God knows who else she could have given a copy to! You won't be safe there, Elise. I want you safe. Just say you'll stay with me?" I ask, almost begging. I don't care if I sound like a pussy, as long as she says yes.

She takes a breath and gives in. "Okay, I'll stay, but only until my mother is better. Let me pay for something—anything," she asks. Is she out of her mind?

I shake my head. "No, absolutely not! You still have to pay for your day-to-day bills while your mom is gone," I remind her. "Elise, have you thought about what you're going to do if your mom refuses to get help?"

Her face immediately pales, and she looks down towards the table. "No," she whispers.

Maybe I shouldn't have brought this up, but it's a possibility. She needs to be prepared just in case. "Hey," I whisper. Elise looks up. "Just know this could be a possibility. I just want you prepared mentally for the fight. No addict wants to believe that they're an addict *or* that they need help. This isn't going to be easy. I'm here for support. We all are."

She reaches over the table to squeeze my hand. "Thanks, Jeff. I really mean it."

"Come on, let's blow this joint!" I say with a wink.

The way home is entertaining. Elise's mood has completely done a 360 since our lunch, thanks to my man, Kyle. He offered the interview to her, and she blew it out of the park. I'm so proud of her. She has a new sparkle in her eyes, and I'm loving it.

I get dinner started while Elise goes upstairs to change. My brother called and is heading over. He hasn't formally met Elise yet, and he wants to get some bro time in. Julian is a crazy little dude. He's the complete opposite of Junior—thank God! I don't know if I could have handled a douche for a brother.

Julian is more on the softer side. He puts off a strong exterior, but he's gentle at heart. He couldn't be a player if he wanted to. That takes a special kind of skill—not giving a crap—and he definitely doesn't have that gene in his body.

The doorbell rings. "I've got it!" Elise screams from the foyer.

I hear them greet each other, and then I hear footsteps towards the kitchen. My brother walks in first, giving me the thumbs up along with a huge shit-eating grin. I want to slap that grin right off his face.

He comes around to slap me up. "What's for dinner? It smells delish!" Julian says.

"I'm making mom's stuffed chicken and vegetables. You wanna help?" I ask, already knowing what his answer will be.

"Hell nah!" he answers, taking a seat on the barstool.

Elise comes around the counter. "I'll help. What do you need me to do?" she offers.

I grin. I can't help it. I could get used to us cooking in the kitchen together. I hand her a knife and push the veggies over to her. "Chop these up into thick pieces so I can steam them," I direct her.

"So Elise, you and Jeff met at work?" Julian questions. I look up to give him the "watch what you say" look. I've never cared before. Of course, I've also never brought a woman around my family members either.

"Yeah, we've worked together for a while now. I work in reception, outside the main office, so I really don't get a chance to see everyone," Elise explains.

I jump in. "That's why I had to stalk her. She couldn't come to me, so I came to her," I add with a wink.

Julian begins laughing as he watches us. "Wow bro, it sounds like you've got it bad!" I fling a piece of chicken at him but just miss. "Elise, just so you know, I've never seen my brother so domesticated. I kind of like it," he admits. "So, you got any hot sisters you could throw my way?"

I roll my eyes. "Don't listen to him," I tell her. "Even if you did, he wouldn't know what to do with them!"

"Screw you, douche!" my brother yells.

Elise giggles. "No, sorry. I'm an only child," she tells him. She's finished with the vegetables. "Where do you want these?"

"Just leave them there. Can you pick a bottle of red from the wine rack?" I ask her.

"So, have you thought about Dad's offer?" Julian asks. Aww man! Not a topic that I want to bring up at the moment. Especially after the conversation Elise and I had earlier today. I want to keep tonight's topics light.

"Nah, man. I really haven't given it much thought. Can we not talk about this now?"

Julian looks aggravated. "You can't avoid him forever. He's still our father."

Elise jumps in, "I told Jeff a couple days ago that he might regret it if he doesn't go." Great, now they can both gang up on me. I give Julian the death stare. He needs to drop this!

"Whoa! Sorry, bro," Julian says with his hands up. "But I think your girl has a point."

Elise looks between the both of us. "Would you like me to leave the room so you can discuss this privately?" she asks.

"No, Elise. You're fine," I say, turning to Julian. "This discussion is over for the night!" I don't know why I even let him come over.

Elise looks to me, annoyed. She then turns to Julian and asks, "How do you feel about this, Julian?"

I finish stuffing the chicken and throw it into the oven. I grab three wineglasses and pour us all a glass while waiting for Julian to respond.

"The truth is, I was young when they split up, so it doesn't affect me as much as it does Jeff. I think everyone needs someone, and I'm glad Dad seems to be finally settling down, even if it's at my mother's expense. I just think it takes less energy to forgive than to hold onto all that resentment. I don't want to be *that* guy, and I don't want Jeff to be either. That's why I think it might do him some good to confront Dad so he can let go of it all," Julian clarifies.

My brother has some valid points, and I completely agree with him. But I just don't have it in me to listen to my father's excuses or reasoning behind it all. Honestly, I think the moment I lay eyes on him, I might just deck him.

I was a boy who needed his father, and he failed me. Yes, he gave me financial stability, but I would have given it all back to have him in my life.

"Julian, if Jeff isn't ready, then maybe you should go. I'm sure Jeff would understand, right?" says Elise. They both look to me for my approval. The truth is, I would feel a little salty, but I would get over it. He's grown. He can do whatever he wants.

I take a sip of my wine. "Yeah man, do what you gotta do. Don't let me stop you," I say. I throw the vegetables in the steamer and start preparing the salad.

"Damn bro, I'm going to have to post a picture on Facebook for Mom to see. This shit smells bangin'!" Julian compliments.

I laugh. "Just don't be posting no pics of me! I hate that Facebook shit!"

"I never got into it either," Elise comments.

Julian shakes his head. "I guess you two are just made for each other," he teases. "So Elise, how do you like working for the Saunders?"

Elise downs some wine first. "Good! Mr. Saunders can be a bit scary, but I really like Mrs. Saunders. Other than that, it's a very nice agency to work for."

I pass by her, squeezing her shoulders, to check on the chicken. "Elise just got interviewed for Kyle's personal assistant position," I brag.

"Oh yeah? Kyle's a cool dude. You're going to like working for him," Julian promises.

Elise's cheeks turn pink. It's adorable. "Well, I didn't get the position yet. I won't find out until next week sometime," she says, playing it down. It's just like her to do so.

After another ten minutes, the chicken and veggies are ready. Julian takes his Facebook pic before we dig in.

The rest of the night is enjoyable. I'm happy my brother came. I see him out while Elise cleans up. Julian turns to me before he heads towards his car. "I'm happy for you, bro," he says, giving me a side hug. "I think she's pretty amazing. Just don't mess it up!" he warns. I give him a quick tap on the shoulder.

"Thanks, fuckhead. I won't!"

I head back into the kitchen. Elise is dancing away to the music off her iPhone. It's cute. I don't want to disturb her, so I lean against the wall, doing my best to hold back my snicker. After another five minutes, she finally looks up, startled.

"Holy crap! How long have you been standing there?" she asks, trying to catch her breath.

I walk up to her and lean down to give her a gentle kiss on her lips. "Long enough. Can you show me that move again?" I taunt. She smacks my chest.

"Do you want any more wine?" I ask, holding up the almost-empty bottle.

She finishes cleaning the counter off. "No thanks, but I am in the mood for something else—" she hints with her brow arched.

I can't seem to grab her fast enough. I yank her upstairs and begin stripping her out of her clothes before we make it into her bedroom. She's a little feisty tonight, and I'm totally, 100 percent turned on!

The moment I plunge inside of her, all warm and snug, I feel at home. All my tension and worries fly out the window as she wraps around me. This is where I'm supposed to be;

there's no other woman made for me. She's it. Now how do I tell her this without her running?

After we finish, I scooch her butt to my hips and wrap my arms tightly around her. I snuggle my nose into the nape of her neck, inhaling deeply. Her scent completely intoxicates me.

"Can we stay like this forever?" she whispers.

"I thought you would never ask," I whisper back.

CHAPTER TWENTY

I close my eyes shut again as the sun rips through the cracks of the curtains. I am exhausted. My body is worn down from all this new sexual activity and all these late nights. All I want to do is doze off again. I look at the alarm clock, and it says quarter to seven. I moan and slam my hands over my eyes.

I feel Jeff stir. "Morning, beautiful," he greets, bringing me closer to him.

"Hey," I say, backing my butt up in antici-pation of his reaction.

He chuckles and kisses my cheek. "You sound tired. Do you want to play hooky today?"

Hmm . . . I've never done that before. Do people really do that? "Won't it be a little obvious if we are both out today?"

"Who freaking cares? That's what we have PTO for. It's personal time, and I would most definitely consider this personal," he says while tickling my waist. I almost kick him off the bed—I'm extremely ticklish.

"Whoa! Okay, I'm done! I'm done!" he screeches, laughing. Now I am awake, but do I feel like getting dressed and heading off to work? No. I definitely don't.

"Okay, let's play hooky," I answer. I feel completely bad to the bone.

Jeff grabs his cell and taps away. "Who are you texting?" I ask.

He finishes and puts the phone back down on the nightstand. "I just sent a quick text to Kyle to let him know we won't be in today."

I sit up quickly. "Wait, you did what?!"

He pokes at my side, trying to get a smile from me, but I refuse. "Jeff, you can't just go around calling me in sick. I just freaking interviewed for him for Christ's sake! What if this ruins my chance of getting the position?" I shriek, totally freaking out. "You should have at least allowed me to call in myself!"

"Shh. Calm down. It's fine. Kyle is completely okay with it. Believe me; if he cared, he would have said it," he tells me. He kisses my bare shoulder with his perfect lips, sending a chill down my spine.

Oh no! This is completely unfair. He's using my body against me. It's clear he knows exactly what buttons to push. "You promise?" I ask.

If I'd somehow messed up this job opportunity, I wouldn't be able to forgive myself. This is such a big step in the right direction for me, and I'm even beginning to consider going back to school so I can have the skills to move up even further in the company. I just haven't mentioned this to anyone yet.

"Yes, sexy. I promise," he tells me, holding up his three fingers for scout's honor. How freaking adorable he is. There's no possible way I can stay upset with him. Regardless, I'm ready for some morning sex and then maybe a morning nap.

I lie back down on the bed. "I believe you. Now, won't you come fuck me?"

His mouth drops open, and he's literally speechless. I'm loving this: the power I hold over him. This is what Maxine and Kinsey are always gloating about.

"Elise, I would be more than happy to fuck you," he replies, moving himself over me. He kisses me deep and hard, pouring all his feelings into this one kiss. Damn, he is so freaking sexy. I feel like I'm living a dream. How can this godlike man want someone like me?

We make love or have hot, passionate sex— whichever describes it best—and fall asleep in each other's arms. It can't get much better than this. Things like this don't happen in my life. I'm just wondering when it's all going to be taken away.

I wake up to the smell of fresh coffee and yummy bacon. My stomach growls. I am starving. I pull on one of Jeff's T-shirts and head downstairs. I walk into the kitchen, and he looks at me as though he wants to eat *me* for breakfast. My cheeks burn up immediately as the heat scorches me between my legs. My body is now prisoner to him; there's no escaping the shackles that bind me to him now.

"Good morning, beautiful," he greets. He holds up a coffee mug. "Coffee?"

My smile broadens. "Yes, please!"

"How did you sleep?"

I sit down on the barstool in front of him. "Wonderful. You drained all the energy from me," I admit, blushing. "You know, you're spoiling me with all this cooking you're doing. I'm going to gain ten pounds from all this delicious food."

He takes a sip of his coffee. "And you'd still be perfect," he says with a wink.

This man and his words—I almost feel beautiful. I almost feel like a desired woman. Who would have ever thought?

Jeff's phones rings. He answers it and locks it with his neck so he can dish out our plates. "Hey, Ma," he says. "What's up? Is that so? I'm gonna kill him!"

My mind is reeling, wondering what's happening on the other end of the line.

"No, I'm not going to see him," he says. "Listen, I'm not discussing this any further. I don't want anything to do with him. I told Julian to go. I'm not stopping him. He's his own person."

He passes me my plate and comes around the counter to sit with me. It's clear they are discussing last night's conversation about visiting his father. Jeff looks irritated that Julian spilled the beans to his mother.

"Okay, Ma. I love you, too," he says before hanging up.

We sit in silence for a moment. I allow him to sort the conversation out before I start asking questions. I pop a piece of bacon in my mouth, and it is delish! Perfectly crisp.

Jeff snickers at me. "Is that bacon good?" he teases.

"It definitely is!" I reply. His mood has shifted a bit. "So tell me, is your mom trying to talk you into seeing your father?"

Jeff takes a sip of his coffee and then looks back at me. "Yes, she thinks it will do me some good to let go of all this resentment I have. I'm going to kick Julian's ass for opening his mouth about it!"

"What if I were to go with you?" I offer. I want to help. I want him to trust me, too.

"I couldn't put you in the middle of it all. Believe me, it won't be a fun time. I don't want you to witness what might go down," he clarifies.

My heart breaks for him. He's afraid of the unknown. I know exactly how he feels. "If I say yes to seeing my father, will you?" I ask. "We can be each other's crutch. It's now or never, Jeff. I'm scared shitless, too, of confronting my father, but with you by my side, I'll feel safe."

He takes a moment to decide. The thought of being face-to-face with the man I haven't seen in all these years stresses me out. It makes me want to run the other way and say screw it, but I know I have to confront this black cloud that hangs over me—first with my mother and then my father. Then maybe I can be free and finally live for myself.

"Okay, I'm in," he tells me.

Thank God he agreed before I had the chance to back out. "Okay, good. Now what's on the agenda for the day?"

I finish my toast and eggs, and down my coffee. I am stuffed! "How about we hang by the pool all day, and I'll make us some frozen drinks?" he proposes.

"That sounds perfect!" It's like he read my mind. But I have one problem. "I don't have a bathing suit."

He finishes the last bite on his plate. "Who said you needed a bathing suit? My pool is 100 percent private. We can go butt-naked, and no one will ever know," he informs me with a wink.

Unfortunately, I'm still not confident enough to pull that off. I smack his arm. "You are funny! How about I just tan in my bra and underwear? The naked thing isn't quite me, but you're more than welcome to do it—"

Man, seeing those buns of steel all dripping wet would be a fantasy come true. He stands up and gives me a kiss on my nose. He grabs our plates and begins cleaning up the kitchen.

"So tell me, how was your night with Kyle? How's he really doing with the baby coming so soon?" I inquire.

Jeff fills up the dishwasher. "I think it's definitely getting real for him. Max is definitely wearing on him, though. She's a demanding pregnant chick," he says, chuckling. "This little girl is going to have him wrapped around her fingers, though."

"Oh, I completely agree. Max has already called it. They just better hope the next one is a boy, or Kyle's life is going to be run by girls," I joke.

Jeff finishes wiping off the counter. "Did I tell you that they asked me to be the godfather?"

I jump up and down on the barstool. "No way! Oh my God, Jeff! That is so freaking exciting! How did you feel when they asked you?"

He grabs the blender out of the cupboard above the stove. "I felt completely blown away. This little girl is going to have me wrapped around her finger, too," he admits, laughing to himself. "Do you want kids?"

Oh whoa! Not the question I was expecting. Especially coming from him. "Um, yeah. Someday. I need to get my life in order before I start thinking about creating another human, but I have dreamed of the white picket fence. I mean, what girl hasn't?" I respond. "What about you?"

"Yes, I definitely see myself married with a bunch of kids running around. If you would have asked me this a couple of years ago, I would have said hell no! But the whole idea of it doesn't sound so horrible any longer. Is that weird?" he asks.

I smile. I just can't help it; he's adorable. I think he'd be an amazing father, too. "No, I don't think it's weird at all, Jeff. It's actually a turn-on. Just don't say it in front of other girls, or I might have to beat some butt!" I joke.

He puts the liquor bottle down. "Damn, Elise. You just made my dick hard! You can't say things like that to me unless you want to get manhandled!"

I laugh as my cheeks flame with heat. When will I ever get used to his mouth? I hate blushing. It gives my inexperience away. It doesn't even allow me to pretend that I'm on his level. It's a constant reminder that I'm an amateur in his world.

"Don't be shy on me now, Elise. Why don't you go upstairs and change while I get these drinks ready?" he says, taking control. His bossiness is cute.

"Okay."

I head upstairs, trying to remember what bras and underwear I've brought. This reminds me that I need to do some laundry. I look through the dresser drawers and can't find anything good. I have boy shorts and comfort bras, nothing remotely sexy. Now what?

And then it dawns on me. Maybe I need to get out of my comfort zone and be the sexy diva he says I am. A pair of white lacy boy shorts with nothing on top should do it. What do I have to lose? This is nothing he hasn't seen before, anyways.

I grab my bath towel to wrap it around me. I exhale one last deep breath, open the door, and head down the stairs. Jeff has already made his way outside, and the frozen drink mess covers the kitchen counter. I stop at the sliding glass door. It's now or never. This is the moment where I transition from a girl to a sexified woman.

I gather the courage to open the door. Jeff is lying back on one of the lounge chairs with our drinks on the table next to him. He looks up at me through his sunglasses. "Hey, you finally made it," he teases.

I stand in front of my lounge chair, holding onto the towel that's wrapped around me. Jeff is watching me closely. I begin to unwrap myself, finally letting go of the towel, and allow it to drop to the deck. It's just me in my lace boy shorts and nothing else. I feel open and vulnerable. Jeff now has a shit-eating grin on his face, but he can't seem to find his words. I smirk at this thought, because usually he is overzealous with his words.

I nonchalantly sit down on the lounge chair, grab my frozen drink, and lie back, allowing my naked virgin skin to bask in the sun. "Wow, babe. You are smoking hot! How am I supposed to concentrate with you over there like that?"

I giggle. "Just pretend I'm not here," I suggest.

He rolls his eyes at me. I must be rubbing off on him. "That's like holding vodka to an alcoholic's lips and telling them not to drink it! Not fair," he whines. I love that I am affecting him this much. "How about some sunscreen?" he says, holding up the bottle with his right eyebrow arched high.

He's good and very determined. I don't think he'll stop until he touches me. This time I roll my eyes. "You stay right over there, mister," I instruct. "No sunscreen for me. I'm getting my tan on."

He pouts like a heartbroken puppy. I'm feeling sort of powerful right at this moment, and I *like* it! "Okay, fine. You win—for now. How's the drink?"

I take a sip of the amazing strawberry daiquiri he made. "It's delish! But I wouldn't expect anything less from you," I tell him with the same wink he always gives me.

"Drink up so we can go for a swim."

I make sure to take my time, sipping *very* slowly. Tantalizing him as much as possible. I *finally* finish and put the glass down. He stands up in between our chairs and stretches. Next thing I know, my body is in his arms, and he's jumping in the pool with the both of us.

I come up for air, and he is right in front of me, grinning from ear to ear. I splash him and back myself up. He dives underwater and pulls my feet under with him. It's just him and I under this clear blue oasis. It's quiet and peaceful. He brings me to him underwater and kisses me. It's cute and different. I like creating these new experiences with him. I would stay in this moment all day except for the fact that we both need oxygen to survive.

We both come up for air. I wrap my legs around him, and we float. I almost forgot that I am topless in his arms, but this wouldn't be the first time, and hopefully not the last.

"I think your confidence is sexy, and I like the fact that you're feeling comfortable around me. Can I be completely honest with you, though?" he asks.

I gulp. "Sure."

"You've had me from day one. Do you remember when Kyle came back from college and started working at the agency?" he asks, swimming with me around the pool.

"Yes."

"I came to visit and take him to lunch, and I saw you. You just sparked something inside of me. I couldn't get you out of my head, and *believe* me, I tried. You were so quiet and shy. I wanted to talk to you so badly, but I didn't know how. I mean, *me*—the king of words— couldn't even form a sentence!" he admits, shaking his head.

I grin, butterflies in my tummy. "That's the moment I decided to work for Saunders Agency. I had to be around you somehow, and I knew eventually I would figure out a way to talk to you. It's clear I don't need the money, but I did need to be in your presence, even if it's just passing the reception desk every day. Being with you and touching you now makes those two years of observing worth every moment. I guess what I'm trying to say is that I only work at the agency for you. My thoughts are consumed by you, and I don't know how to shut them off. Maybe that makes me a pussy, but I could give two shits when it comes to you," he finishes, clearly anticipating my response. I think he is expecting me to run, but his confession has done quite the opposite.

I put my forehead against his and stare into his eyes. He's erupted something from deep inside of me. The feeling is so foreign. I have to take deep breaths because I'm afraid I might have a panic attack. I close my eyes to calm my-self, and when I open them back up, he is watching me intently.

I grab the back of his head, pulling him to me. His lips touch mine. I run my tongue along his flesh to coerce his mouth open, and he obliges with no questions asked. He makes tak-ing the lead easy and satisfying.

I decide to slide my right hand down his chest, over his ripples, and down his swim trunks. He groans into my mouth as I stroke his swollen, stiff shaft. He slides my panties to the side so he can play with my sensitive, aroused skin. I grind myself over his fingers, and my in-sides melt.

I feel his tip at my entrance, so I push against him so he can slide inside me. I need to feel him right now. "Damn, baby," he grunts, closing his eyes so he can concentrate. "You feel so fucking tight."

He grabs a hold of my hips to still me so he can gather his composure. "If I move, I might come," he admits. I kiss his neck and bite on his earlobe while I wait. I swear he just got harder.

I'm finally getting accustomed to his invasion, making each time more and more pleasurable.

He begins easing in and out of me. The water makes me feel weightless and allows me to move with little effort. He brings me to the side of the pool, using the grip from the edge to push into me deep and hard. Every thrust pushes me closer to my release. Heat rushes through my body as the waves come crashing over me, consuming the both of us, one after another.

He leans his forehead against mine as we catch our breaths. I rub my fingers up and down his spine with him still inside of me. "I wish we could stay like this forever. We fit so perfect together," he tells me.

I kiss the tip of his nose, and he pulls out. He hops out of the pool, grabs me a towel, and wraps it around me when I get out. "You're so sexy," he whispers in my ear. I lift my left shoulder and give him a shy smile.

"Another drink?" he asks.

"Yes, please."

"Okay, I'll be right back."

CHAPTER TWENTYONE

Friday was the perfect day to do absolutely nothing. We drank poolside all day, and then she went to her doctor's appointment for birth control. We ordered pizza when she came back and then made love again before we fell asleep. What more could I ask for? And yes, I just called it "making love." Any other title seems sleazy and just plain wrong now.

Unfortunately, she is still adamant about only staying here until her mom gets some help. I better savor these moments while I can, because who knows what's going to happen once she leaves.

A slap to the back of my head jolts me right out of my thoughts. "What the—?" I gripe. I turn around and Kyle is cracking up over my cubicle. "Bro—you're gonna make me slap the shit out of you!" I respond.

"Yeah, if you can catch me first," Kyle snickers.

I fold my hands behind my head and lean back in my chair. "Dude, we've already been through this a million and one times. And every time I whoop your ass," I remind him.

Kyle looks shocked. "Yeah, maybe in your made-up world," he taunts. "So, I came over here to let you know I just offered Elise the position. She'll start with me next Monday."

I fist pump the air. "Wow, that's great news, Kyle!" This is cause for a celebration tonight. "How did she react?"

"She was stoked, man. She'll be sitting in the desk right outside my office. I think she's going to be real beneficial and easy to train.

Now I just have to break it to the others that they didn't get the position. I hate this part of my job."

"Yeah, I don't blame you. But if you want to play boss, you gotta make boss moves," I say.

"Oh, and now that she's my personal assistant, that means no more 'personal days' for the two of you, or I will *personally* come to your house and beat you down. You'll be fucking with my work," he threatens, half-joking and half-serious.

"Blow me, man."

"No thanks. That's your girl's job," Kyle responds as he walks away.

The last couple of days flew by nicely, pretty uneventful. We celebrated her promotion on Monday night and have stayed home every night since, cooking dinner together. We've fallen into a comfortable rhythm, something I am going to miss when she leaves. If only I could get her to stay somehow. I might just have to show her what she would be missing—with my tongue.

Tonight is the big night. The night she will finally confront her father and put all this resentment behind her. I promised her I would be by her side, and that's exactly what I plan on doing. I'll wreck his shit if he says anything out of place.

I pour myself some Jack on the rocks while I wait for Elise to finish getting ready upstairs. She's taking a little longer than usual, but I'm sure she has talked herself out of this 101 times already.

After another ten minutes or so, I hear her descend. I look at my watch, and we're already running a little late. I decide not to mention this to her, because she already has enough on her mind. She comes into the living room looking for me. My breath halts. She looks amazing. She's wearing a short dress that shows off her unbelievable legs, curls in her hair, and just enough black eyeliner to make those baby blues really pop out. How did I get so lucky?

"Hey. You ready?" I ask.

She looks down towards her fingers. "No, I don't think I'll ever be ready."

I get up from the sofa to embrace her in my arms, giving her some of my strength. "I'm here for you, so if at any time you want to leave, just say the word and we're out. Okay?"

She nods her head without speaking. We head out to the car. The air is thick with tension. "You look beautiful tonight." I just had to tell her. She takes my breath away.

She looks at me shyly. "Thank you."

The rest of the ride is driven in silence. It's clear she's nervous as hell and her mind is jam-packed with God knows what. We pull up to his hotel, and I valet the car so we can have a quick getaway if need be. I meet her at her door; she looks to be on the verge of a breakdown. I grab her face so I can look straight into her eyes. "I won't let anything bad happen to you. I promise."

She nods her head and releases her breath. I lock my fingers with hers, and we head in together, hand in hand.

We walk through the crowded lobby, passing a bridal party, and head straight to the bar.

I look around and see a bunch of business suits, some couples, and some of the wedding party. Then I see a man sitting at the bar alone, with salt-and-pepper hair and khakis. My gut tells me this is him.

She squeezes my hand; I squeeze hers back. I allow her to lead the way. We stand directly behind him. "Bruce?" Elise says quietly.

He turns around, and there's no denying it. Elise is the spitting image of him. I thought she looked like her mother, but I was wrong. She looks identical to her father. She must also realize this, because her face drains of all color. I rub my thumb over the top of her hand to bring her back to me. She looks to me, and I mouth to her, "Relax."

She takes a deep breath as he stands up. He must also see the uncanny resemblance, because he's speechless for a moment. "Hello, Elise. I'm so glad you made it."

He looks to me and then back to her. "Yes, I decided to come after all," she says. She directs her attention to me. "This is my boyfriend, Jeff," she introduces. I feel proud of this title. She *finally* said it out loud.

I reach my hand out. "Hi, Mr. Jewels. It's nice to meet you," I tell him.

He has a firm grip on my hand as he shakes it. "Jeff—it's great to meet you as well. I'm glad you came also," he says with a genuine smile. "Do you want to grab a more private table over in the corner?"

"Yes, please," Elise responds.

We take our seats at the table in the corner and order some drinks from the cocktail waitress. It never fails; the waitress is paying extra attention to me. I see the annoyance on Elise's face. It's cute watching her get jealous.

"So, how long have you two been dating?" her father asks.

I pause a moment to wait for Elise to answer, but she doesn't. "Only a short while, but we've known each other about two years now," I answer.

"And how did you two meet?" he asks.

"We work together," I respond again.

Her father smiles and then looks to Elise. "How's your mother?" *Oh shit!* He should have at least warmed up to that question. What a jackass.

Elise's whole body stiffens. "My mother?" she huffs with a pissed chuckle. "My mother is a pill-popping drunk who I've been taking care of since you left."

Damn, good for her! He wants to ask the question, he better be ready to handle the answer. On some realness, though, he actually looks like this affects him. Maybe like he's even a little bit sorry.

"Your mother was a very dependent person. That's why I left in the first place. I'm just sorry I left you behind. If I could do it all over again, I would have taken you," he admits.

"That's why you left in the first place?" she growls. "What the fuck are you talking about, Bruce?" Whoa! I don't think I've ever heard her swear like this before. "You left for another woman. You were cheating on my mother!" she says, raising her voice.

He looks confused but then understands. "Is that what she's told you all these years?"

"Yes!" she snaps.

The waitress comes by with our drinks and asks if we would like to see a food menu. "No!"

Elise barks. I laugh inside. She's cute when she takes charge. The waitress walks away.

"Are you trying to tell me that isn't the truth?" she questions.

He looks her straight in the eyes. "Yes, that is exactly what I'm telling you."

She continues to stare at him as she takes it all in. "That's not how I quite remember it. I remember her being lonely, constantly waiting for you to come home, and you not being pleased with her, because something wasn't exactly to your liking. She was always sad, and you were never there to comfort her."

He nods his head. "Yes, you're right. I wasn't home very much. I did work a lot, and I can admit I treated her poorly. I emotionally abused her and sought some help after I left. I'm okay with taking the blame for that, but I *won't* take the blame for her addiction. She did well hiding her problem for a long time, but I knew. I threatened her many times to stop or I would leave, but she was too far addicted by then.

"I'm not sure if you remember, but she hurt her back when you were younger and was prescribed pain pills for the problem. Back then, doctors would hand the prescriptions out like candy, a quick fix. Unfortunately, it ruined her. I asked her to get help. As a matter of fact, I *begged* her to get help, but she refused. I should have tried harder. I should have done something more, but I didn't and that is something I have to live with for the rest of my life," he confesses.

I almost feel sorry for him—almost. But he still made the choice to leave Elise behind. He's a coward.

"Why didn't you ever try to contact me?"

"You don't think I tried? I called, I wrote, and I even came to the house recently, but she told me you went off to college. She wouldn't tell me where, though. I thought about hiring a PI to find you, but I also figured you might have already contacted me if you really wanted to see me," he says sadly.

"I didn't know how to reach you. She's been taking my mail. I'm only here because I found your letter on the nightstand in her room," she explains with a tear slipping down her cheek. I gently rub it off her face. "Did you get remarried?"

His eyes sparkle. "Yes, you would like her. Her name is Julia. You also have two younger sisters: Katie is ten, and Emma is eight."

I put my arm around her to squeeze her shoulder and whisper in her ear. "Do you need to leave?" I ask. I have to make sure she can handle all the bombs being dropped.

She looks at me and shakes her head. "Do they know about me?" she asks her father.

Bruce's smile brightens. "Of course they do. They're waiting on the day they can finally meet you. Elise, I'm sorry I didn't protect you from all of this, and I'm sorry I didn't try harder. There isn't a day goes by that you're not in my thoughts. I would like to see you again if it's okay with you."

She looks down to her fingers as she contemplates this. This all makes me think of my father and what reasons he may have for never coming to visit my brother and I. Will I be able to forgive him once I know the truth? Will his truth even be worth listening to? I don't know, but after years of pure hate, I think I may have some hope after listening to Bruce.

"You know, this is a lot to take in. I need some time to process all of this. I need to deal with my mother first, though. She needs to get help, and I can't move on until she does," Elise says honestly.

He finishes his drink. "That's fair enough," he responds with relief. I'm sure he was prepared to hear her say she never wanted to see him again.

We all stand up. I shake his hand goodbye, and he turns to Elise. It's clear they're both not quite sure what to do, so thank goodness he makes the first move. He goes for the hug. Elise is unsure at first, but then she gives in. The look on his face is priceless, and I truly believe he is a man of his word.

Tears fall down her cheeks, one after another. Bruce wipes them away and then gives her a kiss to her forehead before leaving. I immediately take his place. She hides her face into my neck as we walk out of the bar; she doesn't want to cause a spectacle of herself.

I give the valet my ticket. I embrace her while she quietly sobs into my chest. This is years of pent-up emotions being released. This is needed in order for her to heal and forgive. I put her into the car and walk around to the driver's side.

"Let's go home," I say.

She wipes the tears away and straightens her shoulders. "No, I need to go see my mother. Can you take me there right now? It's time I confront her."

CHAPTER TWENTY TWO

We sit in my driveway, neither of us saying a word. It's a silence filled with doubt and trepidation. I'm mentally pumping myself up for what's about to happen. Facing my father is one of the hardest things I've ever had to do, but dealing with my mother is far more excruciating.

"Will you come in with me?" I ask Jeff.

He looks relieved. "I thought you would never ask. Of course I will."

I get my keys ready as we head up to the front door. I'm not truly ready for this, but I know I have no choice. It's now or never. I'm here, so I have to suck my fears up. It's time to be a woman now.

I unlock the door and push it open. It's dark, stale, and stuffy in here. The air is thick with the smell of cigarettes and booze. I see empty bottles of liquor and beer cans strewn about the coffee table. Great—it's obvious Reggie has been here. I look over to the couch, and my mother is passed out. Nothing new. She looks as though she hasn't showered in days; her hair is pasted to her head, and she's still in her dingy robe.

I look back to Jeff, and he is just taking everything in. He looks livid, but I can't concentrate on his anger right now. I enter the kitchen, and it is no different from the rest of the house: filthy and completely unlivable. It's clear she hasn't been eating. I fill up a large pan of cold water, walk over to my mother, and splash it on her head. She immediately sits up, catching her breath.

"What the hell, Elise?" she screams, wiping the water from her face.

I back up. "Get up, Mom. We need to talk," I demand.

She grabs her head and moans. "Go get me my pills," she commands.

I cross my arms over my chest. "*No!* No more pills!" I yell.

"Why are you screaming?" she asks with her head in her hands.

I calm myself down. "I want you to get help, Mama," I tell her, suddenly full of composure. "You have an addiction, and you need to stop before you kill yourself."

She glares up at me. "Oh, now you give a shit about me?" She turns her attention to Jeff. "You left me for *him*. That's just like you to act like a little whore! You chose a man over me, and for what? He's just going to leave you anyways," she spits out.

I look over to Jeff and shake my head. I don't want him to respond to her; it won't help. "I'm not here to discuss my relationship. I'm here to take you to rehab. I found a nice place for you, somewhere I think you'll like."

"I don't need help. What I need is a new daughter! You're a traitor. I know you went and saw *him* . I'm sure he turned you against me with all his lies!" she shouts.

I take a seat on the edge of the chair across from her. This isn't going to be an easy fight. "Yes, I went and saw my father. He told me the truth—something you should have done in the first place. There was no other woman, Mom. The problem was between the two of you. I know, and he knows, that he didn't treat you right. But he also asked you to get help. Why didn't you? And if you couldn't do it for him, why not for me? I needed you! I needed you to be a mother to me. Was I not enough?"

She looks at me with eyes of stone. "It wasn't your father who didn't want you; it was me," she says so matter-of-factly. My heart finally shatters after holding on for so long. I put my hand over my mouth to catch my sob.

Jeff rushes to me. "Now this is enough!" he yells. "You're a sick excuse for a human being! You should be ashamed of yourself! You don't deserve to have anyone in your life, let alone your own daughter! You're going to die alone, just like you are meant to," he growls, slamming the rehab pamphlet down on the coffee table.

He stands me up, but I can't even walk. My legs are shaking and weak, but I am determined to walk out of here with my pride intact. Jeff lends me a hand as I head to the door and head to my new future. "Get yourself some help, lady!"

I can no longer hold myself together. She purposely stabbed me in the heart, and she did a good job of it. She's chipped at the walls of my heart for years now, and she finally sent them crashing down. I no longer sob for her; I cry for myself. I am now shutting this door to my life as another has opened. One full of promises and hope. I'm turning my back to the dark and walking towards the light.

Jeff helps me in the passenger seat, buckles me in, and kisses my forehead. "I'm so sorry this happened. No one should ever have to go through this."

I look up at him through my tear-filled eyes. "I'm okay. Really I am. I've done all I can. It's up to her to do the rest. Thank you for being here with me," I tell him. I'm overly grateful for him at this moment.

"You're welcome, beautiful. I'm glad I was here for you, too. I won't let anyone hurt you," he declares. He shuts my door so we can head home.

I must have fallen asleep on the ride over. I feel groggy when I wake up in my bed. I try to sit up, but can't. I realize Jeff's arm is around me tightly. I squint at the clock, and it says two in the morning. I gently remove his arm from my grip and slide out of bed. I tiptoe down the hallway, down the stairs, and into the kitchen.

I grab a glass of water and head over to look out into the night. The moon is shining brightly in the dark night sky. It's mesmerizingly beautiful and brings a calming serenity over me. I open the sliding glass door to walk out onto the balcony. A chill sweeps over me. I wrap my arms around myself and lean against the railing.

I allow my mind to wonder through last night's events. I concentrate on all that was said. Even though I got nowhere with my mother, I still feel good that I tried. She said some horrible things to me, but I know deep down inside she was being spiteful, because I went to see my father. I'm not excusing her behavior, but I know she doesn't hate me. Now I need to figure out my next step. I can't stay here forever, either.

I gaze at the moon a while longer until I feel hands slide up my T-shirt to my naked breasts. Jeff cups them and tweaks his thumbs over my nipples, sending a vibration all the way down, straight between my legs. He rubs his hard dick against my booty as he kisses the back of my neck. Ugh, that feels so good.

I curve my back, pushing my chest against his hands while pushing my butt out. He nips at my ear, and I moan loudly. I don't give a damn who hears us anymore. I'm done caring. He slowly slides his hand down the front of my panties and strokes my little nub gently in tiny circles. I moan even louder. "Damn, Elise, I like when you do that," he whispers in my ear.

He slips his fingers through my wet folds and plunges deep into my sex while still grazing my clit with his thumb. I grind myself on his fingers as he massages me from the inside. He finds his perfect rhythm, completely driving me mad. I feel my inner walls begin to clench, but before he can send me over the edge, he stops. My body screams obscenities.

I whimper, begging him to continue. He begins slowly again, applying his precise pressure, working me up, until the heat scorches over my body and I am coming hard over his fingers. He brings me right over my climax, and now I feel like Jell-O against him.

"How'd that feel?" he asks.

I can barely form a sentence. "Amazing."

I hear a foil packet rip and feel his hand rolling the condom over himself. He turns me around and lifts me up, wrapping my legs around him. He brings us over to the couch and sits down, with me straddling him on top. He must love this position.

I'm sitting right above him. The head of his shaft waits right at my dripping wet entrance. I am about to sit down, but he stops me, holding my hips in place. He looks at me with intense, drunken eyes. My heart slams against my chest; he's making me nervous. I've never seen this look from him before.

"I don't know what you have done to me, but my world only makes sense when I'm with you. You are forever ingrained on my soul. I am madly in love with you. I have been since the day I laid eyes on you," he confesses. I'm stunned. Speechless. My heart overflows with emotion, but I'm scared. I don't know what these feelings exactly mean. I lean down and kiss him deeply. He has taken my breath away with this confession.

I slowly sink down on him, filling myself to the max. He digs his fingers into my hips in extreme pleasure. Our tongues collide and dance into a sexy rhythm as I grind myself over and around his manhood.

I lean my head back, completely en-gulfed in this sweet feeling. I never want it to end. If this is a dream, I never want to wake up. He reaches in between us to stroke my most delicate spot. It ignites my flame, and my or-gasm explodes. I completely let go, basking in the feel of him and my body while screaming his name.

He follows right after, both of us trying to catch our breaths. He gives me tiny kisses all over my face. I can't help smirking at his cuteness. I lie against his chest, still connected to him, listening to his heartbeat as the time passes by.

"Come on, babe. Let's get to bed," he says.

My muscles are stiff as I stretch in the morning. The blinds are cracked open, the sun is luminously bright, and Jeff is not lying next to me. I have to admit that I'm a little bummed that I'm not waking up to his beautiful face, but lying on his pillow is a single pink rose—the next best thing. I can forgive him now.

I yank on my sweatpants and head downstairs. The waft of coffee drifts under my nose. This is exactly what I need after a long night of sex. The kitchen is empty, but a coffee cup is laid out for me. I pour and dress my coffee and head out to the veranda where I know Jeff will be. This seems to be his wakeup spot. It's magical watching the sun come up from here. I understand why he loves it.

"Morning," I greet him, bending down to kiss him.

Jeff smiles up at me like I'm the sun in his sky. "Good morning. How did you sleep?"

He winks at me, and I roll my eyes. "I slept good, but I'm sore," I tell him, stretching my neck from side to side.

"Well then, I guess that calls for a massage later."

He's too good to me. My phone rings, breaking the conversation, and it's an unfamiliar number. "Who is it?" Jeff must see the hesitation on my face.

I shake my head. "I don't know."

I press the answer button. "Hello?"

"Hey sweetheart, it's Bruce."

My brows furrow. "Oh, hey. Is everything okay?"

"Listen, I'm sorry to bother you. I really don't know how to break this to you, but I spoke with your mother last night. She was extremely upset—a little hysterical, actually—that we met, so I went to see her last night," he explains.

Whoa! He did what? "Wait, you went to my house?"

"Yes, to be honest, she was scaring me a little. She's still your mother, and I couldn't just sit by and let her hurt herself, so I went to check on her."

I snap up, almost spilling my coffee all over. "What do you mean hurt herself?"

"As you know, she's not well. Whatever was said last night between you affected her—and by the time I got there, her wrists were slit."

I put my hand over my mouth. "Oh my God! Is she OK? Where is she?" I screech, panicked.

"She's OK, I rushed her to the hospital, and they bandaged her up. They have her under observation right now, but she has agreed to rehab, finally."

"I'm on my way," I quickly say.

"No, Elise. She wanted me to tell you not to come," he informs me. Tears fall down my cheeks, and I begin sobbing like a baby. Jeff quickly comes over to me. "Elise, what has happened is not your fault. She wanted me to tell you she was sorry for what was said. She was upset. As soon as they release her, they will be transporting her to the rehab facility. You've done everything you could do, Elise. Now it's time for you to move on with your life while she gets some help," my father says.

"Ok, thank you for calling me," I get out between sniffles.

"Listen, I'll text you and update you once she's transferred. I know this was a lot to drop on you, but I figured you would want to know. Please call me if you need anything."

"Okay, I will."

We hang up. I feel as though I've been crying for days. I feel somewhat at fault for what has happened, but this tragedy has played a role in helping her agree to rehab, and I am grateful for that. For once, things are oddly starting to look up and fall into place. It's a miracle that my mother not only agreed to rehab but is taking some responsibility for her actions as well.

"What did your father have to say?" Jeff asks while rubbing my back.

I wipe my sniffles. "My mother is in the hospital right now. She slit her wrists," I tell him.

"Is she going to be OK?" he asks.

"Yes, she's under observation right now, but she agreed to rehab. Once she's released, they will send her there. She also wanted me to know she was sorry about what she said last night," I inform him.

"Wow! That was a big step for her. I pray she gets the help she needs in there."

I look up at him, finally understanding what I've been feeling all this time. It's love. I am foolishly in love with this man, and I have to tell him. "I love you, Jeff. If it wasn't for you, I would have never had the courage to do *any* of this. Thank you for being here with me. I'll never be able to repay you."

There goes that shit-eating grin, spreading its way across his face. "Wait—did you just tell me that you love me?" he asks.

I giggle. "Yes, silly. I love you."

He grabs me and brings me over to him so I am now sitting on his lap. "I love you too, beautiful! And you're the one with the courage. I've learned something from watching you. You are fucking amazing!" he adds loudly. I laugh at his goofiness. "Let's celebrate! What would you like to do?"

I have an idea. "Anything?"

"Yes, anything—"

"Can we have everyone over for some pizza and beer tonight? It would be great to spend some time with them all on our turf," I ask, praying he'll say yes.

He thinks about it for a quick moment. "That actually sounds like a great idea. I am totally down with that! You call the girls, and I'll talk with Junior and my brother to see if they want to hang too."

I kiss him gently on the lips. "Thank you."

CHAPTER TWENTY THREE

Jeff

Sunday night was epic. The guys hung out while the girls gossiped. Elise and I played hosts for the night, and it just felt so damn right. I can truly say I have everything I could possibly want *except* Elise living here with me full time. I don't want to wait, and I sure as hell don't care if it's too soon to move in together.

I totally have noticed a difference in her persona. She's more relaxed and carefree. Two huge burdens have been lifted off her, and I can see it reflected in her smile. I'm falling more and more in love with her with every day that goes by. It still scares the shit out of me, but what scares me most is not having her in my life.

I talked with Kyle one-on-one Sunday about my confession earlier that day. He looked proud and slapped me on the back, welcoming me to the club. He said that all it takes is "the one" to change all thoughts and foolish ways. Life as I know it will never be the same; she's changed me without even trying. Now that's one hell of a woman.

I get taken from my thoughts by some soft lips against my neck. I smirk and reach behind me to bring her to my lap for a real morning kiss, a kiss that makes my dick hard each and every time. "Morning. How did you sleep?" I ask, already knowing the answer. We didn't get much sleep at all last night.

She yawns. "Hmm, good question. Somebody couldn't keep his hands to himself. I think I may have to take a vow of chastity in order to get some sleep tonight," she teases with a wink.

She's learning from the best. I love that my humor is rubbing off on her. I pout. "That definitely won't stop me," I tell her. But what I can do is allow her to have a good night's sleep tonight. "How about an early dinner so we can get to bed a little earlier?" I try to bargain.

She walks around the counter to pour a cup of coffee. "I would love that, except for the fact I promised Kinsey we would go out for some drinks after work."

Damn! That was not what I was hoping to hear. "Oh, okay. When were you planning on telling me?"

She looks up at me with a glare. Oh, fuck! It's clear I have pissed her off. Not good. "It slipped my mind, but I am telling you now. That's all that matters," she growls. Dang, she's hot when she's feisty.

I have to recover—and quick. "Okay, no biggie. I'll just have a night out with the guys then." Screw that! My butt is not staying home while she's out. "Where do you plan on going?"

She puts her cream and sugar in her coffee and answers without looking up at me. "Not too sure yet. Are you planning on stalking me or something?" Wow. Where the heck is this coming from?

This is a first. This is one thing I've never been called—a stalker. "I don't want you driving when you have been drinking. If you don't want me driving, can you at least both take a taxi? Or maybe have Max be the DD?"

She considers this for a moment. "If Max isn't up to it, we'll be fine. It's not like we're going to be choking down shots of Patrón like you boys do."

"Okay, fine. But can you call me if you need me to come get you?" I plead.

She takes a sip of her coffee and eyes me over the rim. "Okay, if that will make you feel better, I'll call if I need you. But just so you know—I'm a big girl, Jeff. I've been taking care of myself for a long time now. I'd like to think I'm pretty responsible."

Aww, man! I don't want her to think I doubt her. I get off the stool and walk around the counter to her. "I feel protective of you, that's all. I would go crazy if something were to happen to you. I'm sorry if I'm coming across as overbearing and not believing in you. That's not it at all. I just want to keep you safe," I explain.

Her face softens, and she wraps her arms around me while nestling her face into my chest. "I love you, Jeff. I'm sorry for being on the defense. I'm just a little extra tired this morning," she explains.

My heart explodes with these three little words. "I love you too, Elise," I reply back. I almost feel a little cheesy, but who cares? "You ready to get going? Kyle will kill me if you're late."

She takes her last sip of coffee, and we head out.

The rest of the day goes by slowly. Elise has been too busy these past couple of days, learning the ropes in her new position, to leave for lunch. So it's just been Junior and I. Junior and Kyle did a good job keeping the tension at bay when they were over Sunday night. There was no back-and-forth bickering, which is a step in the right direction, I must say. I had already planned on locking their asses in a room together if they would have started, but luckily for all of us, that was avoided.

It's finally five o'clock, time to clock out. I don't wait a second longer before heading over to Elise's new desk. "Hey beautiful, you ready?"

She seems a little off. I'm getting a strange, tense vibe from her. Weird. "Actually, I'm going to leave with Kinsey, so you can go ahead. I'll see you later tonight," she tells me, trying to hide her nervousness.

What the hell is going on? "*Okay*—is everything alright?"

"Of course! Why do you ask?" she questions pretty quickly. I see Kinsey walking up.

I shrug. "You just seem a little preoccupied is all."

"I'm fine. Just tired. I'll call you if I need you later," she informs, brushing me off.

I give her a kiss on the cheek and head out to my car. I'll give her the benefit of the doubt. Maybe she's just overworked.

As I walk through the parking lot, I notice a familiar car. It's Kroy's car. What the fuck is he doing here? Didn't Elise tell him there was no chance of them getting together and to back off? Or is he here on a stalking mission? Either way, I don't like it one bit.

I stomp up to the driver's side of his car. "What's up, man? What are you doing here?" I grill.

He looks up at me with his stupid, nervous smirk. I want to slap it right off his face. "I'm here for Elise. She should be coming out any moment."

Those words sting like a jellyfish. "She knows you're here waiting for her?" I question, hoping he won't give me the wrong answer.

"Yeah, I just spoke with her." Definitely the wrong answer.

I keep my cool as best as I can. "Listen, bro. I'm gonna only tell you this one time. Elise is mine. We're together, and there's no shot for you two. So I suggest you mosey on out of here before we have some problems," I tell him straight up, no sugarcoating it.

"That's great and all, but I'd rather hear it from her lips, not yours," he says, full of nerve. Fucking prick. I guess he wants my foot up his rear.

I've had enough. "If you don't leave, I'm going to bash your face in just like before. Plain and simple. You choose," I growl.

"Jeff?" I hear Elise's voice from behind me, "What are you doing?" Kinsey stands next to her, taking this all in.

She really has the nerve to ask me what the hell I am doing? "What's going on Elise? You told him to meet you here? I thought you told him to stop contacting you?"

She looks down at her fingers. "I thought telling him in person would be nicer. I didn't want you to be involved, because I knew you would freak out."

"Oh, come on!" Kroy yells. "Elise, you don't have to do what he says. He's not your keeper. You still want to see me, right?" He looks over to her, completely ignoring me.

My hands ball up into fists. I'm about to lose it. "Did you not just hear her say she was going to tell you to get lost? Get it through your perverted little skull—she does not want to see you anymore!" I scream.

"Jeff, calm down. People are starting to watch," Kinsey warns.

"I don't give a fuck!" I snap at her. She looks pissed, but she shuts her mouth.

Elise finally speaks up. "Kroy, Jeff is right. I was coming out to tell you that I can't see you anymore. I'm with Jeff now."

Kroy blows out a deep breath. "How about you just call me when everyone leaves so we can talk? I like you Elise. I thought we had something good going."

That's it. I bring my hand back, ready to deck him in the face right through his open window. The girls immediately begin screaming, and Elise grabs my waist to pull me back. Every inch of me wants to just let go and smash my fist into his face. "Jeff! Stop! You don't have to do this!" Elise yells. I step back, and Kroy is holding a smirk across his face like he's enjoying this. I should have just wiped that smile off his face. If it was the younger me, I would have.

"What the heck, Jeff?" Elise screams. "Stop acting like a psycho!"

Kinsey goes up to Kroy to baby him, making sure he's ok. Does she not see the huge grin on his face? It's clear he's enjoying himself. "Jeff, you need to just get out of here! You've done enough!" Kinsey yells.

"Thank yourself for this! You should've just told him, and none of this would have happened," I bark at Elise.

She straightens herself up and stands right up to me. "Don't put this on me! I was taking care of all this my way! I didn't need your help." Her words burn me.

"Fine. Go ahead. Deal with that piece of shit yourself. I sure hope you can handle him, because he's one sick fuck. I'll see you at home," I spit out. I get into my car and squeal off loudly.

I am fuming. My blood is boiling over and smoke must be coming out of my ears. I'm gripping the steering wheel so tight that I can hear the leather squeak underneath my flesh. I can't stop replaying the conversation over and over in my head, and each time I do, I get more pissed. This all could have been avoided if she just would have told him over the phone. What the hell did she think she was going to accomplish by doing it in person?

Kroy is sick and twisted. Didn't she hear anything I told her before? God, she was so mad when I didn't tell her about his past, and now this? Who knows what he could have done if he would have gotten her in the car alone. I can't even go back to the house. I feel like smashing everything in sight.

I pick up the phone and scroll to find Junior's number. He answers. "Bro, meet me at McGregor's. I almost smashed Kroy in the face just now, and I'm ready to drink."

"Whoa! OK, on my way."

Jenny takes one look at my face as I sit down, cracks open a Heineken, and pours me a shot of Patrón. "Thanks, Jenny. Keep them coming."

"Okay, boss! You got it."

I slam back the shot, feeling the liquid fire burn down my esophagus. It deflates my anger as it nestles in. I pick up my Heineken and chug it until it's empty, slamming it back down on the bar. I whistle for Jenny, and she grabs me another.

The barstool beside me squeals as Junior takes a seat. Jenny puts down my beer and asks Junior what he'll be having. "Hey, Jenny. I'll have what he's having, and two shots of Patrón."

Jenny nods and gets to it. I take another long pull. "Dude, what happened? What was Kroy doing at our work?"

I hang my head down. "Elise and Kroy went on one freaking date before her and I got serious. He's been calling her, and I told her to tell him we were together and to stop calling."

"And did she?"

"Elise is just Elise. She didn't know how to break it to him, so she told him to meet her at work so she could tell that prick face-to-face. The only problem is she didn't warn me. Instead of telling me, she tried to keep it from me, man," I explain with complete disgust. Just re-telling the story pisses me off all over again.

Jenny sets our shots down. We both clink the shot glasses and throw them back. This time it doesn't burn; it glides down with ease.

"Damn, I didn't even know her and Kroy knew each other," Junior says.

"Yeah, thanks to Maxine; they met at her baby shower. Max doesn't know about mine and Kroy's past. I'm sure if she did, she would have never tried to set them up. What pisses me off is that I told Elise what he had done, and she still wanted to meet with him in person. What if they were alone, and he didn't want to take no for an answer just like the girl in high school? My visions went back to that night, and I saw red. If Elise, Kinsey, and all the other onlookers weren't there, I would have snapped. I probably would've ended up right back in jail," I tell him before throwing back the rest of my beer.

Junior sips his beer and shakes his head. "Yeah, man. That wouldn't have been good. So where did you guys leave everything?"

"I don't fucking know, man. I yelled at her like a jerkoff and took off before I could cause any more harm. She's probably pissed at me. Let's order some more shots. I'm not feeling it yet," I lie.

We spend the next two hours going shot for shot like dumbasses. My words are slurring, and my vision is now double. I fucked up. I'm totally missing Elise, and she probably hates me. I notice Beth and her girls standing near the pool table, gawking. Not good. They look like tigers on the prowl.

Carrie steps out of the group and walks towards me. *Shit!* I nudge Junior, and when he sees her, he groans. "Man, why are they always here?" he whines.

"Hey, Jeff. Long time no see. Where've you been?" she asks me, trying to seduce me with her eyes.

I know what I want to say, but my lips won't follow. "Been busy."

She now leans towards me with her tits in my face. "You don't look busy right now," she whispers with one brow arched.

Everything about her is wrong: her smell, her voice, her eyes. She's no Elise. "I'm busy drinking. Go back to your friends, Carrie." Junior chuckles at my bluntness.

She gets even closer, putting her hand on my leg and wrapping her arm around me. "Well maybe we can get busy drinking together—at my place?" she says in my ear.

"Uh-oh!" Junior says, looking to the door and nudging me.

"What?" I snap. I look past him. I immediately sit up straight and push Carrie away from me.

"Hey!" she yells.

"Elise!" I scream after her as she runs out the door. I stumble off my stool and head after her until I reach Kinsey, who's in front of me like a brick wall.

"Don't you dare! How could you, Jeff?" Kinsey hisses. "I thought you changed. You had us all fooled! You're a piece of crap!"

"Kins, it's not what it seems. Let me explain!" I beg.

"There's nothing left to explain. Just stay the hell away from her!" she screams at the top of her lungs. The whole bar goes silent as she stomps off.

I stand here, frozen and completely off-kilter. What the hell just happened? Why the hell did I just let her leave without explaining myself to her? Oh heck no! I run out the door, but I'm too late. Kinsey is already screeching out of the parking lot.

CHAPTER TWENTY FOUR

I'm completely numb: no feeling, no emotion. I feel like my whole body and spirit is dead. I can't even cry. I think I'm in shock. Everything around me is muffled as though I'm deep underwater. I hear a voice from afar as though I'm dreaming. I hear my name—I think.

"Elise? Elise!" Kinsey yells, still sounding a distance away.

I look over at her like I'm seeing her for the first time today. I blink and look around. I'm in front of Jeff's house. My stomach coils, and I think I might puke. The last couple minutes come crashing down on me and tears begin to slide down my cheeks.

Kinsey shakes me gently. "Elise, do you have the key to get your things?"

My mouth snaps open, but nothing comes out. I just nod my head. "Come on. You need to snap out of it before he gets here!" she yells.

I open the door and drag myself out. What if he shows up here? What will I do? What will I say? Shoot! I don't want to see him. I *can't* see him right now. If I do, I will fall apart. I hurry to the door and fumble to get my key out.

I have to grab my stuff and get out of here fast, but where will I go? Back home? The house will be so empty. I'm not sure if I can handle that right now.

I get the door open, and she follows me to my room. "Do you have a suitcase or bag?" she asks me.

I nod and go into the closet. I grab the small suitcase that I brought my belongings in. She begins taking things out of the drawers as I empty the closet. I feel like a walking zombie, like none of this is real. I grab all my toiletries and just shove them into the bag as fast as I can.

Finally, everything is packed up, and Kinsey helps me bring it all to the car. I take one last look at the house that has been my sanctuary for so many weeks and begin to sob. I feel as though my heart has just been ripped out of my chest. My light is now fading into the darkness and there's nothing I can do to stop it.

Kinsey gives me a quick hug and then backs up and heads out of the driveway. I feel relieved we made it out without confrontation, but now what? I finally find the words to speak. "Where are we going?" This isn't the route to my house.

"You're coming to stay with me," she says bluntly. I know she won't take no for an answer.

"But Junior. He was with Jeff—" I remind her.

"If he knows what's best for him, he'll know not to allow him over. Don't worry about Junior, I'll handle him."

I watch life pass by the passenger window— dog owners walking their dogs, couples strolling hand-in-hand—as we drive through the town to the expressway. My life has been turned upside down in seconds while everyone else still goes on with their lives. We make it downtown within twenty minutes thanks to Kinsey's driving. I just need to lock the world out and smother myself with darkness.

Kinsey pulls into the parking garage and parks. She presses the trunk door opener so we can grab my bags. Everything I do feels staged and robotic. I'm afraid everything's going to come crashing down all at once. If I even allow myself to think about what I walked into earlier, my heart will break even more until nothing will be left to salvage.

We take the long elevator ride up in silence. I know she wants to say something. It's Kinsey; she always has something to say. Once we're inside her beautiful apartment, she brings me to her bedroom. "I want you to stay in my room. I know you could use the privacy. I'll sleep on the couch," she instructs. She comes towards me with open arms in a motherly gesture. "Elise, everything's going to be okay. You will get through this. I'm here for you, and you can stay here as long as you need," she sweetly says.

She wipes the tears from my face. "Thank you, Kinsey."

"Anytime, Elise. You know that. Why don't you go take a nice hot shower, and I'll order something for us to eat. I'm starving, and I need to speak with Junior to give him the heads up."

I wrap my arms around myself and nod. She closes the door behind her, leaving me alone. Completely and utterly alone with my thoughts. Maybe this isn't such a good idea quite yet.

I get in the shower and let the scalding hot water beat down on my skin. This pain is nothing compared to what my heart is feeling. When I get out, I wrap the towel around my hair, throw on my comfy clothes, and lie down on the bed. I curl up into a tiny ball. My phone notification light is blinking at me, and every ten minutes, my phone vibrates as someone tries to call. I know exactly who it is. What was left of my spirit shatters even more. A hurricane engulfs me, and I begin to drown in my own tears. There's no way to stop it now. Sob after sob comes rushing out. I can't even see in front of me; the floodgates have opened.

I finally drift asleep, but nightmares haunt my dreams and I am awakened. "Elise, wake up. You're having a bad dream," Kinsey says softly. "Come, get up. I ordered Chinese food. You need to eat."

I nod my head. "Okay, I'll be out in a minute." I just need a moment to gather myself together.

"Okay, see you out there."

I drag myself out of bed to the bathroom and wash my tear-stained face. My eyes are swollen and red, and my hair looks like I've just been electrified. I don't even recognize myself. If this is what a broken heart looks like, I never want to be in love again.

Kinsey has everything set up on the coffee table with pillows around to sit on. I take a seat, and she makes me a plate. It smells divine. My stomach immediately growls. I take my first bite, and it's heaven. I didn't realize how hungry I actually was until now.

"So, I spoke with Junior, and he's staying at Jeff's tonight. I'm not too sure about tomorrow though," she advises.

"What did he have to say for Jeff?" I ask, still not sure if I really want to know the answer.

She rolls her eyes. "Oh, just the normal shit. You know, the whole 'it wasn't what it seemed' and 'you need to hear him out' bull. But don't worry; I took care of it. I told him to tell Jeff to fuck off, and if he shows his face here, I will rip his balls off and feed them to him."

I giggle for the first time in hours.

"Max has called a couple of times. I filled her in, I hope you don't mind."

I shake my head. "No, I don't mind. I'm surprised she hasn't busted through the door by now," I say, attempting to crack a joke.

Kinsey chuckles. "Believe me, she was going to, but I told her you need some rest."

"Thank you."

After we eat, I go back to bed. Acting like a normal human being is just way too difficult at the moment, and it's extremely tiring. I just want to sleep.

Kinsey wakes me up to see if I'm coming into work. I shake my head and roll back over. I fall asleep for another couple hours, and again I am awakened by Kinsey.

"Hey, did you eat?"

I shake my head. "Okay, I'm going to go whip us up something. Junior won't be here tonight, so you don't have to worry about running into him."

I spend the next couple of days like this, but I know eventually I'm going to have to face the music. I can't hide forever, and I need to go back to work at some point. The bills need to get paid and I'm done dipping into my vacation time.

I know Kinsey will cause a fit if I leave, but I'm ready to be on my own. I can't take up her life forever. So I pack my crap up and take a taxi home. She already had my car dropped off to the house. I send her a text to let her know where I have gone. She's not happy about it, but she knows she can't force me to stay. I'm a grown woman, and I need to start acting like one.

My cell continues to buzz off the hook, and texts from Jeff flood my phone at all hours of each day. I throw my phone on the coffee table and continue to clean. My mother left this place a dump. It's going to take me more than just a couple of days to put it back together again.

It's late on Saturday night. I'm in my sweats, nestled on the couch with a blanket while watching Lifetime movies. I've been like this all day. My hair is unwashed, thrown back into a bun, and I could give two shits. I left my house only once this week to get some groceries to survive on, but a shower is the last thing on my mind.

I hear the noise of a key being slipped into my front door. I look over and watch the knob twist. My heart is pounding against my chest, and the door flies open. I quickly get up, grab my phone, and back up to the far living room wall.

"Well hello, beautiful. What a great surprise," Reggie says as he stumbles into the living room. It's clear he is drunk out of his mind, because he can barely stand.

"You need to get out of here! This isn't your house, and my mother isn't here!" I demand.

He smirks crookedly, and it sends chills down my spine. I don't feel safe. He's giving off a dangerous vibe, and my gut is telling me to get out of here. I wrap the blanket around me tighter.

He stalks towards me. "But *you* are!" he says with a raspy voice.

I put my phone up. "Don't move any closer, or I will call the police! You need to leave *now*!" I scream, now deathly afraid. I look around quickly to see how to make a fast getaway, but I'm trapped.

"You can't run from me this time, Elise. There's nobody here to rescue you," he tells me with a wicked grin.

My heart is going to beat out of my throat. My whole body is shaking. I look down towards my phone to dial 911, and I'm ambushed. The wind is completely knocked out of me, and I'm gasping for air. Reggie has me pinned on the floor, facedown. He's on top of me, and I can't move. My world begins to play in slow mode. I zero in on my phone; it flew across the room, completely out of my reach. I pray for a miracle. I pray for this to be a nightmare that I will wake up from. I pray for Jeff.

His breath is at my ear, tears slide over my face, and the smell of whiskey and cigarettes slither past my nose. I want to vomit. I can't stop myself from crying hysterically. "Please, don't. Please just let me go, and I won't go to the police," I beg over and over, but it makes it worse. He screams at me to shut up.

He pins my head down with his forearm. My adrenaline is at an all-time high, and he begins ripping down my sweatpants. I can't stop begging and pleading. I scream for help, but I know nobody can hear me. I try to squirm as hard as I can, but he just holds me down tighter and grips my wrist behind my head. A sharp pain goes down my arm the more I struggle.

I rapidly search for anything in my reach, but it's no use. My sweatpants are down past my thighs, and he rips my underwear off. I am completely exposed to him as he spreads my legs even farther with his knees. My cries and pleas are louder as I beg him to stop. I'm just not strong enough to fight him. He has liquid power in his blood. This is it. He's going to force himself inside of me.

"Damn, you look so pretty. Just sit back and enjoy this, you little stuck-up bitch! I know I'm going to," he whispers before licking my ear. I whimper in disgust and squeeze my eyes shut. I can't believe this is happening to me. Please God, just take me away. I feel his fingers at my thighs and his tip at my entrance. I keep my eyes closed, trying to pretend this isn't going to happen. I try to send myself somewhere else mentally.

But before he can force himself into me, he is ripped off of me.

CHAPTER TWENTY FIVE

" Where is she, Kinsey?" I yell, searching around the apartment.

"Jeff, calm down!" she screams back. "She's not here! She went back to her house days ago."

"Wait, what? Are you serious?" I ask, trying to make sure I heard this right.

"Yes, she's fine. I just spoke with her earlier."

I run towards the door. "She's not okay! Her mother's boyfriend is still out there!" I tell her on my way out.

"Jeff—what are you talking about? Jeff!" she questions. I don't have time to answer her or explain anymore. I need to get to Elise.

Junior runs behind me. "I'm coming with you, bro!"

I do a hundred on the expressway, making it to her house in record time. Everything seems quiet on the outside, so maybe this is a good sign. When I get up to the door, I hear a scream. It sounds like it's coming from Elise. The door is unlocked. I slam it open and walk over the threshold. What I see is disturbing and vile, and my whole world comes crashing down on me. My adrenaline kicks into overload, and all I see is blood red. I'm ready to kill!

Reggie has Elise pinned to the ground, on top of her, with her legs spread and her lower half naked. Elise is struggling and crying. I can't move fast enough. I rip him off of her and throw him across the room. I'm going to fucking kill him! I bash his head through the wall by the neck and squeeze as hard as I can. He's gasping for air, face turning from red to blue. I want this disgusting piece of crap dead! I could give two shits if I end up in jail.

I can't stop slamming his head through the wall and against the floor. The anger is raging through me. Junior is now behind me, trying to rip me off of him. "Jeff, stop! You're going to kill him!" he screams at the top of his lungs. I can't let go. I start punching his face until blood is all over him and I. I can't bring myself to stop.

Junior finally tears me off of him just as the police arrive. Reggie is lying unconscious on the floor. I try to go at him again, but Junior and the police officers hold me back.

One officer cuffs me as another bends down to feel Reggie's pulse. "He's still alive! Get an ambulance in here and fast!" he barks to his men. I hear them radio it in over the speaker.

I look over at Elise, so small and fragile. I promised I would protect her, and I failed. Tears flood my eyes. "Let go!" I demand, struggling to get out of the officer's grip.

"Sir! If you don't calm down, I'm going to have to put you in the car," the officer yells.

Junior quickly begins to fill the officer in on what just happened, and after a lot of questioning and explaining, he finally releases me from the cuffs.

I rush over to Elise, and swoop her into my arms. I cradle her against me as she buries herself into my chest. I rub her hair and tell her everything will be okay as she bawls uncontrollably in my arms. I wrap the blanket around her tighter. God, I should have been here! I should have protected her. Why did I even give her space? I shouldn't have listened to everyone else when they told me to give her time.

Minutes go by. The ambulance takes Reggie away, and then the EMTs come over to look at Elise. "Elise, we need to take a report and get you to the hospital," the female officer says softly.

Elise shakes her head. "I don't want to go," she whimpers.

"It's protocol. The doctors need to check you out," the officer informs.

I rub her back. "I'm not leaving you. I'll be right here with you, and I won't leave your side, OK?"

Elise finally nods her head. After I explain to the cops what went down, we leave in the ambulance, and Junior follows us in the car. It's clear he called everyone, because a crowd shows up at the hospital shortly after. Elise doesn't want to be seen by anyone, so they all sit in the waiting room until the doctor is finished.

Visiting hours finally come to an end, and our friends exit, leaving us alone. I sit on the bed with her, squeezing her tightly. "Jeff, I'm sorry I didn't give you the chance to hear you out. "

I shush her immediately. "Elise, don't. I don't care about any of that."

"I looked at your texts even though I tried not to. I was just so mad at you that I didn't want to believe them, but deep down inside, I knew you were telling me the truth," she admits. I smile.

She yawns. She's getting sleepy from the sedative the doctor gave her. I lay her down on the bed and wrap myself around her. "I'm just glad I made it there in time," I whisper. "If he would have hurt you, I would have never forgiven myself."

This time she comforts me. "Shh." She puts her finger to my lips. "But he didn't, and I have you to thank for that," she says, looking up at me. "I love you, Jeff."

My eyes water, threatening to spill over. This is what love does. I never cry. Just having her in my arms makes me the happiest man alive. "I love you too, Elise," I reply, kissing her on the tip of her nose.

She's my world, the air I breathe, and I could not live in this world any longer if I didn't have her by my side, loving me with every inch of her soul.

CHAPTER TWENTY SIX

I've finally stopped having nightmares. It's been months. Jeff's been so patient and supportive through this hard time. He's allowed me to heal, and slowly but surely, we are back in the game with our amazing sex life. I don't know what I would've done without him. He has healed me from the inside out. He's my best friend and my soul mate.

My mother is still in rehab, going strong. I talk to her every week on the phone and have been to two of her therapy sessions, which is needed so the both of us can heal. We have a long way to go, but tiny steps are still steps in the right direction. She feels consumed with guilt over what happened, and we are working through that as well. I feel optimistic that someday I will have my mother back.

Bruce and I are getting close. Jeff and I have met my dad's wife and my siblings, and they honestly bring light to my life. My sisters already look up to me, and I feel a deep need to be a strong role model for them. We have plans to visit Jeff's father down in South Carolina next month. Julian just came back from his visit, and he seems happy and more at peace. I can only hope our trip turns out as good.

Maxine and Kyle finally had their baby girl, Penelope. And I have to admit—I am so in love. She is gorgeous and already has Jeff wrapped around her little finger. He now has two women in his life that he's head over heels in love with. His gentleness with her shows me that he is going to be an amazing father—when that time comes.

We've packed up the last of my house. I am finally selling it and "officially" moving in with

Jeff. My mother agreed to move into an apartment when she leaves rehab. She's going to be getting some assistance, and I offered to help with the rest until she can get on her feet. This separation has been good for the both of us. She is working on her independence, as am I. I no longer feel like the shy, weak Elise that I was months ago. I feel strong and confident in all my decisions.

Jeff and I stand in the doorway as I look around my house one last time. Jeff wraps his arms around me for comfort and strength. "We're starting a whole new chapter together, beautiful. Are you ready?"

I look up at him. "Without a doubt. Thank you for being here for me," I tell him.

"There's nowhere else I'd rather be. You are my life now."

My heart swells. "And you are my world. Forever and always."

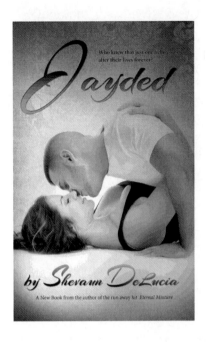

Turn the page for a sample chapter of
Jayed, Book #1, of *A Forbidden Romance Series*.
Available from:
Amazon
Barnes & Nobels
iBooks
Kobo
ISBN: 9780986395109

SAMPLE CHAPTER

Jayded

CHAPTER ONE: KYLE

A breeze rushes over me, sending goose bumps across the surface of my skin and chilling me to the bone. I pull my tangled covers up over my shoulder and bury my face deep into the warmth. Ahh, so snug.

Just then, my alarm shrieks loudly through the room. I don't want to move. Fuck work today. Ugh! If only I could lie in bed all day and get paid for it, life would be perfect. On second thought, I could do that as a male escort! I laugh at my dirty mind, shake my head, and smile. The things I come up with.

I tae one last breath and blow it out forcefully before I push the covers off and feel the breeze glide over me once more. Brr! I jump across my bed to shut the darn thing off, almost falling on my face when my foot catches on the sheet.

It's the middle of January, and still, to this day, I cannot fall asleep without my fan on. It is an old habit acquired from childhood. The sounds of the whipping blades drowned out the noise of Junior, my older brother, snoring—something I had to endure when sharing a room with him as a kid. I've needed it ever since. It's one of my weird addictions.

I rub the sleep from my eyes, a parting gift from the good ole Sandman. I just hate morning time. I think I've been up no more than five minutes before my phone rings. I don't even need to look at the caller ID to know who it is.

I press the green button and put the phone up to my ear as I walk to the bathroom. "Hey, Ma. Why must you always call me this early in the morning?" I grumble. I grab the washcloth from the towel rack and hold it under the hot, steaming water.

"Well good morning to you too, son! I just wanted to remind you to dress up today. We have a possible partner coming in to visit. Your father is going to be on his shitstorm-rampage getting the office prepared," my mother says. I sigh knowing today will be a rough one. I can hear her take the phone from her ear as she orders her french vanilla coffee with sugar and extra cream. She stops at the Dunkin Donuts drive-thru each morning. "Did you need me to grab you one?" she asks.

I finish wiping off my face with the steamy washcloth. "Nah. I'm good, Ma. I'll grab one on my way there."

"Ok, love. I'll see you in a few."

I put my phone on the counter and finish my normal morning bathroom routine. I can't help but feel a little stoked that it's business casual dress attire today. That means the girls are going to be on fire, dressed in pumps, tight dress pants, or maybe even some nice, tight ass-grabbing skirts—*yeah buddy*!

I work down the street at my parents' publishing company: Saunders Literary Agency. My parents both built the company from the ground up. They have made it into a very successful business that's going on ten years now. Just last year, I decided to join the team after finishing my last semester at college.

Believe me, being twenty-four and working for my parents is not my ultimate goal in life, but I had to keep the money flowing. There was no way in hell I was going back home to live under my parents' roof while I figured out what to do with myself.

There are a couple of girls at the office who have caught my eye, but nothing worth talking about. They were more like wham-bam-thank-you-ma'ams. Elizabeth, the long-legged wonder with a nice rack—I just had to get my mouth on that. I dated her on and off for a couple of months, but she wanted too much from me. She wanted to be exclusive, and when I told her we needed to cool off for a while, she went all stalker-mode on me. She turned into a stage-five clinger! So I ran.

Bottom line is I'm twenty-four, for Christ's sake! Who the hell wants to settle down at twenty-four? One piece of ass for the rest of my life? That shit isn't happening! At least, not anytime soon. I've been lucky enough to have parents who've stayed together all these years. I've gotten to watch what true love looks like through them. But for me—I'm just happy living as a bachelor.

My parents met at the same age I'm at now, and they are the small percentage who've made it, stuck with it. They've been together almost thirty years, and they're still going strong. My childhood was nice. It was textbook normal, with some occasional hiccups. But marriage and family is pretty much non-existent in my future, at least for now.

I finish a quick shave and head back to my closet to put on my dress clothes. I have a studio apartment. It's small but efficient, and the rent is cheap. I have my bed, leather sofa, breakfast nook looking over the small kitchen, and a nice big window looking out on the busy downtown streets. But the best part of it is—there are no parents!

I check the thermostat before I head out, making sure it's set to turn on by five in the evening so I can come home to a nice, snug apartment, and then I head out the door.

Work's going to be a little crazy today. It always is when we have clients or prospective agents who may join our company. My parents have some big clients that are very loyal because my father is very good at what he does. He is usually extra tense and extra snippy on these days. He's fighting for traditional publishing versus the self-publishing trend that authors seem to take to lately. So keeping our clients happy is extremely important to our company.

Me, I try to stay out of Dodge when my father is in his moods, and my mother gets the short end of the deal. She has no choice but to deal with the lion head-on.

I hustle my butt getting into my car. It feels like ten below outside. Really, it's only about thirty-two degrees. At least that is what the radio man just said. Mental note: Get a car starter installed! I say this every winter. And each time I finally get down to making a move on it, it's already spring and I let it wait until the next winter. Yes, I know; I am a major procrastinator.

What can I say?

I turn the key and the motor hums to life. I pat the dashboard and whisper her sweet nothings. My car is a beauty: a black 2014 Cadillac, CTS-V luxury sports coupe. It was a graduation gift from my parents. They may have gone a little overboard, but nothing's too good for their "little baby boy," as my mom would say.

I pull up to work and park to the back. The less cars, the better. I would crush someone if they scratched or nicked this baby. Now, if only I could find a girl who is just as sleek and sexy, my world would be perfect. Yeah, I'm a little crazy. I shake my head with a grin while looking around to make sure no one is seeing my craziness.

I buzz myself in and walk past the secretary, Elise. She's quiet and shy—pretty in a natural, bland sort of way. Every time I walk past her, I make sure to give her an extra special smile. "*Hello*, Elise. You're looking very pretty today," I tell her as I walk by. I like to see her cheeks redden.

She giggles. "Thank you, Kyle." I give her a wink, she buzzes me in, and I stroll toward my desk.

As I walk past my coworkers, I nod my head and charm my way through the office. I finally reach my desk and clock in. Jeff Bauer, a longtime friend, comes to visit, hanging against the outside of my cubicle. "Hey, man. What's up?"

Jeff's my dude. He's a blast to party with. We've known each other since eighth grade when he moved here from South Carolina with his mom. He is one loyal friend. When he's got your back, he's got your back. He's proved this many times during our drunken party nights. He never leaves a soldier behind, and he has bailed my ass out a thousand times. A true wingman.

I slap him up. "So, we still on for tonight?"

His face lights up with the thought of some free booze. "Hell yeah! I'm totally in. Where we at tonight?" Jeff asks.

I can't help but laugh. He kills me. "It's a McGregor's night tonight. My parents have to schmooze a possible new agent. You know how that shit goes," I say, rolling my eyes to add some extra affect.

"Alright, man. It's on and poppin'!" He smacks the back of my head and takes off.

"Douche!" I yell as quietly as possible. I get smacked upside the head again. "Ouch! What the—?"

"Watch the language, Kyle. We have a guest!" my mother whispers vehemently.

"Yeah, yeah," I respond, annoyed. I have to find another job. Getting scolded at work at eight thirty in the morning fucking sucks!

My mother eases up a bit, noticing my reaction. "I have Maxine in my office. Do you mind showing her around a little? Take her to the kitchen to grab some coffee, please?"

She always makes me the errand boy while Junior, my older brother, gets to be in on the important meetings and conferences. Yes, he's worked here since right out of high school and knows the business in and out, but *I* have a degree under my belt now. I am way more qualified than he could ever be. My father tells me I need to earn my spot in the business, which, in my opinion, is total bullshit. I could go work at any one of these top agencies with my background. I may be the baby of the family, but sometimes I feel more like the black sheep.

I grunt like a child about to throw a tantrum. "Fine. Not a problem."

My mother gives me a pat on my shoulder and walks away. I push my chair in a little harder than normal and begin my touring duty.

Before I can make it to my mom's office, Elizabeth stops me. She sticks her chest out just enough for "the girls" to poke out, front and center. I can't help but look for just a quick moment. "Good morning, Kyle," she greets me with what she thinks is a seductive smile. I'm totally on to her, and her smile irks me like nails on a chalkboard.

"Morning, Beth. Listen, I can't talk right now." I try to scoot around her, hoping she'll get the hint.

"Kyle, wait! Will you be at McGregor's tonight?" she asks. Great. Stalker chick's gonna be there. Awesome.

"Yeah." I turn and walk away.

"I'll see you there!" she yells from behind.

I stroll up to my mother's office and knock on the door before opening it. A woman sits in front of my mom's desk with her back to me, typing furiously on her laptop. I look at her boringly. Most agents seem to be dull, boring, snooty, and all about business. Their idea of fun is reading a book. Or maybe it's just that any woman dressed in a dress suit reminds me of my mother.

"Uh, good *morning*," I say, trying not to startle her. She looks to be very concentrated on her work.

Maxine turns in her seat. My mouth hangs open. It's like time freezes, and all I can think is *holy fuck*! I'm speechless. Never in my life have I been speechless or caught off-guard to this magnitude. The woman in front of me is fucking hot! On fire! I slowly take her in, starting with her high red pumps, long legs, and tight red skirt reaching her knees, hugging one amazing ass and some unGodly shaped hips. Man, those hips though. I can already see my hands being at home on those hips. My eyes drift up to her tiny waist and voluptuous breasts. *Yum.* Her face is flawless: lips plush and eyes a beautiful iridescent blue, which completely contrasts against her darker complexion and the brown of her hair. Simple perfection.

I must be standing here like a doof, making an ass of myself, because she smiles with a tiny bit of amusement. She reaches her hand out to me. "Hello. You must be Kyle?"

I continue to stare, completely mesmerized. It takes me a moment to snap out of it. "Uh, yes, I'm Kyle. You must be Maxine." I grab her hand, immediately feeling the softness of her skin. "It's nice to meet you," I say with a smile.

"It's just Max," she informs me.

I scream at myself from within, trying to get a grip. She's just a woman, for God's sake! An amazingly attractive woman who undoubtedly has already, within seconds, caused a stir from down below. A woman with long, shapely legs that I would kill to trail kisses up and have wrapped around me. A woman with hips I could grab perfectly while watching her grind on top of me.

Her amusement has now traveled to her sparkling eyes. "Your mother, Connie, told me you would be giving me a tour?"

She turns to close her laptop. I almost reach my hand out to grab that beautiful ass of hers, but I slap it away before she turns back around. Man, what I could do with that ass in my hands. Shit! Okay, okay. Stay focused.

I pull the door wider and hold out my hand for her to go first. "After you," I say.

She walks past me, her eyes meeting mine as she crosses my path. Our eyes stay connected for a moment, energy rampages through every limb of my body, gathering at the southern region. I'm unable to part from her gaze until she finally disconnects from me. The air whirls around me, leaving me with the fragrance of flowers and cucumber melon. It's intoxicating. I lean in, without realizing it, to smell the air left from her trail. Shit! What the hell am I doing? I'm losing my mind, that's what I'm doing. I can't help it, though. I've only spent a couple minutes in her presence, and I'm already addicted.

ABOUT THE AUTHOR

Shevaun DeLucia, author of the *Eternal Mixture* series, lives in upstate New York with her husband, four children, and two dogs. As a stay-at-home mom while her children were young, she fell in love with reading. She indulged in the small moments that took her away from the reality of her loud, rambunctious household, bringing her into a world of fantasy. When reading wasn't enough to satisfy her, she turned to writing, determined to create the perfect ending of her own.

Acknowledgements

First and foremost, I would like to thank George Parulski, graphic designer/photographer for *Transcendent*. This book wouldn't be possible without you. Your creations are extraordinary, and I couldn't have asked for anything better! Secondly, to my editor Jinelle Shengulette, thank you for translating my words perfectly! We make a great team!

Next, I want to thank my PR team: The Next Step PR, including Kiki Chatfield and Ruth Martin. Thanks for all your amazingness! You both have taught me *so* much, and I am lucky to have you two by my side! I don't know what I would do without you. I look forward to what lies ahead in our working relationship and, most importantly, our new friendship. You ladies rock!

To Jesse and Miranda—thank you for bringing on the hotness! It was a fun shoot, and I'm so glad you both took a chance on it!

And of course, I have to thank my family for all their support and patience as I continue to follow my dreams. They are my rock, and because of them, I will never give up on my dreams.

Last but not least, I want to thank all my new readers! Without you, I wouldn't be working as hard as I do on the daily. I've met some amazing people this year, and I look forward to the years to come!